Acclaim for Paul M. Deadlines

"The themes of Paul McHugh's companionable, rock-solid and soul-satisfying mystery could not be more modern and relevant. But it is his wonderful character, the has-been alcoholic newspaper columnist Colm MacCay, who will stay with you, and who channels McHugh's considerable writing talent into a voice that surprises and delights with all the narrative panache of the classic Irish storyteller. Deadlines _is a superior story, not to be missed._"

— John Lescroart, _New York Times_ best-selling author

"With Deadlines, _Paul McHugh nails the desperation of new-millennium newsrooms and the quirky crusaders of the Bay Area. He also has a lot of fun with the unlikely culprits in this land-and-money murder mystery. As you learn from the very first page,_ Deadlines _is not a 'who' done it but a 'why and how will our heroes find out' done it. The fact that those heroes are journalists, and that McHugh's prose uses humor to great effect, are welcome twists indeed._"

— Farai Chideya, author, _Kiss the Sky_ and _The Color of Our Future_

"Every reporter worth his or her notepad is a sleuth at heart. Paul McHugh brings this truth to life with crackling suspense and a true, ink-stained veteran's eye for the newsroom.

— Dan Rather, journalist, managing editor and anchor, _Dan Rather Reports_

"People who love San Francisco and appreciate a good mystery will find Paul McHugh's Deadlines _a page-turner with unforgettable characters and a realistic view of crime. McHugh creates an eccentric figure who epitomizes an endangered species — a reporter who can connect the dots. My wife Beverly and I couldn't put it down._"

— Sheriff Mike Hennessey, City and County of San Francisco

Also by Paul McHugh

The Search for Goodbye-To-Rains

Wild Places: 20 Journeys
Into the North American Outdoors
(editor)

Deadlines

a novel

Paul McHugh

LOST
COAST
PRESS

Deadlines

A Novel

Copyright © 2010 by Paul McHugh

Lost Coast Press
155 Cypress Street
Fort Bragg, CA 95437
(800) 773-7782
www.cypresshouse.com

Book production by Cypress House
Book and cover design by Michael Brechner / Cypress House

Library of Congress Cataloging-in-Publication Data

McHugh, Paul, 1950-
    Deadlines : a novel / Paul McHugh. -- 1st ed.
        p. cm.
        ISBN 978-1-935448-04-4 (pbk. : alk. paper)
        1. Journalists--Fiction. 2. Fraud investigation--Fiction. [1.
California--Fiction.] I. Title.
        PS3563.A31163D43 2010
        813'.54--dc22

                                        2009043632

Printed in the USA

9 8 7 6 5 4 3 2

First Edition

To Dawn, my light

The lunatic, the lover, and the poet
Are of imagination all compact.

— Wm. Shakespeare,
A Midsummer Night's Dream

Prelude

A horse stood on a rough balcony of rock that jutted out above the sea. The man riding the horse sat upright and immobile in the saddle. A molten sun hovered above the misty horizon, like a spotlight aimed down through a scrim of gauze.

It was late afternoon on an August day. A breeze blew inland, ferrying a briny reek of low tide, and thin ghosts of fog and spray.

At this moment, the man on the horse did not look like a killer. He seemed like a bronze statue placed in a park. Then a cell phone chirped. The rider's hand shot up to tug the phone out of his vest. He flipped it open, glanced at the calling number, closed it, shoved the chromium slab back in his pocket without answering.

The man clicked his tongue, touched the horse with his heels. Its thick neck arched and bent, it turned out of the overlook on the coastal ridge. He directed it onto a path that led down into a valley thick with live oaks. The horse was a big white stallion, its shoulders and haunches roped by muscle. Black hooves thudded against dirt of the trail.

As they moved, the noise of distant surf rose and fell, like rhythmic roars from a stadium crowd, then slowly faded to a background mutter. Filtered by the dense green foliage, light grew soft.

The rider had broad shoulders, a thick chest. Square hands lightly held the reins. He wore tall boots, jodhpurs, a black vest over a white polo shirt, and a riding helmet. Beneath his helmet jutted a face with dark brows, prominent nose, a thin-lipped mouth, and a square jaw with a cleft chin.

He bore some signs of age. Deep creases fanned out from his eyes and lips, flesh along his jaw line and chin sagged. Still, his face would have seemed handsome except for a strange blankness. He stared coldly down the trail, showing a passionless intensity, a nearly robotic demeanor.

The sea could no longer be heard. Three sounds reverberated through the still forest—faint creak of saddle and stirrup leathers, blasts of breath out of the stallion's nostrils, muffled thud of its hooves.

A quarter of a mile below the horse and rider, the same trail wound downhill to enter a grassy valley.

Making her way upward through tall grass on that pathway, a gray-haired woman walked. She led a small dog on a leash. Glasses with large, round, green frames emphasized the thin length of her face. A shabby wool coat was clasped at her waist by a single button, a purple knit cap was tugged low on her forehead.

The dog, a cocker spaniel, constantly fought her control, zigzagging on the leash. She tugged back, rebuking him in a low, exasperated voice that also held notes of amusement and affection. As they went up the hill, she used her other hand to poke at the earth with a carved cane of rattan. They reached the rim of the forest, then vanished among the trees.

Immediately, a golf cart hummed out of the fog, rolling along atop the grass. It halted at the spot where the woman had disappeared. A paunchy man in a brown uniform swung out. He had a mustache trimmed close, military-style, but uncut hair dangled from the back of his cap, hanging down over his collar. From the bed of the cart, he pulled orange traffic cones, and a sawhorse with a sign wired to it. He arranged all these across the path.

In red letters, the sign announced, TRAIL CLOSED TODAY – FOR MAINTENANCE.

The security guard jumped back in his cart, steered around the sign, and drove up the trail.

A few hundred yards onward, the spaniel poked his nose into a clump of sword fern, then started to lift a fluffy leg. He abruptly put it down, jumped sideways, barked.

"What's up, Mr. Jessup?" the woman asked. "Seen a deer?"

The dog barked again, more excitedly. Out of the thickening

mist, the horse and rider loomed. The woman stared hard at them. Anger swept over her face.

"Go back!" she yelled. "You don't belong here! This is a walking trail."

She waved her cane. Her dog, yapping excitedly, ran in circles at the end of its leash.

The rider's ominous advance continued.

"Erik Eiger! You goddamn fool! Get out of here!"

"Shut up, old bitch." The rider's voice bore a heavy, yet unidentifiable, European accent. "You it is who must go now."

The woman's anger advanced to pop-eyed rage. Widening her stance on the pathway, she stood her ground, then brandished her cane.

"This was my father's land! His plan stays in force! Everybody must—"

"You will be quiet!" he shouted, biting off the words.

The rider's heavy brows knit together, his eyes glittered. He goaded the stallion with abrupt signals from reins and legs. The horse reared up to an astonishing height, punching its broad front hooves out into the misty air.

The woman was shocked. She jumped aside as best she could, stumbling and hobbling. She made it off the trail, but continued to shout at the rider.

"I'll get you thrown out, by God! Barred from Cornu Point!"

The rider turned his mount toward her. He made the horse rear again. Broad, black hooves flailed at her face like the fists of a sparring boxer.

"You want that? Those stupid last words?"

The woman gasped. Her mouth made an astonished "O."

The rider aped her expression, mocking her.

Her eyes bulged, her jaw tightened. "Okay, buster!" she said.

She dropped her dog's leash to grip her cane with both hands. When the stallion's forequarters dropped down, she whacked the horse hard atop its muzzle with her stick, trying to make it panic and bolt. But the stallion barely flinched. It snaked its neck forward, open mouth displaying large square teeth, stretching out to bite the woman. She snatched her arms away and back in the nick of time.

The rider spurred the horse forward. The woman retreated before it, staggering as she retreated, thrashing through brush below the trees. Still the rider pursued her, step by step. The stallion, aroused, arched its thick neck, made plunging strides with its great hooves.

"Stop this, stop, stop, Erik!" the woman yelped. "You gone nuts?!"

As she stumbled back, the woman swung her cane about wildly, but landed no more blows. She staggered into a thicket, dense and springy as a trampoline, and could move no farther.

The rider spun his horse end for end. He gave more signals. The stallion hopped, leapt upward, then kicked powerfully outward with both back hooves. One huge hoof struck the woman full in the head—a fan of ruby droplets sprayed out into the green blur of shadow below the trees—while the other hoof crashed into her upper chest.

The old woman flew like a flung doll. She hit high on the mound of stiff brush. Her limp body hung for a moment, cruciform. A long sigh escaped from her lungs, her thin muscles convulsed. She slipped, twisted, slid downward, to the faint snap of twigs.

Cheek pressed to damp earth, a shattered face came to rest. The woman's brown eyes were open, dull, and staring. The little dog's leash had tangled in the brush. At the end of that tether, it continued to leap, spin, and frantically yap.

A smile of triumph flickered upon the rider's lips. He rode the stallion back out to the trail. He dismounted, patted the horse on the neck, praising it. From a bulging pocket on his vest, the rider tugged out a halter and lead line, and tied his animal to a tree.

The golf cart rolled up. The guard in the dark uniform nodded at the rider. He glanced down the tunnel that had been battered through the undergrowth. The old woman's form lay at its dim end, a heap of colored wool from which poked pale, still hands, half a staring face. The guard snorted a laugh.

"Target eliminated!" The guard said. "And so's a big problem. Finally!" He cupped a hand to his ear. "Is it me, or does it seem kind of quiet all of a sudden?"

He pointed at the rider. Then he banged palms of his hands together, miming applause. "May I say, sir, another splendid performance! Terrific job."

The rider's thin lips parted in a gap-toothed grin, and he bowed ceremoniously.

The guard went to the rear of the cart and yanked out a blue plastic tarp, lashed into a roll by white nylon cord.

And so Beverly Bancroft departed from our world. That feisty old dame had fought her last battle, just as her killers planned, among the shadows. And there, the specific nature of her death might well have remained hidden. Her passing did not go unremarked, but the fact that it was a murder came to light only due to determined snooping by a rather unlikely team — Sebastian and Elle.

Well, okay. And me. I did join their squad, later. But they got the big investigative ball rolling. Started me up too, by the way. They deserve all credit.

However, I was the one in best position to witness the events, or speak to people who witnessed things I didn't, or visualize certain other happenings by simply extrapolating from all our knowns. So, it seems up to me to tell the tale.

Chapter 1

Sebastian Palmer blew into The City late in the summer of 2007. By City, I actually mean California's "Babylon-by-the-Bay" — as a *Post-Dispatch* newspaper columnist once dubbed it — San Francisco. A metropolis often chilled by fog, regularly heated up by nightlife, and forever promising its citizens a dose of dulcet love, as in a classic Tony Bennett tune. On occasion, that still occurs. Hell, it even happened to me once.

Palmer sprang from a small burg on Florida's panhandle. After graduating from the Medill journalism school at Northwestern University, he'd gotten swindled into signing on as an intern at my paper. That would be the *San Francisco Post-Dispatch,* a faltering daily, newly acquired by a multimedia firm. The aim of our new overlords was to transform our rag into the semblance of a scrappy crusader, then spark an ad revenue and circulation war with the *San Francisco Chronicle.*

Instead, both papers ended up fighting like alley cats over scraps of the shrinking regional media biz. Life's just a parade of discoveries.

Palmer was a slender young man who slouched up to an altitude around six feet. He was rather casual about matters of dress and appearance. His speech had a pleasant lilt, since corners of his consonants had been sanded off by his birthplace. All this might give an observer the sense of a slacker. Yet below Palmer's relaxed surface, I soon saw, stretched some rather steely nerves.

At first, I regarded his refusal to be daunted as naiveté. Later,

I saw it revealed inner grit, more than I had at his age. Ultimately, I perceived this trait as a legacy of Southern manhood. Palmer sprang from a family with a venerable military tradition. He'd inherited the grit of Lee's butternut troops. That attitude of 90-proof stubbornness with a twist of endurance explains why Grant and Sherman needed so much time, and blood and powder, to get those guys to admit they'd been beat.

Palmer also displayed a taste for danger. I don't mean the flashy, moth-to-flame compulsion you see in daredevils. It might be better to say that he was heedless of risk. He let curiosity pull him deep into situations before he fully comprehended what was happening. Which was why, as he drove out from his Florida home to this new San Francisco job, then paused in Yosemite for rest and exercise, he wound up damn near killing himself on a steep slab of granite.

Most newcomers to San Francisco promptly tour our town's art museums and galleries, surfing beaches and green parks, fabled bistros, clubs, theaters and pubs, or our splendid restaurants serving every conceivable fare. People can eat their way around the world just by dining for a month in The City.

In my day, acquitting oneself as a gourmand was the mark of a bon vivant. You had to master drinking too, navigate the night by sipping fine wines at Top of the Mark, then Bruno's martinis at his Aub Zam Zam bar in the Haight, a Bloody Mary or two amid a breezy ferry ride over to Sausalito for breakfast. Finally, Irish coffees at the Buena Vista cafe just after you got back to town, before rushing off to work. Here's mud in your eye!

None of that for Palmer. He checked in at that venerable SoMa (South of Market Street) hotel where our newspaper maintained a lofty penthouse for VIPs, as well as mini-studios in the basement for interns or other visitors of scant status. Such as Palmer. But before unpacking all his bags, Palmer plugged in his laptop, found a climbing gym, consulted a Google map, then strapped on the inline skates he'd brought with him, and scooted on over there.

Cliffhanger Gym was built in an old Mission District movie theater, just off Cesar Chavez Street. Perfect site, due to its soaring ceilings. After climbing structures went in, the place itself resembled a movie set. There was a curve of artificial boulders, towers lumped with folds and ledges. All had been slathered in a rough plaster meant to mimic natural rock. Convoluted surfaces were dotted by protruding handholds and festooned with bright climbing ropes. A visitor might reasonably expect to see a platoon of cartoon dwarves in there, singing and swinging picks as they dug out diamonds big as softballs.

But on that weekday morning, just one lissome human occupied all the faux rock. Elle Jatobá hung off an artificial boulder, defying gravity while she zipped along like a spider. Her movements were graceful, and synched to beats that poured into her skull from iPod earbuds.

Palmer stood at the front desk, paid money, filled in liability forms. Elle was summoned from the walls and assigned to him as an instructor. When they stood face to face, he saw a copper-haired lass with clear, slate-gray eyes and a spray of freckles sprinkled across the bridge of a straight, Grecian nose. Her lower jaw was a bit long and strong for a woman—a feature that made her more plain than pretty.

But her body was attractive, "ripped" or "buffed" as they say, qualities revealed by sports bra and tights. As a quirky fashion detail, a yellow bandanna was tied about her left leg, just below the knee.

Elle studied our young man. She noted his hazel eyes, the thatch of curly dark hair that arrowed down his forehead in a pronounced widow's peak, and the way a well-meaning stylist had frosted the upper tips of his hair into a series of bleached tufts. She also saw slits in his earlobes, resulting from recent removal of a pair of largish decorative plugs. (One does hesitate, does one not, to name such ornamentation earrings?)

But what really commanded her attention were red scabs on torn skin that welted the right side of Palmer's face.

"Jesus! What the hell happened to you?" she blurted.

I should explain. Elle was curt in her speech, as well as everything else. To her, tact was a time-waster.

"Oh, I took a fall on Half Dome," he said.

"I guess!" Elle said. "How?"

"Know those cables up the back side?"

She nodded.

"I tried using those, for my first climb ever. See, I'm from Florida—"

"I was so *not* thinking, hey, this guy's from Jersey!"

"Um, yeah. So, it got strange quick. A clump of folks jammed the route. In the middle of 'em there's this woman in a panic. Panting and slobbering about how scared she is. Can't go up, won't go down. Her hands are on the cables with this total death grip. "I ask, can I help? Everyone yells no. She'd been plain stuck for half an hour. Folks around her are totally cranked. She blocks them all, except anyone willing to duck under her arms. That line looks slow, so I jump outside the cables. But I keep a hand sliding along on one. Then something sharp rips me in the finger."

"Loose strand of steel wire," Elle said.

Palmer nodded.

"Why didn't you grab gloves from that pile at the base?"

"Didn't think I'd need 'em."

Elle shook her head, rolled her eyes.

"So, I raise my hand, see a cut, just oozing blood," Palmer continued. "As I look down, my feet slip. Before I even realize it, I go sliding. My butt hits, my face hits. I'm about two hundred feet up. If I can't stop, I'm screwed! But I don't have any notion how. Bust up my fingernails trying. But I have on these old cotton sweats and a cut-off shirt, and they tear and snag on the rock. Slow me down enough so I grab onto one of those posts that hold up the cable."

"Lucky man!" Elle said. "What kind of shoes?"

"That I had on? Just my old running shoes."

Elle's face went sour. "The worst. Those soles are made to wear, not stick." She looked him up and down. "So. Why come here? I'd think you'd never want to be on rock again."

Palmer's gaze was earnest. "Judgment. Need that, first. Then technique. Shit, there's a ton I don't know. Like, I mean, what you said about my shoes. Never had a clue. Around Tallahassee, there was no place to climb. Read a lot about it, couldn't try it anywhere. Me and my pals slid around down in limestone caves." He shrugged. "'Bout all we had."

Elle nodded. "Okay. Just so you know, that cable route up the back of Half Dome isn't a real climb." She swept an arm, indicating walls of her gym. "This isn't much like real rock either. Come to a gym to get fit, learn the gear, nail a move. But it's all controlled. If wild rock is what you're after, you need serious chops.

But you start out by taking baby steps. Don't throw yourself at it!"

Silver eyes scanned Palmer, then drilled into him. Her brusque tone sent a shiver down his back.

"You all cool with that?"

"Sure."

She showed him how to fit a climber's harness around his hips, double the strap through the buckle. She bound his feet into sticky-soled climbing shoes that felt nastily cramped. She demonstrated the belay device, with a backup line that anchored a belayer's harness to a floor bolt. Then Elle had him belay her on a top-rope while she scampered up a wall.

"Ready?"

Before he could respond, she pitched herself toward the floor. Palmer felt himself lurch up, desperately threw his anchoring hand down and behind the belay device. He stopped her at eye level. She spun on the end of the rope.

"Almost good enough," Elle said.

Swiftly and surely, Palmer dove toward love. He possessed a far more genteel approach to communication than Elle did. Still, they both were straightforward people, and approved that quality in each other. What can I say? Likely, Palmer was also seduced by watching Elle's sweet shape stretch from hold to hold.

When it was his turn to ascend, Elle belted out instructions.

"No! Don't haul with your arms! Climb with your legs, balance with your hands. Bone that right leg out. Yeah, straight. Drop your heel. Breathe. Now, rise up, stand on those toes. Curl fingers of your left hand into that jug. Feel that? Solid! Cool. See, any limb not in use can rest. Higher you go, the more methodical you are. Get it?"

After the hour of training ended, they plopped down on chairs in the gym's snack bar to sip from chilled bottles of Odwalla juice.

"Nice," Palmer said. "Thanks. A bunch!"

"Sure," Elle replied. "So. What brings you all the way out to San Francisco?"

"Oh, my bucket. A beat-up ol' Toyota Corolla."

"Right." She rolled her eyes. "And?"

"A job. At a newspaper, the *Post-Dispatch*."

"Cool."

Palmer made a face. "Not so much. One of my profs told me he wanted to quit teaching, launch an online news venture. Said I should join up. Suddenly he messages me, wait, I needed to try a gig in old-school media before I qualify for his startup. Couldn't see the point in it, but anyway, I said, sure, fine, let's do it your way. So I applied, and won my internship at the *Dispatch*."

"I'm guessing there's now a problem?"

"Before I left Florida, I saw Professor Kruger had a site up. Way different from that news site idea. Calls it 'LoveBabies.net.' For first-time parents? Send in your pix, he'll do a digital mash-up of what your baby might look like. He'll sell you a thousand-dollar stroller, or discount a year's supply of diapers. All kinds of infant services. Must be making money. He's too busy to answer my calls."

"Bummer."

"Nah, it's all good." Palmer said. "I always dreamed of driving out to visit San Francisco. Might as well see what's up with the newspapers, too."

"Sure. Why not? Have some fun."

Palmer let his eyes wander over Elle, taking all of her in. Somehow he missed a slight flush that rose to her cheeks, the way her gray eyes sparked, the manner in which her lips compressed. Or he utterly misread these signals. It wasn't mutual appreciation. She was irritated.

Palmer drained his juice bottle. Then his fingertips touched Elle's hand.

"Hey, you ready to eat? Can I take you to lunch? Any great place to go?"

Elle gazed at him steadily. "Sebastian," she said slowly. "You just arrived from Florida, huh?"

"Yep."

"All right. Clue me in on something, here. Happen to have a girlfriend back home?"

Palmer thought for a moment. "Nope," he said.

"Well, I do," Elle told him.

Chapter 2

I would not call the WestWorld media mavens "bottom feeders." Well, they *do* like to lunch on carrion. If major stockholders approach in a threatening way, they *do* tend to scuttle off sideways. On occasion, however, they can exhibit nobler traits. Their transfusion of cash *did* keep the *San Francisco Post-Dispatch* (my professional home and Palmer's destination) from slamming its doors and chaining them shut.

By 2007, America's newspapers already had started to "twirl 'round the gurgler" (as a nifty Aussie idiom goes). That twirling soon accelerated to giddy velocity. Edgar Allan Poe's yarn, "Descent into the Maelstrom," is a close description of what the ride was like for those of us still on staff at newspapers during that period.

Before WestWorld came to the rescue, the O'Higgins brothers, William and Terrance—floundering spawn of the newspaper's founding family—had long felt overmatched by their leadership duties. Their residual ability steadily drained off, due to bad habits that can afflict the wealthy, indolent, and dissipated. Stints in rehab did help Willie and Terry reevaluate. When a decent offer for the paper was trolled past their snouts, they sold out instantly. A lifetime supply of methadone was thereby assured.

WestWorld snapped up the faltering journal at a bargain price. Its corporate executives fancied they might seize an opening, and by a few shrewd moves, knock the *Chronicle* off its high horse, then build a new paper of record for San Francisco, perhaps the entire Pacific Coast. They even fantasized they might pry the prevailing media tone in our region from blithe, liberal delusion over to a profound, thoughtful, sober conservatism.

I have no idea what sort of drugs *they* were on.

Once the *Dispatch* was in their grasp, they pondered: How best to initiate such a substantial shift?

For openers, they chose to dry-gulch the paper's lead columnist. On the same day that Sebastian Palmer came to San Francisco, one Colm MacCay found himself summoned to meet with our spanking-new top editor, freshly jetted in from WestWorld's airstrip outside Denver.

Tom Brotmann was tall, tanned, elegantly dressed and coiffed. The starched collar on his bespoke shirt rose a tad higher than the norm. His thin face settled down upon this collar, producing a wattle below his jaw. It was the only ripple of spare flesh to be found anywhere on his parched, gecko's body. He resembled a somewhat more youthful version of the senior senator from Utah, Orrin Hatch.

Brotmann had been ordered to slash expenses, tighten production, cut staff, and otherwise flog the *Dispatch* toward profitability. No problem. Inflicting fiscal discipline was a prime entertainment for his brand of editorial suite martinet.

—

"Have a seat, Mr. MacCay," Brotmann said.

Colm MacCay settled down on soft gold leather upholstery, on one side of a desk built of oaken timbers taken from the first clipper ship to sail into San Francisco Bay. He'd faced many other executive editors across this desk, but always found his skills adequate to the task. He did not look especially worried.

Rounded and corpulent, MacCay had a classic appearance for an Irishman in middle age. Silver hair slanted back from a round face sheathed with pale, fine, even delicate skin. What at first seemed a ruddy bloom of health on those cheeks could be seen, on closer inspection, to be a cobweb of tiny shattered veins—resulting from a daily ritual of drinking to excess.

Beneath furry black brows that semaphored to each other like friendly centipedes as he spoke, MacCay's blue eyes gazed out upon life with an expression that was simultaneously bemused, pained, and bellicose.

Brotmann poked at two sheets of paper with a long finger. "MacCay, before me is a draft of your column. Here are my thoughts: Such juvenile maundering won't see print in this paper on Sunday. Nor any other day."

Brotmann leaned back in his chair to await a response.

MacCay pursed his loose, wide mouth. He plucked at the lapels of his Harris tweed blazer, ran a finger under the tip of his nose. He crossed his legs. Trousers hiked up, exposing black socks bagging down into scuffed shoes with worn heels.

"Say it straight, Mr. Brotmann." A sneer lightly anointed that 'mister.' "What in my copy do you fail to appreciate?"

"Besides everything, you mean?" Brotmann said. He picked up the printout as though pinching a dot of lint from his Hermès tie. He cleared his throat, read the column's lead: "'The Bush administration now collapses like a house of cads.'"

He glanced up. "MacCay. Since that day when you first curled a chubby fist around a pencil, did no one ever explain that puns are the lowest form of humor?"

"Wow. Thanks!" MacCay said. "That must be why Shakespeare uses them—stop people from being overly impressed by all the rest of his scribbling."

"You trot out this lowlife Joseph Pujol." Brotmann continued steadily, "And he was, what, some idiot who purged himself of gas on the Paris stage? Really. Vile toilet humor. Comparing him to President Bush? Schoolyard name-calling."

"Le Petomane!" MacCay said. "You're altogether mistaken, Brotmann. Pujol was a star. He could play the Marseillaise onstage by breaking wind."

"What does that—"

"Look. What you seem to miss here is how much Bush suffers by comparison. Pujol made coherent sounds. When Bush talks, all we get is the bad smell. Print this, then everybody, pro or con, yacks about it all week. Isn't that what we want?"

Brotmann tapped the manicured nail of his right index finger on the desk.

"*You* look," he said. "I arrived here to a pile of angry letters and e-mails from Catholics. You claim the Church's good works are demolished by its stance on condoms!"

MacCay uncrossed his legs. "Mr. Brotmann" he said. "In my book, a condom is God's mercy made manifest in latex. If Dark-Agers can't adapt to modern life, they should quit the salvation business, try to find honest work."

Brotmann's pursed lips formed a puckered circle.

"You claim our war on drugs creates gangs, in the same way that Prohibition produced Al Capone. You also recently called Cuba the Monaco of communism. You suggest we let it flourish unmolested to see if a Marxist system has any useful parts."

"Absolutely! Socialized medicine. Of that, we should not be so terrified. Our present system is welfare for corporate bureaucrats. Their only expertise is denial of coverage."

"Mr. MacCay. Do you think we're having a discussion?"

"Shouldn't we be?"

Brotmann leaned forward. "MacCay, you're a hack. Blowing gas? You're a champ! You called the pope feudalism's living fossil. Your mockery of Rush Limbaugh as a cartoon figure—'Ayatollah Lushbimbo'—is not amusing. You insult Vice President Cheney as 'Mr. Balderdash-with-Gravitas.' You said he should be tried as a war criminal!"

"Brotmann, to see Devious Dicky frog-marched into the Hague would provide grand theater, yes? Millions would applaud."

"That's a fantasy for some mumbling nutcase who lives in his bathrobe. My job is to renew this newspaper, help it survive the twenty-first century. Translation: I need your space for real writing. Our readers don't need you! I've got stats to prove it. 'Dear Abby' outpulls you two-to-one."

MacCay lurched to his feet, face turning beet red. He opened and closed his mouth, then said, "You forget that I'm a Pulitzer Prize-nominated columnist. Three times!"

Brotmann smirked. "Always the bridesmaid, eh, MacCay?"

MacCay gaped. Then, abruptly, as if a switch had been flipped, he regained control. He reached back, located the arms of the chair, lowered his bulk. He crossed his legs at the ankles, nodded.

MacCay leveled a finger at Brotmann.

"Hope I'll stomp out, hmm?" he said. "You need a scalp to nail above your door. Terrorize the staff into submission. That's it, isn't it? Hope I'll quit. I'm Guild, so I can't be fired. Not without a fight."

"True. I can't fire you easily." Brotmann leaned back again, lacing his hands over his lean stomach. His smile was icy. "But shifting a work assignment? That, I can do. Your space here, too. Mailroom personnel are boxing up your corner office even as we speak. You'll go to a far more appropriate space. Next, you get a new assignment. If we can figure out something that fits your... talents. That concludes my prepared remarks. Can't waste any more time on you, MacCay! And so, good day."

Brotmann clamped his bony lizard fingers around the unpublished "Colm's Column" manuscript. He bunched up its pages, pitched the wad into his wastebasket.

MacCay reared onto his feet. He glowered as he slapped meaty hands on the edge of the desk. Brotmann ignored him. Instead, he picked up his phone, kicked his swivel chair around, and casually tapped buttons.

MacCay's watery blue eyes shone balefully. He departed Brotmann's office in a lumbering, pigeon-toed stride.

—

Earlier, you met Sebastian Palmer and Elle Jatobá. Now I must inform you that you've just met me. Um, no, not Brotmann. Yes. I'm Colm MacCay.

Immodestly, I've let you glimpse me at a moment when my cozy yet crazed world split open. A long-ignored chasm gaped at my toe-tips. Or perhaps "abyss" would be more apt, since I'd sedulously hollowed my life out. Over decades, I'd gotten that pit rather deep. Consequently, my columnist's role meant much more to me than a mere job. For far too long, it had formed my sole lifeline. Yet I now found it turning to rotten thread.

Upon my chasm's jagged lip, I teetered.

Chapter 3

His second morning in town, Sebastian Palmer strolled two blocks north to Market Street, hopped on an "F" streetcar, rode three blocks east, then walked a block south to Mission and Seventh Street. Of course, he might've saved money and time by strolling straight from his hotel to his destination, but on the previous afternoon, after his class with Elle at Cliffhanger Gym, he'd skated all around, exploring his new city.

Soon as he saw vintage streetcars rattle up Market and the Embarcadero, he felt impressed. Cable cars and ferries were San Francisco icons, nearly clichés. But old electric streetcars, he figured, constituted a real find. Riding one could launch his new job with a degree of real 'Frisco style.

Early on a foggy Tuesday morn, Palmer caught a Milan Tram, a streetcar glowing in Italian orange, jolted a short distance along Market Street, then jumped back off and went south.

The main building of the *San Francisco Post-Dispatch* was a sandstone hulk. Four fluted pillars flanked its main entry. Up by the roof, letters of corroded bronze in a Times New Roman font spelled the paper's name.

The O'Higgins family, in its publishing heyday, hired an architect of middling ability. His true talent lay in squandering other people's money like an admiral on leave. The result, erected in 1915, was a tall, square behemoth that bellowed clout and permanence.

But Palmer already knew, not much went well behind the facade. A decades-long model for funding newsrooms had been shattered. Newspapers, TV stations, and radio news bureaus were all rapidly cutting back, searching for any remnant puddle of that great sea of black ink on which the ships of their enterprise had formerly sailed.

Palmer believed, as his professors at Northwestern had sworn, journalism could only survive via clever new ventures designed to fully exploit digital media. The trick—as with any online effort—would be coaxing viewers to cough up payment. Info itself may indeed wish to be free, as Stewart Brand declared, but its providers still must be paid. How else can they manage to buy themselves a mug of decent coffee?

Palmer yanked open a glass door below the portico of that sandstone edifice. A security guard pointed out Human Resources. Palmer filled out forms, picked up a magnetic card key, was handed a dim, much-photocopied map to the newspaper's departments.

The travel section of the paper was his goal. He'd been hired to help create a new page with a local focus, meant to stanch ebbing readership among Bay Area youth. He also was invited to jazz up content by creating related podcasts and videocasts, and by blogging on the *Dispatch*'s floundering website.

A walnut-paneled elevator creaked him up to the third floor. Palmer homed in on a warren of cubicles that sprawled below acoustic paneling and fluorescent lights. As he deciphered the maze of aisles, his ears picked up a crinkling, then a snuffling sound.

He went around a partition, saw a large red sign suspended: TRAVEL.

A round man hunched above a desk, munching on a breakfast Croissandwich. Another pastry swathed in Burger King livery sat at his elbow. The man sensed an alien presence. His volleyball-sized head swiveled to look at Palmer. Flakes of crust dribbled off his wispy goatee.

"Who're you?" he mumbled through a mouthful.

"I'm Sebastian Palmer. Here to begin my internship! And you must be...Artie Davis?"

Davis' eyes flicked toward the wall clock. "You're early."

"Better than arriving late, coming to a new job, hey?"

Davis seemed dubious. He yanked open a desk drawer, found a crumpled napkin, wiped his lips, then his right hand. He extended it. Palmer reluctantly took the greasy fingers.

"Anyway, welcome!" Davis said, abruptly deploying a shallow bonhomie. "Come. I'll show you the ropes. And what happened there?" He gestured at his own moon face, indicating places where Palmer's scabs were visible.

"Oh, I fell. On some rocks. I'm fine."

Davis led him to a smaller cubicle equipped with a Dell work station, the beige plastic cases of its monitor and tower scarred and dingy from use. But some new material, fresh office supplies, notebooks, pens, paper clips, colored highlighters, tape dispenser, and stapler, sat ready and waiting for him alongside the keyboard.

"Tech support set you up with a phone, voicemail, and e-mail. Call 7247 to get it activated. Dewayne, our mailroom guy, brought you the supplies. If you need anything else, just ask. Someone will come to train you on CCI—the system we use to put out the paper."

Davis' porcine eyes blinked. "Y'know, I just realized, actually, it's fabulous that you're here early! Something I need. Just a minute." He waddled off, returned with a cardboard box burdened with a mound of multicolored press releases and faxes. He thumped the box down on Palmer's desk.

"Sort out these coming events," Davis said. His tone suddenly turned curt. "Pick out the good ones. Write a paragraph on each. Only a paragraph. But include everything a reader must know to attend."

Palmer, dismayed, stalled. "How do I select which ones are good?"

Davis flapped a hand impatiently. "Write as many as you can. Items I run will be good. Stuff I spike will be bad. It's an educational process. Clear enough?"

"Mr. Davis," Palmer said. "Got to tell you, it's not what I signed up for." His voice grew firm. "This is scut work. My training is in reporting and writing."

"Yeah, yeah, I know!" Davis' voice abruptly shifted to a whine, pled for sympathy. "But our new kingpins just kidnapped my E.A. and sent him to Sports. I must have these items entered by three o'clock." Davis gaped at him owlishly, then bobbed his head up and down. "Come on, Palmer. All jobs have crappy parts, to some degree."

"Can't we talk about actual news stories? When we last spoke on the phone, y'know, we agreed I'd be able to try some enterprise. For Metro."

Davis waved his hand again. "Sure, sure. Can't discuss it now, though. I'm due for a travel writer's brunch, at the Hyatt. We'll yack when I get back."

Davis bobbed his head more vigorously, seeking to compel Palmer's submission by inducing him to nod in return. This very well might have been tip number 47, lifted by Davis from a dog-eared paperback, *Body Language Secrets of Top Managers*.

"You're heading to a brunch? After eating that?" Palmer pointed at the wrapper-littered surface of Davis' desk.

Davis flushed. "A trick I use to suppress my appetite. Before I go out. Not that it's any of your business!"

"Of course not. But you know, if serious hunger damping is what you're after, I'll let you in on a secret. What you do is, get yourself some white bread? Then put on a big ol' scoop of Crisco. Add mayonnaise for flavor! Just one sandwich like that should do the trick."

To Davis' initial blush of embarrassment was added the stiffening cheeks of high dudgeon. Even hairs on his sparse goatee seemed to bristle.

"Think you're being funny?" he demanded.

"No, no," Palmer said earnestly. "Helpful, is all."

"Well keep it to yourself, goddammit! I'm not interested. Do your work! If this assignment is not completed, your internship might not go well. Understand? You get one chance to make a first impression with me. You can take that to the bank!"

———

Ultimately, Palmer did as requested. Putting this chore in the best light — as a primer on California recreation — he read all the press releases thoughtfully, sorted them, then composed descriptive 'graphs. The task was still monstrously tedious.

Palmer fingered the final pages. He now could scoot out and score a bite himself. He'd seen Tu Lan, a Vietnamese restaurant, about a block away—

His phone rang. Folks from back home? Maybe they'd tracked

him to his new extension, and were phoning with congrats! Or could it be Professor Kruger, calling to apologize, then announce an actual startup for a news site after all?

Palmer snatched up the receiver.

"*San Francisco Post-Dispatch,* Travel," Palmer said. That sounded professional.

"Goody. A real, live person! Tell me your name, fella!" He heard the gravelly voice of an elderly woman, clearly upset.

"My name is Sebastian Palmer. What do you want?"

"You a reporter?"

"Yes," he said. Sounded pretentious to say it.

"Palmer. I've spoken to five people at your rag this morning. Five! Didn't accomplish doodly-squat. Two even hung up! The rest spun me all around your phone tree till I felt like a goddamn hamster on an exercise wheel. So, I end up with you. Going to be any help?"

"I'll try. What's—"

"Listen. I'm a subscriber. For forty years! And I—"

"Ma'am, if there's a subscription problem, that's not my department. I'll—"

"Goddammit, sonny! You dare transfer me again, so help me Moses I'll come down there and whap the holy crap outta you with my cane!"

Palmer held the phone from his ear, regarded it in disbelief, fought to stifle laughter. This was his first call as a newspaper reporter! Amazing.

"Do I hear you laughing?" she demanded. A tendril of weariness crept into her tone.

"No, no," he protested. "Tell me the problem. I'll help any way I can."

She was Beverly Bancroft. She'd lived near Cornu Point, at the south end of Half Moon Bay, since the 1950s, on an estate she had inherited from her father, Max Bancroft. Max, a Bay Area banking tycoon, had a longtime buddy in Rudy Wyatt, a silent screen-era cowboy. Together, the pair donated a substantial hunk of coastal acreage to the California State Parks. But that land did not end up being managed by park rangers. Instead, under special contract, a nonprofit association of local businessmen now ran a large, equestrian-themed resort on the site.

For years, Miss Bancroft enjoyed walking her dogs across this resort to Cornu Cove—a sandy beach just north of the point. But yesterday, out on her customary stroll with her cocker spaniel (the most recent in a long line of these fluffy pups, the third to be named Jessup, she informed him), Beverly found herself stopped by a security guard. He demanded to know why she was there. Said she couldn't have access now, not unless she wore the ID tag of a dues-paying "member."

"It's public land, Palmer! That's what my dad and his pal Rudy Wyatt always intended. They made it a state park, for God's sake! How can I or any member of the public be shoved off? It's not right!"

"I'll look into it," Palmer promised.

"Heads up, kiddo! Won't be easy! Used to be able to shove my way into meetings of the Cornu Point Association. Now all gatherings are private. Closed door! It's those stinking horse people," she accused. "Trying to grab everything. With their muscle-bound phony, Erik Eiger, in the lead. Thinks he's Der Führer! Really, he's only Dick's stable boy." She snickered. "But none of 'em give a rat's ass about anyone. Dog people, bird watchers, picnickers, cyclists, campers—we can all go pound sand. They want total control, and they don't care how evil they act to—"

"What's that mean, 'evil acts'?"

She paused. "I've been getting threats," she said darkly.

"What sort?"

"You tell me! It started last week. Dead rat left on the hood of my car. Next, a dead raccoon stuffed in our mailbox. Dead deer in our driveway. Any roadkill the Cornu Point staff find anywhere, they must drag it over to my place. I think they're trying to scare me away. Either that or drive me nuts!

"I called our county cops. They say if I had a problem with wildlife dying, I need to call the Department of Fish and Game. Like maybe that raccoon decided to crawl into our mailbox and commit suicide?"

"Well, they can't drive me nuts. I'm nuts already! And I'm madder than a sack of bobcats over what they're doing to my dad's dream. I'm telling you, I've about had it. But I've got a stick of dynamite in my back pocket that'll blow their little scheme sky-high!

I know I need to do it in a smart way. Got to enlist a reporter to help me out."

"Hmm. Okay, I'll come see you. Could you send me an e-mail, with names and contacts for the resort managers, maybe some of those board members?"

"E-mail? Well, I don't bother with that new bullshit, sonny. I'm goddamn old, get it? From me, you get a letter. With a postage stamp. Know what those are? Ever seen 'em?"

"Of course. Well, send me your information, I'll check it out."

"Do that, Sebastian Palmer. Don't just try, do it! Or stop saying you're a reporter, okay?"

She hung up.

Palmer thought it over. He clicked open a new Word file, started to type in everything Beverly Bancroft had said. Then he reconsidered. That stack of "Reporter's Note Book" pads beckoned to him strangely.

"When you're marooned in the old school..." he muttered.

He ripped the cellophane off the stack, flipped open the brown cardboard cover on a virgin pad, and began to jot his notes in tiny, neat block letters.

Chapter 4

A rumpled herd of copyeditors and reporters garnered from both the *Post-Dispatch* and the *Chronicle*, wreathed in oracular plumes of cigarette and cigar smoke, stood near a brick wall outside the S&S Pub. Acknowledging their pariah status, they usually clumped together here, just beyond the saloon doors. As they conversed, they gestured with their nicotine-delivery systems to emphasize major points.

The S&S, located on Tulip Alley midway between both papers, became a watering hole for newsies in San Francisco on that sad day when the city's downtown Black Cat Press Club went paws up. Whether employed in radio, magazines, or papers, many city media types now gathered at this SoMa tavern on weekday evenings to blow off steam, shoot the breeze, swap choice gossip, and savage the shortcomings of their bosses.

After his third day at the *Post-Dispatch*, Sebastian Palmer decided it was time to poke his nose into this after-deadline gathering of practitioners of the craft. Badgering Artie Davis for meaningful assignments had proved fruitless. And Davis had shown utter disinterest in hearing anything about problems out at Cornu Point. Palmer felt like he could use a cold brew. Maybe a few.

Palmer nodded to the sidewalk smokers as he went past. Two were folks he had glimpsed in the Metro newsroom on the paper's top floor: Tod Ericson, a balding man with a fringe of ginger hair and a maroon bow tie; and Ken Stein, a sharp-faced younger man with a coiffed mane of chestnut hair. They had been pointed out to Palmer as a hard-charging duo that led the state-affairs lead investigative team. They nodded back, vaguely recognizing him. Palmer put a shoulder against the swinging door, leaned his way in.

The bar was a long, dimly lit warren, abuzz with chatter and laughter. Knots of people sat clustered around tables. Four older men shouted as they thunked leather cups of liar's dice against the top of the bar. Young men from the neighborhood, dark-skinned, of indeterminate race, slapped away at a line of antique pinball machines set against the far wall. Those bing-bong casino noises rang through the general din.

At the saloon's epicenter stood an elliptical bar. Its well held a matched set of skinny, elderly, white-shirted bartenders. They shuffled energetically about, tugging down taps and shaking up cocktails. The rim of their universe was constructed of stout oak, smeared in varnish so ancient it resembled brown paint. The bar looked as if it might once have been attacked with an ax, then had ink rubbed in its wounds.

Palmer peered at framed black-and-white photos hung on the wall nearest him. They showed abuses the bar had suffered. There were shots of union pressmen, garbed in black-stained aprons and elaborately folded hats of paper, leaning on the bar, pounding on it with their fists, and—under a sagging banner that proclaimed, "Happy New Year!"—hurling cocktail glasses right at it as barkeeps ducked for cover.

Above these hung a row of larger, more majestic frames, bearing crisp veloxes of big-type front pages: the Great San Francisco Earthquake; Pearl Harbor; VE Day; the assassinations of Kennedy, of Martin Luther King; the first walk on the moon; the 9/11 attack on the World Trade Center twin towers.

"Hey, it's our newbie newsy!" A woman's voice pierced the dense haze of sound.

Sally Sartoris, a tall, flat-chested woman with a chiseled face framed by a bell of dyed brown hair, beckoned to Palmer from her table. She patted a chair beside her, one of the few empty seats in the place. As Palmer approached, he saw one smoker enter from outside, a chunky, grizzled older dude, unlit cigar stub clenched in his whiskered jaw. He snatched a chair from another table, dragging it along. He also headed for Sally. His chair bounced over the lumpy floor of painted concrete.

Palmer had heard that Sally, one of the *Dispatch*'s top city reporters, also was the paper's leading union activist.

"Sebastian Palmer!" she said. "Do I have that right? Hey, you met Kurt Vreeland? Guy's been plugging away here, at either the *Dispatch* or *Chronicle*, twice as long as I have! Kurt's a fabulous resource for local stuff. What he doesn't have dialed about the Bay Area probably ain't worth knowing. 'At right, Kurt?"

Vreeland plucked the cigar from a horizontal gap in his clipped beard, muttered something unintelligible, then reinserted the tattered, spongy, ash-tipped plug. His wary eyes gave Palmer a going-over. His handshake was firm and brief.

A short, stout, harried waitress with a Latina accent took their orders for beer.

"How's it goin'?" Sally asked Palmer.

"Well, I'm getting lots of chores done for Artie Davis," he said, "but I'm not learning a damn thing about reporting. Not yet, anyhow."

Vreeland mumbled a few syllables around his cigar stub, and his eyes glinted.

Palmer cupped an ear. "What?"

"He says, Davis is a fat old whore," Sally interpreted. "Under our new regime, Artie's days are numbered."

"No kidding!" Palmer was impressed. "You mean, does it have anything to do with, like—okay, this is just between us—all those deals I hear him making on the phone—"

"Absolutely! A pay-to-play man," Sally confirmed. "Takes a salary from the paper, then tries to score extra baksheesh—free flights, meals, gifts, trips, clothes, memberships. He wants it all."

"How in hell does anyone get away with that? I mean, what about ethics—"

"Travel Section has long been a moneymaker on ads. Our former managers were lax, so they turned a blind eye. Also, Davis does what I call the skunk defense. Makes himself so obnoxious no one wants a thing to do with him. Including oversight."

"So, by me working with Davis—"

"Your reputation is not burnished," Sally grinned. "But if Davis doesn't quit, he'll soon be fired for cause. Probably wants to plump up his kitty before he scoots. But keep your own nose clean. Show independence and some initiative. You should be fine.

"Our new owners claim they'll be strict on ethics. Down where we grunts make our way, that seems true. Can't say the same for the suits up in the suites. But I know they'll use new rules to chop away the deadwood.

"You, Palmer, should stay tuned. Bet their next move will be to set up two-tier compensation—a worse deal for newbies. But WestWorld will find out they can't cut their way to success. Tony Ridder tried that at The Murky. Look what happened to them."

"The what?" Palmer was confused. He'd never heard of a paper called The Murky.

"The *San Jose Mercury News*. Around here, we call the *Post-Dispatch* the Patch. The *Chronicle* is either the Chron or the Comicle."

At that moment, a loud shout was heard at the end of the bar where the four men played dice. A large, silver-haired man had tumbled off his barstool. He now was being helped off the floor by the others.

"Ah, Mac's back at it," Sally said. "Poor guy's always had one major reason to pound the hooch. But they just gave him another. Bastards yanked away his column, without a word of warning."

Vreeland muttered. This time, to his surprise, Palmer partially understood him—something about MacCay being given an Empty Drawer Exit.

"Kurt means, when a boss makes you sit at a desk, but you get nothing to do," Sally explained. "They hope you'll take a hint, and head for the door."

—

More than a bit in my cups, I, MacCay, steered my bulk haphazardly through the scattered tables, leaving a mumbled trail of "'Scuse me's," in my wake. As I shambled for the saloon's front door, I saw good old Sally and Kurt. I hoisted up my arm in greeting, and lurched over.

"Genulmen," I said. "And lady. I salute you! The looming iceberg of fiscal disaster has gashed our hull. Yet here ye be, high on the poopdeck, fortifying for the long swim ahead. Makes perfect shense. Man is the animal who drinks, then snaps his fingers in the face of cash... cash... catashtrophe. Do carry on."

Sally and Kurt lightly clinked their pint glasses together, smiled wanly, but did not drink.

I smirked at them, then gazed down at Palmer.

"Ho!" I said. "And this strapping youth? A fresh recruit for our SS *Lost Cause*, hmm?"

"Colm, this is Sebastian Palmer," Sally said, patting the young man on the shoulder. "A Medill grad. He's come out from Florida to intern at Travel. But I understand he knows podcasts and blogs and video and all that. Maybe he can give you some tips. Then you can blow Brotmann's mind by showing you know how to reinvent yourself."

"Ah, the media's wonder drug, digitalis," I wheezed. "You possess salable skill, m'boy. Here's my best tip: Row away from our wreck! You've come west. Now launch your own opportunity. Facebook may have been done, but there're other body parts. How about creating Boob-book for us gents to visit online? Or Buttbook for the gals?"

Three faces stared up at me with dubious expressions. Did I alter course? Not in the slightest. Perhaps you wonder what deeds I had done to hollow out my life? Here's one category. I throve on shocking and dismaying people, especially during one of my rampaging binges. It was a way to prove I did not want what I actually thought I could not get: their respect. I suppose I felt unworthy of it, so, perversely, I charged the opposite way. Objectionable they might find me, but forgettable I would never be. Such behavior let me matter in a different way.

"Digital videos!" I exclaimed. "Sure, college gals and starlets have been overexposed. But how about 'Grannies Gone Wild,' eh? Heck, make softcore of all stripes. I flatter myself as an expert. Go there, young man, and I can direct your course. Our best is yet to come. No pun intended. And none taken, I am sure. Goo'night lady and laddies. Goo'night, goo'night."

Their jaws started to slacken, their expressions grew alarmed. Clearly, my work was done. I hauled anchor, came about, piled on canvas, and careened toward the saloon door.

Behind me, Vreeland plucked the cigar stub from his mouth and said something. For once, his diction was clear. I could overhear him. And briefly, the others.

"O what a noble mind is here o'erthrown," he said.

"He's a columnist?" Palmer asked.

"Actually, Mac was good!" Sally said. "Less so, of late."

—

Well past 10 p.m., Palmer returned to the *Dispatch* building to retrieve his Timbuk2 messenger bag, stashed below his desk. His mind whirled with tales Sartoris and Vreeland had told about the paper's snarled internal politics and the threat of economics that could whipsaw the whole news business.

Then, there was MacCay to ponder. What a lush!

Palmer reflected, maybe he should take notes on life at the Patch. Could be a popular blog in it, like Diablo Cody's stuff about stripping, or Chris Allbritton on "BackToIraq." He could post what a young newcomer finds while he flails his way through an American media empire in chaos! Something along those lines... .

Just before he departed, Palmer decided to head up to the newsroom to see what might be transpiring out in the broader world.

Two desks on the fourth floor were brightly lit and occupied. One belonged to the night city editor, a man with a curly shock of black hair who wore sandals, shorts, and a loud aloha shirt. At a nearby desk sat a young but weary-looking woman, working the phones, as well as AP and Reuters online feeds. These two were assigned to fill the last available corners of the five-star edition, a bullet column for spot news that ran on page three.

Near the desks, black steel brackets descended from the acoustical tile ceiling, and from them hung three lit TV screens tuned to CNN, FOX News, and Oakland's KTVU. Their sound feeds mingled into a soft babble.

"Cop shot in San Francisco," the reporter said.

"Sure, why not?" the editor replied.

"How many inches?"

"Two. Unless he's dead. Then three."

"All right. I'll call over to S.F. General. Oh, man, now here's a thing."

"What?"

"A woman did die. Old gal at a park near Half Moon Bay. This afternoon. She wandered onto a horse trail. Yelled and waved her arms. Trying to make a protest, they say. Unfortunately, she spooked a horse and got herself kicked. Right in the head."

Palmer surged out of shadows of the newsroom aisle. "Hey! Did they say what her name was?" he blurted.

The reporter and editor, both startled, studied him.

"Who might you be?" the editor asked

"Palmer. Sebastian Palmer. Intern. I just started here. Down in Travel."

They exchanged a glance. Palmer couldn't read it. Something amused them. He bet it had to do with the infamous Davis.

The reporter hid her smile by glancing down at her computer screen. "Name, Beverly Bancroft," she said. "Age, 78. Her family donated all the land to establish the park, years ago. She had some repute as an activist. Various causes. Looks like she argued a lot with the people running the park. Tweaked about some kind of heritage issue."

The editor tapped buttons, checked his own screen. "Cornu Point?" he asked. "One with the new polo field. Down past Half Moon Bay. Where that old muscle-boy movie star hangs out?"

"Erik Eiger? Yep," the reporter said.

Palmer stood still, shocked. Couldn't get his mind around it.

The editor looked at him. "What's your interest?" he asked.

"Oh, well, she called me up!" Palmer blurted. "That woman, Miss Bancroft. My God. I just spoke to her on the phone two days ago!"

The editor shrugged. " Buddy. Lotsa folks croak," he said. "All the time. Some, you might happen to know. But don't worry. There'll be plenty that you won't."

Palmer had been prepared to say that Beverly Bancroft had told him she was being threatened. But the night editor's snide, dismissive attitude made him hesitate. Maybe this was not the right guy to tell. But if he wasn't, who was?

"How many inches for her?" the reporter asked.

"Depends on how good your headline is."

"You are supposed to write 'em!"

The editor chuckled. He pointed to a corkboard behind his desk, bearing the legend "Hedline Hall of Fame." A clutter of short strips of newsprint were pinned to it, including: OAKLAND OFFICER KILLS SUICIDAL MAN, FLATULENT PIGS FORCE AIRLINER DOWN, WOMEN DIE WHEN LAUGHING GAS CANNISTER BLOWS UP CAR, DAHMER BODY CREMATED AS PARENTS FIGHT OVER BRAIN, DISNEY COMPANY SUED FOR EXPOSING REALITY.

"C'mon, c'mon," he said. "Gimme your best shot."

"Er ... 'Hoof Hit Halts Horsepark Heir?'" the reporter hazarded.

"You can do better than that," the editor scoffed.

Baffled, Palmer turned slowly around. Frowning, he stalked off.

Chapter 5

A gray wash of sunrise seeped across the Santa Cruz Mountains as Palmer coaxed his weary sedan over the hump of Highway 92. On the winding descent toward Half Moon Bay, he observed a string of commuter headlights coming the opposite way, writhing toward him like a python made of glowing beads.

At Coast Highway 1 he bore left. Going south, he passed a town, a small farm, then an ornate sign announcing a Ritz-Carlton resort and a golf course.

Next a dense patch of houses appeared, on the tip of the northern arm of a wide bay. And finally, he drove out on top of a broad peninsula that swept out to sea to form the southern arm of the bay.

From his map, Palmer knew this was Cornu Point, so that wide swatch of water down there must be Cornu Cove. On the spine of the peninsula, an access road writhed westward. A hundred yards off the highway, a gateway stood flanked by two massive pillars faced with umber stonework. Between these blunt columns, a gate of black steel bars ran on a track across the pavement. Just past the gate stood a lit guard shack. Palmer could see someone inside, puffing on a cigarette while he read a magazine.

Palmer pulled in, parked about fifty yards away from the gate. He looked around. Near the driveway stood a painted plywood sign with hand-carved wooden letters that announced Cornu Point. Below that phrase, he could see cryptic runes. Other letters had recently been pried off. A ghostly slogan was left, rendered in slightly brighter background paint.

As his car roughly idled, Palmer clambered out, went over to the sign. Now he could read the imprint left by words that had been removed: "A unit of the California Department of Parks and Recreation."

When he returned to his Corolla, Palmer saw the guard's head poke out of the shack door. The guard stared. Palmer waved at the man, got no response, then hopped in his car and drove off.

Half a mile south, on the far side of the peninsula, Palmer passed a gravel turnout that looked just about big enough for his car. He checked the mirrors, whipped through two U-turns, and wedged the car into the spot. A narrow, single-track trail leading from it looked like it might go out onto Cornu Point. *Perfect,* Palmer thought.

He walked down the rough trail, which soon forked. One branch angled left down a steep, crumbling slope toward a rocky shore where languid surf heaved and hissed. The other headed up onto the forested plateau. Palmer went right. He thrashed through overhanging brush, found himself on a wide trail. Beneath his feet, the firm earth was pocked by the crescent marks of horses' hooves.

He walked farther, came upon a square wood post with a red-and-white symbol tacked on. It showed a hiker with a walking stick. A much narrower trail slanted away from there, and on that side of the post was a symbol of a horse.

Palmer continued down the designated equestrian trail. Trees parted, and a striking ocean vista sprang into view, framed by a long curve of misty shore. The brightening sky and the wrinkled sea glowed in the same shade of royal blue, so Palmer could hardly make out a horizon line. An immense blue bowl offered a vision of serene, windswept eternity.

Other trails periodically linked to the one he walked on. Palmer then noticed the wide tracks of golf-cart tires. This cart had printed a pair of fresh stripes over the many old hoof prints. He heard a murmur of voices ahead.

Stepping around a bend, he saw two uniformed men standing beside a white golf cart with a Cornu Point logo on it. A sheriff's deputy, arms akimbo, rested his hands atop his Batman utility belt. Beside him, a paunchy guy in a brown security guard's uniform, his open coat gaudy with epaulets and gold piping, talked vociferously, waving his arms. He seemed to be enacting some sort of story. The guard wore a close-cropped brown mustache. From the rim of his cap, russet-brown hair hung down to his collar.

Right in front of the two men was a plot of ground marked off by multiple lines of yellow plastic police tape tied to the tree trunks.

The paunchy security guard noticed Palmer. His eyes bulged, his jaw thrust out. "Who the hell are you?" he demanded. "Where d'ya think you're going?"

The deputy, older, dark-haired and olive-skinned, frowned at Palmer, but said nothing.

"Me? Just out for a walk," Palmer said amicably. "Why? Anything wrong?"

The men glanced at each other. "Number one," the guard said, "this is a private club. I can tell just by looking, you ain't a member. Number two, if this was still a public park, our gate still wouldn't be open, not until eight o'clock. Three, you're on an equestrian-only route. Even if you were a member, you'd be cited."

"Four," the deputy put in, "you're at the scene of a death, one still being investigated. Can't really have anyone disturb things up here. Not till we're done."

"Oh," Palmer said. "Sorry. What happened?"

"Go buy a newspaper!" the guard said hotly. "Read all about it! Do it after you raise bail, kid, because I'm gonna nail you for trespass."

"Hey, I didn't know!" Palmer protested, holding up his hands, palms out. "I'm visiting here from the East Coast. I just saw a trail from the highway, thought it would be a good walk. There was no sign saying I couldn't."

"And no sign saying you can, either." the guard groused. "That path is illegal. The fucking mountain bikers built it. You know how to spell 'assume'?"

The deputy laid a hand on the guard's sleeve. "Come on, Dick," he said. "Ease up. No wonder you get our locals so riled." He looked at Palmer. "Son, you got some ID to show us?"

"Sure."

Palmer pulled a worn leather wallet from his hip pocket, handed over his driver's license. The deputy glanced at it, then swept it past the guard's irate glare.

"See? He is from Florida. How can you expect him to know any of this? Look," he continued. "We've got work to do." He handed back the license. "Turn around, go on out of here the exact same way you came in."

"He can't! He'd be on a horses-only trail!"

The deputy rolled his eyes.

"He's gotta stay on pedestrian paths," the guard insisted. "Only! That's how all this trouble got started!" He plucked a radio from his coat pocket. "I'll call ahead." He jabbed his finger at Palmer, then at a narrow side trail. "You take that downhill. You get to the pavement, stop. Security will meet you there and show you to the main gate. Try anything else, you're arrested! Understand?"

Palmer nodded amiably. He set off down the trail the guard had indicated. He walked downhill through coast live oaks with curls of lichen hanging from their branches like wisps of moss. It was pleasant enough for a park. But he truly wasn't looking forward to meeting another member of its truly annoying security force.

Something struck Palmer as odd about this trail, though. He paused, trying to identify the strange element. Then he got it. All the dirt below his feet had been swept clean of tracks. The path looked like someone had recently pulled a swath of chain-link or a harrow drag over it, the way maintenance crews sweep a ballpark infield. The sole tracks marring the trail's brushed surface now were his own fresh prints, marking his footsteps down the hill.

Without understanding exactly why, Palmer began to examine all his surroundings more carefully. He felt reminded of his boyhood, the way he and his buddies had chased around in oak woods much like these, trying to figure out places to hide and ways to find each other, while they pretended to be Army Rangers and Green Berets.

Farther off the trail, in undergrowth just past the bend where he stood, Palmer noticed a long strip of white stem ends. Bushes in a corridor that led out between the trees had been trimmed severely, slashed close to the ground. That too looked strange. It was the only place where the forest showed any such activity. Palmer walked toward the cleared space to scout more closely.

Amber sap wept from the ends of freshly clipped stems. He now saw long gouges in the earth. Leaf litter had been raked over them, but the marks hadn't been fully buried. Palmer knelt, and gently dragged duff away with his fingertips. He saw that the scuff mark he probed ended in a broad, sharp crescent.

"Umph!" he said to himself. A hoof had been driven deep into a patch of soft earth.

He stood. Yards off, in the intact underbrush, he noted an alien glint of bright green. Palmer waded with difficulty through the interlaced twigs. Lying upon the forest floor, he saw a set of plastic-framed glasses, with a long black keeper-chain clipped to one earpiece. He looked the glasses over, checked the size against his own temples. This eyeware was small, maybe a good fit for a woman or a child. But what kid uses a keeper-cord? The prescription was pretty strong, too—likely for someone older.

Palmer weighed the glasses in his hand. He looked back up the trail. He reached a decision, folded the glasses, wrapped the chain around them, and stuck them in his pocket. Then he continued downhill, in the direction he had been told to go. He assumed another uniformed bully would be at the end, impatiently awaiting his arrival.

Chapter 6

"What bothers you about it?"

Sally Sartoris gave Palmer a probing look. They sat knee to knee in her large cubicle, decorated with long swatches of sumptuous, exotic-looking brocades, and cheap posters that touted travel destinations in Asia.

"All we ran on Beverly Bancroft's death was a tiny sketch!" Palmer said. "Taken off of a Cornu Point press release. Tarted it up with an empty quote, to make it sound like a real report."

Palmer held up a folded page from the morning's *Post-Dispatch*. "Why don't we say whose horse kicked her? Who the rider was? I mean, that's gotta be relevant, right?"

"Full details will be released following the investigation." Sally quoted. She scanned again the six short paragraphs that ran below a photo of Beverly Bancroft.

Beverly had been a narrow-faced woman, with a fluffy buzz-cut of gray hair. In this photo, the old woman stared belligerently at the photographer as if challenging his right to point a lens in her direction. The photo credit cited Cornu Point Association.

"Underage victims are supposed to get their names held back. Not perps!"

"Perps." Sally repeated dryly. "What makes you think there's a perpetrator? What if it really was an accident? Ol' Bev happened to be in the wrong place at the wrong time?"

Palmer wondered how much to give up. His treatment by the night city editor and Artie Davis made him wary. Much as he liked Sally, and appreciated her help in getting him ramped up for work here, he felt an impulse to keep his cards face down. Don't show until you know the status of your hand.

"Never leap at conclusions," one of his older profs had admonished him. "Always stroll."

"The thing is, who's investigating?" Palmer said. "The Patch hasn't put a reporter on it. Looks like the Murky and Comical also rewrote the release."

Sally sighed, then gazed up at the ceiling as if beseeching heaven. Her brown bangs slid aside. In the harsh glare of fluorescence, Palmer could see fans of tiny wrinkles at the corners of her eyes and mouth.

"Back when I began here," Sally said, "all departments in the city and county of San Francisco had a reporter assigned. True, most of us beat people were just out of school, or fresh from regional rags. But together, we constituted a real set of eyeballs. City honchos knew they were watched. Well, with all our cutbacks, blanket coverage like that is a goner. I don't see how it can ever return.

"Don't get me wrong, I hope it does!" She looked at him. "May sound pompous, but without media providing that level of insight, America's voters will go blind. Most folks don't even get it, that's what's happening now. Brights on Britney and Miley and Brangelina get shoved up their noses, they think they've just snorted some news. Then, for so-called hard reporting, they inundate you with sensational street crime. Don't even notice that you're not hearing much about local white-collar crime. But which class of criminals steals more?"

"Well, I do want to look into Cornu Point," Palmer proclaimed. "Some real bizarre shit is going down at a place meant to be a public park."

"Attaboy!" Sally smiled wanly. "Have at it."

Palmer hesitated. "So, what do I do next? Davis won't let me work on this. He only wants me to be his hack assistant."

Sally stretched out her lanky length, and laced her fingers behind her neck.

"Professionally, Davis is a dead man walking," she said. "So no harm in going higher. Talk to Bob Porteous or Brotmann. Work this. Dig, see if there's any real dirt to be found. If you do, ask them to partner you with an experienced investigative reporter.

Maybe they can pick someone. But we're stretched thin. I just got pulled off a prison guard series so I could go whack corrupt building inspectors."

She stifled a yawn with her fist. "God. That's so *Groundhog Day*. Those bozos straighten up for a year, then go right back on the take."

"Can you help me with one more thing?"

"What?"

"Any quick way to find out where Beverly Bancroft lived? Close relatives she might have?"

"Easy. Do a LexisNexis," Sally said. She spun her swivel chair. Her fingers blurred over her keyboard, then she pointed at the computer screen. "See? It's all right here. I'll print it out. Grab it over there."

"Hey, thanks."

"No problemo. Stop by if you have more questions. Just never again, please, right before deadline!"

———

"You've got four minutes," Brotmann told him. "Start by telling me why we are speaking today, without an appointment made by your supervisor. He's Arthur Davis, isn't that correct?"

"Yes, sir." Palmer said. *Jeez,* he thought. Even though he was from the South, he'd stopped calling adult men *sir* in his teens. But he didn't really know how to talk to Brotmann. Palmer felt like he was trapped in some executive-suite theme park, trying to chat up an Audio-Animatronic Calvin Coolidge.

"Mr. Davis wants me to write up calendar items," Palmer told him. "I told him I went to journalism school to do more than that."

Elbows propped on his desktop, Brotmann steepled his fingertips.

"You realize there's not many new jobs in journalism? Of any sort?"

"Yes. But I'm saying, I can get my regular tasks done at Travel, then add more value to the paper with my other projects." Brotmann seemed to like that. Palmer took a deep breath, plunged onward. "There's a big park out on the coast. Looks like the public is being cut out of the picture. Nobody seems to really understand why. The place is well within the Patch—excuse me—our *Post-Dispatch* distribution area. Our readers should be informed."

"What park?"

"Cornu Point. Just south of Half Moon Bay."

Brotmann tapped his index fingers together.

"Where that old lady was killed," he said. "By a horse."

"Yes, sir. Might be some odd stuff about that, too."

Brotmann's eyes narrowed.

"Are you saying her death was not an accident?"

"Not necessarily. But this woman, Beverly Bancroft, was a thorn in the side of the park managers. Must be easier for them now, with her gone. Even that is a story."

"I see." Brotmann pinched his lower lip between his thumb and forefinger, and stared at his desktop. Then he looked up. "Very well. I'll chat with Davis. But if your work for Travel suffers, you're off this other thing. It's an elective. On all our parts. See?"

"Yes, sir. One more thing, if you don't mind. I asked Sally Sartoris for advice. She said it would be best if I teamed up with an experienced reporter. Would that be... I mean, Sally and I do get along pretty well. And, then there's Kurt—"

"That will be discussed." His pale eyes fastened upon Palmer. "Anything else?"

Palmer saw that his minutes with the eminence had expired.

"No, sir. But thank you."

—

Davis was off on one of his jaunts. Man spent more time away from his desk than at it! Fine. It did mean Palmer had to perform many of Davis' rote tasks. But, he figured, extra work was a small price to pay to be able to enjoy the peace and quiet of the man's absence.

"The skunk defense," Sally had called it. Palmer smiled.

He had everything wrapped up by midafternoon. Time for more research out at Cornu Point. With Sally's LexisNexis info, and a printout of his own from Google Maps in hand, Palmer bolted out the door. He drove down Coast Highway 1 to scout around for Beverly Bancroft's home.

Across the highway, on the east side of the big peninsula, a final corner of the once-sprawling Bancroft estate could be found. Supposedly. Here Beverly had lived with her elder sister, Olivia, age eighty-five.

Eventually, Palmer found his way to a large, flat lot, carpeted by the rusty needles of redwood trees. Tall columns of their shaggy trunks stood in ragged ranks around a small, two-story, green-painted house. Dots of moss flecked its shingle roof. An old Chevy station wagon, its red paint gone dingy, sat out front.

A hundred yards off, steeped in the denser shade of trees, Palmer saw a broad, mossy stone wall. From that low rocky rectangle, two slim stone fingers poked high into the gloom. He realized that he was looking at ruins of a mansion. Only that pair of forlorn chimneys and the ring of the foundation remained. The grand home itself must've burnt down long ago.

The last surviving structure on the estate looked to be the guest cottage. No lights were visible within it, nor was there any other sign of life. Palmer clomped up the brick steps, lifted a corroded brass knocker, sent raps echoing into its interior. He tried again. No answer. He was about to leave when the knob suddenly rattled. The door creaked open, only to be jerked to a stop by a chain. That dark slot exhaled warm air, freighted with smells of mildew and mothballs. Through the gap, a dim eye, veiled behind a thick lens of plastic, seemed to regard Palmer with alarm. He could also see a long nose with a bead of clear moisture clinging to the tip of it, and a wild tuft of white hair.

"What do you want?" a thin voice quavered.

"Are you Olivia?" No answer. "Olivia Bancroft?"

"What do you want?" she repeated.

"Can I come in?"

"No."

"Well, can you help me with something? It's about Beverly. Your sister."

"No!"

Feeling vaguely foolish, not knowing what else to try, Palmer tugged the green eyeglasses out of his pocket. He raised them up to the crack in the doorway.

"Can you please say if these happen to be Beverly's eyeglasses?"

A spotted hand, horribly gnarled with arthritis, trembled out of the gap. It plucked the glasses out of Palmer's fingers, slowly drew them back inside the house. Then the door slammed shut. He heard a lock snick.

"Hey." Palmer tapped with the knocker. "Hey!"

"Go away." A muffled voice drifted out to him.

"I need to get those back! Those glasses could be real important."

"You go away. Or I'll call the police!"

Following that exchange, nothing Palmer did produced any response from the wizened occupant of the house.

"Shit!"

He kicked the front steps in frustration, then stalked back to his Corolla. He also kicked its front bumper, for good measure. Oh, well, he thought. At least those glasses now resided in a safe spot. But if it turned out they were important evidence, could Olivia Bancroft be prompted to remember how she'd gotten them?

Another thought occurred to him. Had Olivia been left to cope with things all by herself? Should he notify someone about that? There must be some sort of county agency that dealt with lonely, abandoned old people. He checked his watch. Too late to try calling anyone now. Might as well return to the office.

—

Palmer finished up at his desk, then trudged upstairs to Metro to survey the goings-on. The night city editor and his pet reporter were absent, perhaps off on a break of some sort.

However, a tall man wearing a Basque beret stood near the city desk. He had a porcelain face of nearly albino pallor, decorated by a trimmed fringe of blond beard along the jawline. He gazed up at the babbling TV monitors, wearing a smile.

"Hey, what's up?" Palmer said. "I'm a new guy. Sebastian. Down in Travel."

"Hi. Leiff Jensen, A&E," he said. "I do reviews. Many different kinds. We're so shorthanded I stretch out all the time. Whether I know a field or not. 'We wing it, for you' should be our new motto. Whoa, this is cool. Check it out!"

"What?"

"It's Erik Eiger! Dude used to rule the sword-and-sandal genre.

Eiger did his thing between Steve Reeves, Victor Mature, and Arnold Schwarzenegger. Pirates with shirts open down to the short hairs, Viking chieftains, centurions who ran off with the emperor's mistress—he played it all. Channel 8 aired a short with him at six, said there'd be more at ten."

"Why's he on the news?"

"Oh, Erik's now Mister Horse Mogul at Cornu Point. And guess what? It was his stallion that kicked that old biddy into kingdom come!"

"What?"

"Shhh!"

"Hello. My fellow Californians. We come here now to speak to you at a sad time."

Palmer saw a man with square, bulky shoulders, dark orange hair, light orange skin, a prognathous jaw, and a manner of utmost gravity, peer directly into the camera. He wore a tan suit and a white tie.

"Yes. It is true. Something bad happens out here, only two days ago. And we take full responsibility, and we are here to tell you the full truth about dat.

"A human being died, at Cornu Point. Dis was a person who cared many things about the environment, and dose places where families might attend to have fun," Eiger intoned. "We are zo deeply sorry for all dis many loss."

He stared into the camera again. "And now, I must confess. Yes! It was my horse, the one dat I rode upon, who dealt Miss Bancroft her deathblow. How I regret dat moment.

"But Miss Bancroft should not have been dere!" Eiger continued. "For she knows dis place where we are just horses! Quickly, she jumps out for us, all arms waving. She yell, 'No! Not here!' And I understand she is wrong, but my horse Franz, what does he know? Only dere is person who swing around her arms and yell. What now? She is threat! So he frightens, den kick out. Very sad, what happens."

Eiger bowed his head in sorrow. The camera frame slowly widened, and now took in two men in gray suits, seated on either side of Eiger. One wore a red tie, the other blue. One had a receding hairline, the other wore glasses with thick black frames.

"With me here today are Mr. Don Bates, the general manager of Cornu Point, and Mr. Larry Wheeler, our executive director," Eiger said. Both men, wearing faint, sad smiles, nodded in greeting.

"Dey have announce new rules, and Cornu Point takes dem to deal with dis unneeded tragedy. Number one, all pedestrian trails must be closed immediate, to stop any at all repeat of dis unfortunateness." Eiger had some difficulty pronouncing this last phrase, and had to run at it twice. "From now, we offer instead guided monthly walks for bird watchers and you nature lovers out dere, and we will call this program the Beverly Bancroft Memorial Walks. You can register for it by telephone to our front desk.

"Also, Cornu Point will hold a celebration of the life of Miss Bancroft at dis very site where she passed away, at 9 a.m. on Sunday morning. As some of you may know, we sometimes have difference with Miss Bancroft about how to run Cornu Point. But always we respect her opinion, and we do agree dis magnificent resource should be operate the best possible way for California."

Eiger leveled his gaze at the TV camera. "Cornu Point Association now hereby take responsibility for seeing Miss Bancroft to her eternal rest. And we will provide caring assistance to her sister Olivia, the last surviving member of her family, and—"

At that instant, a blonde, fluffy dog ran onto the screen, yipping enthusiastically. It leapt up onto Eiger's lap, and began trying to lick his nose. Eiger laughed while struggling to control the small, writhing animal.

"And dis too! Is Miss Bancroft's dog Ketchup, who was out walking with her on dat sad day. I myself will adopt little Ketchup, to make sure he has good home."

Leiff Jensen, the pale man who stood at Palmer's elbow, doubled over with laughter "Jesus!" he snorted. "Shameless bastards. Fucking hambones."

"Isn't anyone going to ask him any questions?"

Jensen stared at him. "What, you think that was a press conference? No, no, only a video press release. Not all that professional, either! Channel 8 airs crap like that all the time. Calls 'em special reports. Same thing the Bushies did. Had reports made by a PR firm, that they distributed from Washington. Local TV stations loved 'em because they looked kinda news-like, plus they were entirely free to air.

"On this one, more dough should have been spent. That puppy shtick was pure cheese. But still, kinda fun, eh? I love seeing has-beens vamping as corporate shills. Just gives me goose bumps. Probably shouldn't think too hard about why that is."

Jensen blew a kiss at the screen. "You still got it, Erik, baby!" Jensen noted Palmer looking at him in consternation. "I'm a real big fan of his early work," Jensen said, and winked.

"What do you mean?"

Jensen just shook his head and chuckled.

"Cornu Point is about to go big-time," he said. "Be interesting to see if they keep Eiger on as frontman. Or maybe, trade up, to a star with more juice."

"Why's Cornu going big?"

Jensen said. "Ah, you must be new to the Bay Area as well as new at the Patch. There's a huge CalTrans project. They're drilling a Highway 1 tunnel through the coastal hills so they can get around this huge crumbly spot, Devil's Slide, where the road sometimes dumped into the sea. When it fell down, the only other road, Highway 92, got totally crushed with commuters. But after that tunnel's built, you'll have all-weather, year-round access. Real estate down there's gonna zoom!"

A melancholy look settled on Jensen's face.

"Man, if I'd only been able to grab a bare acre around Princeton or El Granada or Cornu Point, I'd be made in the shade! But soon as I began to look, I discovered Cornu Point Association guys, and some sharp cookies called Velocity Trader, were way-y-y ahead. And 3CD too, using straw buyers. About got it all locked up. Except for that funky fishermen's town, on the cove's north side. Those boys are holdouts."

"I have a cousin who got into the real estate game when it went hot," Jensen continued. "Started off with these effin' killer loans from Countrywide. Flipped houses like flapjacks all over Stockton and Vallejo during the last two years. Now he's got a cool four million placed with Madoff Investments! Aw, man, it's such a pisser. Shoulda been me! But I was just half a beat late."

An infomercial for Bowflex came onscreen. A chiseled young

stud in a Speedo chatted up the virtues of the exercise machine while working his pectorals and rippling abs. Jensen snatched up the remote control from the city editor's desk and muted the sound, but he continued to gaze raptly at the screen.

Palmer saw the night city editor and the reporter coming down the aisle.

"Hey," he said coolly. "How are you guys doin' tonight?"

The editor grinned. "Not bad," he said.

The reporter gave Palmer a smile of recognition, a slight twitch at the corner of her lips. She tossed her hair, smoothed her skirt, and sat down at her desk.

"What up, Jensen?" the editor asked.

"Not too awful much," Jensen said. He clicked the TV back to Channel 2, put the remote down. "Nice to meetcha, kid," he said to Palmer, then strolled away. "Want to try your hand at book reviews? We could use 'em," he said over his shoulder.

"Heard anything new on the Beverly Bancroft death?" Palmer asked the editor.

He yawned, then said, "Nope. Coroner's report likely come out soon, though. Tell you all you want to know—and much, much more."

Chapter 7

"**O**kay, you flashed that! So let's make it harder! Only use the holds marked with purple tape," Elle Jatobá told Palmer.

He soon reached the top of the climbing wall once more, a lofty perch where dust and cobwebs frosted the steel trusses below the roof of the gym. He kicked outward. Elle lowered him on the rope as he made giant steps down to the floor. He landed on black shards of shredded auto tires heaped at the base of the walls to cushion falls.

"*E aí, companheiro?* You *sent* that thing!" Elle praised. "Only at it a week, and you make 5.10 look sick. Usually, the only ones can learn this quick are small kids. And they're way in touch with their inner monkey."

"Ah, I'm burning off frustration," Palmer said. "Climbing's so clean, so logical! Do right, up you go; blow it, down you come. I wish more of life was that simple."

"You and me both, brother," Elle said.

Once they had gotten the romance issue straight—i.e., there wouldn't be any, since Elle was an unwavering lesbian—Palmer and Elle proceeded to become pals. Over the course of his first week in town, Palmer managed to score gym workouts half a dozen times. When possible, he sought to train with Elle, and they soon settled into a sibling-like ease.

After lessons, they'd hit the gym's juice bar. One evening, they went out for pizza. Palmer learned Elle's significant other was an older woman, Cheryl Bullock. Cheryl had been one of Elle's teachers, a sociology prof. They fell in love soon after meeting, but waited until after Elle's graduation to become involved. Then Cheryl had left teaching to pursue her big dream, founding her own nonprofit, a group called C.A.P., that fought child abuse. "Women go dyke all sorts of ways," Elle told him. "For me, too easy. Just born like that. Always dug girls more! Cheryl walked a tougher road. She grew up in rural Louisiana, got abused by her male relatives. Things didn't improve until she escaped, ran away, left the state. She earned degrees in sociology, since she wanted to try to help screwed-up families.

"Cheryl did try marriage to a dude one time, but it was, like, a complete fiasco."

Palmer chose not to air his own sexual history. Seemed so vanilla compared to hers. He did ruminate on why Elle wanted to relate her story to him in such detail. When she revealed that Cheryl was recovering from surgery for ovarian cancer, and Elle now had to nurse her through chemotherapy, he got it: Elle was loaded with stress, which meant the climbing gym was now a place of refuge for her, just as it was becoming for him. Telling him about her relationship with her partner let Elle blow off steam.

Instead, Palmer reciprocated by telling Elle about something that weighed on him: his probe into Beverly Bancroft's death. Since Elle was not a media type, and had no link to Cornu Point, he figured it would probably be cool. He lacked hard experience with investigation, and was feeling his way along with this. He needed a confidante, a confederate, someone outside the paper on whom to test his ideas. He felt vindicated when Elle proved fascinated by the tale. Her silver eyes widened, her long jaw dropped, as he related what he had found out so far.

"Poked around a bit online," Palmer said. "Small, local news stories came out three, five, and even ten years ago, about disputes over the direction Cornu Point was going. Becoming less like a public park, more like a fancy resort. Beverly was quoted, raising hell. But since last year, nothing."

"Which means?"

"She was being sidelined."

"But how far? Like, fully into a ditch?"

"Exactly. It's real clear she died out there. Everyone admits that.

But what if somebody actively caused it? Camouflaging it as an accident might just be a smart way to cover it up.

"Looks to me like they tried to conceal where it happened. If that's so, they probably also want to hide how and why it happened. "Thing is, they didn't need to shut her up. Beverly's public support began to go dry after locals saw development around Cornu Point as a big chance to cash in. Prime shoreline went nuts after that tunnel started. God knows how much more it'll jump when it's done."

"Okay, but Cornu Point needs to stay on the map as a top horse-people resort, too. Right? Otherwise why would horse owners fork over the bucks for any lots?"

"Yep. So there's a core issue. How can land originally donated for public use get shunted into a private operation? Is it kosher? What happens if we discover it's not? With Beverly out of the picture, who else cares about challenging the surrounding development? Damn few. I've heard a little village up on the north side may put up a fight."

"Oh, yeah—Castello!" Elle gave a rueful chuckle. "Those bone-heads won't go along with any plan but their own."

"Castello, huh? What do you know about it?"

"Plenty! I've surfed all along that cove. But I only tried the point break at the village once. Real bad treatment. Localism, dude, carried to an extreme."

"Elle, you climb, you surf! What else?"

"Run. Triathlons. That got me more interested in biking, so I'm training for my first century ride. And I do capoeira, too."

"What?"

"An Afro-Brazilian deal. Part martial art, part dance, and part gymnastics. My dad teaches it all over the East Bay. Mestre Ja-tobá. Big-time capoeira star from Rio. He met my mom when she was down there one time on vacation. She watched him in a *rota*—which is both a workout and a ritual—and was blown away by him and all he could do."

"You're amazing!"

Elle shrugged. "Feels normal. Always was a total tomboy." She grinned. "Guess I just grew up into a tom-woman."

"So, what about this village?"

"Castello was a beachhead where smugglers brought in Canadian whisky during Prohibition. Back then it was just a bunch of fishermen's shacks, used by skippers who ran salmon boats out of Half Moon Bay. They could land cargo any time of day or night. "After Prohibition, they spent a bunch of their cash. The road in got paved, real houses went up. But you know, Devil's Slide ain't the only place where highways melt into the sea. Those cliffs are all Franciscan Formation crap—basically, old mud. Comes apart when you so much as pull on it. Wouldn't want to ever try to climb out there.

"So now there's no road out to Castello, only a footpath. People in the village push handcarts to get their stuff in and out. They've got phone and power lines, but that path's their only access. And man, they've got this droopy gate in front of it, and barbed wire all over, and warning signs, some with skull and crossbones! If you're not a Castello resident, it's real clear you're not wanted.

"Surfers who don't know the deal, if they park at the gate, get grabbed and have their boards broken, or come back to find their windshields shattered and tires slashed. That's what happened to me! Not the board, but my car. Used to be you could get beaten too, but I think county deputies told them they'd kick ass and take names if the muggings kept up.

"Anyhow, Castello is still rough. I can see why those corporate bozos at Cornu Point might have a hard time dealing with them. On just about anything."

"Hmm. Even so, I should probably go out there. Try to talk to them."

"I wouldn't."

"I'll take it easy. Go slow."

Elle cocked her head. "Those pointy teeth of yours are sunk way deep into this, Sebastian. A warning from me won't make a difference, will it?"

Palmer grinned. "Nope."

"All right," she sighed. "Got to admit, I'm intrigued. Just say if you think you need my help."

"Sweet," he said.

"Y'know, I've always had a nutty idea ..." Elle hesitated. "I might want to try being a cop someday." Those last words came in a rush.

She glanced at Palmer.

Palmer blinked. "No foolin'!" he said, then smiled, imagining her in SWAT gear. "You'd be great at it, I bet."

—

When Palmer hit the office, Davis still wasn't in. Good. In Palmer's view, Davis' absence beat his presence by a huge margin.

Palmer snatched the Travel section mail out of its slot in the mailroom, brought the wad back, riffling through it. He stopped, shocked, at the sight of a letter addressed to him, Beverly Bancroft's name and return address scrawled in its upper left corner.

"Holy shit!" Palmer said. He'd forgotten it would be coming. He laid that envelope by itself atop his keyboard, then just sat there, contemplating this missive from the grave. He noted that his heart was beating faster.

Suddenly, Davis' bulk hove around the corner of the partition. Something was new about his appearance: most of his salt-and-pepper hair had been dyed jet-black, leaving distinguished wedges of gray at his temples. And he looked upset. Above bulging cheeks and wobbling jowls, his eyes had narrowed to slits.

"What are you trying to pull?" Davis demanded. "Going over my head and talking to Brotmann!"

"Had to talk to somebody," Palmer said mildly. "You haven't been around."

"There's a chain of command here!" Davis bawled. "I– I direct all your work assignments!"

"Brotmann told me to cover my work in Travel. Which I do. Then, he said, I'd be free to pursue this enterprise. He's the big dog, isn't he?"

"Just wait and see what your new assignments look like!" Davis sneered. "I've got my ways to show displeasure. You insubordinate little snot."

"You want to punish me for trying to be a reporter?"

"Shut up," Davis advised. "Right now I've got to lunch with the port about the city's plans for a cruise-ship pier. When I get back, you and I will chat. Guaranteed: you won't enjoy it!"

Palmer felt tempted to say, "This will differ from our other chats how?" But he stopped himself, and just silently stared back at Davis—hoping the man would not be his boss much longer. Even if Davis stuck around, Palmer planned to be gone. Proving himself with a hot Cornu Point story might be his ticket out to the Metro desk and a real reporter's job.

Davis shot him a malignant glare and waddled away. Palmer took a deep breath. He blinked several times. Then he picked up Beverly's envelope, slit it open. He unfolded the pages of a letter in blue fountain-pen ink.

Dear Sebastian,
Sorry I was short with you on the phone the other day. I do apologize. Kindly forgive. But I'm feeling quite cranky. This stuff hurting my father's bequest drives me bonkers! I think many of the people blessed to live on this coast have been blinded by greed. They fantasize that development around Cornu Point will bring them an incredible payout.

Even the Coastal Commission got snowed. They like seeing Cornu Point's plan to keep so much of their ground in open space, and intact coastal forest. The Sierra Club loves seeing shoreline exclusion zones and habitat for endangered species.

But the key thing to keep your eye on here is human access. That's growing more exclusive. For members only. Well, there's another meaning to that word "members," which is the one I'll use right now. In my opinion, the Cornu Point Association is a mob of arrogant dicks!

Way back when, my dad's idea was that Cornu Point Park would be a public-private partnership, directed by a local board. See, Pa was friendly with George Deukmejian, our governor at that time. Well, it seemed like a fine arrangement, at first. State parks department was short-handed, low on funds. They needed pro help to run a big, new unit. But soon, the board, the Cornu Point Association, pushed out ordinary citizens. It became all business guys and Realtors and whatnot. They began to see this place as their little fief. They passed more rules, made meetings secret. Everything began to go to hell.

Know what? These honchos at Cornu now, Bates and Wheeler, they're not even from around here! Those turnips actually came from some outfit in Nevada. Their company thinks it's calling the shots now, I suppose! Well, sir, I've got a big surprise for them. I still own a notarized copy of the founding document. My sister Olivia and I are sole trustees, named in the deed of gift. We can revoke that land transfer if we ever think it's abused. And it doesn't end with us, because we have a right to appoint our successors.

They've ignored me long enough! I've talked to my lawyer about how to drop my bomb on these boneheads. I think I want you, Sebastian, to break the news that their scheme to snatch that land won't work. So, how's that? Think there might be a front-page story in it?

Use our home phone number below to ring me up. We'll pick out a time, real soon, for you to visit with me and Olivia. We can sort all this out. Don't let me down, Sebastian! I need the San Francisco Post-Dispatch's help, because whatever else these idiots may be, they aren't wimps! If we're gonna take 'em down, it's gotta be done right. In the press, in the Legislature, and in the courts.

Please see the enclosed list of the names and best personal contacts for all current Cornu Point Association board members. And I've got P-L-E-N-T-Y of juicy files to show you when you get here!

Love,
Beverly Bancroft

That loopy sign-off, "love," got to Palmer. Probably, it was just default wording, stuck at the end of her every letter purely from habit. Still, it brought tears to his eyes. He might, he thought, be the last living human to receive that word from her.

"Sure, Beverly," Sebastian muttered as he folded her letter. "I'll go there."

"What's going on, young man?" A hearty voice boomed into the cubicle.

Palmer wiped his eyes with the back of his hand. He looked up to see the tall, silver-haired form of MacCay looming above him.

"Just working," Palmer said.

"Yes!" I told him. "We tug on the oars, while management ogres pound the drum. And that's what I came to speak to you about. We need to get some old-fashioned beat reporting done around here. Mind if I sit?"

"Help yourself," Palmer said, displaying a distinct lack of enthusiasm.

I reached around the partition, grabbed Davis' swivel chair, pulled it up, then plopped into it. The worn suspension let me sag down a long way—felt like I was about to get dumped on the floor. Palmer regarded me warily. He looked as if he couldn't wait for me to jump up again and leave. Which wouldn't be that easy, now that my tail had settled to a point eighteen inches off the linoleum.

Assessing Palmer's coolness, I realized that I had perhaps overdone my obnoxious routine that night at the S&S. *Which night? Did that happen last night?* I pondered. Oh, well, no matter. On to the pressing matters at hand!

"Seems you and I have won a chance to work together," I announced.

Palmer's smooth brow puckered, but his look of astonishment didn't last long. It quickly shifted to utter consternation.

"Your boss, Artie Davis, and our imperious chief, Brotmann, hoped to find you a coach for some project or other," I said. "Davis nominated me for that role, Brotmann agreed, and," I beamed, "here I am!"

Palmer blanched. I could almost see his mind race, could even imagine his thoughts. *What? Work with this drunk? I'd rather be shackled to a drowning man!* Could Palmer refuse? If so, how might that play? Would Brotmann then sink the project? There was likely a triumphant sneer on Artie Davis' face, now. If Davis was in fact so discredited, how could he pull off this nasty trick? Clearly, his power had not yet waned. What else was up his sleeve?

Palmer did need to say something to me, because, for a large and swelling heap of seconds, it had been his turn.

"Well," he hedged, "I don't know if my topic holds any interest for you. If it doesn't, that won't hurt my feelings. You can turn the coaching gig down. Must be more important stuff you have to do."

Now that Palmer's reluctance lay exposed, I fastened upon my goal. The less he wanted to work beside me, the more I wished to force him to. Besides, Sally was entirely correct about one thing: If I hoped to stick around the Patch and keep collecting a check, I had to prove to Brotmann that I could accomplish a task resembling actual work. Coaching a ditzy freshman with fantasies of becoming a star muckraker should be as easy as falling off a barstool—a feat at which I've amply demonstrated my proficiency.

"Yes!" I said. "Matters of grand import do await my pen." I hitched Davis' sloppy chair up closer to my quarry. "Since I'm here right now, however, we might as well talk this over. So, spill. Whaddya got?"

Palmer then sketched out the Cornu Point deal for me, but he tried to make it seem boring as hell. He left out any notion of a cover-up in Miss Bancroft's death. He left out his fresh receipt of her letter. I'm guessing that he figured if it all sounded like a wrangle over land management in some coastal backwater, my interest would wane and I'd wander off.

But I didn't. Actually, my curiosity had been tickled. I could tell that Palmer knew much more than he was telling. That alone made it interesting. Also, durable instincts suggested there could be a story in Cornu Point. When serious money can be made, it's amazing what sort of vermin scamper out from beneath the woodwork. And the death-of-a-lonely-crusader bit could contribute a compelling strain of human interest.

Add it up and it gave me a sudden urge to reach way back into a mental closet, push old garments aside as wire hangers shrieked across the scabrous pole. I hauled out a cracked and cobwebbed satchel, heavy with tools. Inside it were items that I had not touched in quite a while. I popped it open, stared for a bit, then tugged out a rusty screwdriver—so to speak. I vaguely recalled how that implement used to be used.

"Go find some paper," I advised Palmer. "See what docs are on file at state archives in Sacramento. You can find the place online. Search out original agreements on Cornu Point, old reports, audits and the like. Comb through it. A picture can emerge. You might get decent raw material for a few good questions. Even if you don't, when you speak with Cornu Point people, you'll sound more like you know what you're talking about. Works best if you hint you know more history on the place than they do. Which can unsettle them. Next, you pound that seam. Get me?"

Palmer looked quizzical, then impressed. "Sounds like a good tip," he admitted.

I decided not to quit while I was ahead.

"Another thing: Even with Miss Bancroft gone, don't be shy about meeting what's left of the loyal opposition. Could be other rebels won't stay in the game for long either. They might not possess useful facts, but they could provide some leads to useful facts."

"Who do you mean?"

"That village? Castello?"

"Yeah," he said. "I was thinking about going there. Should I just walk right in?"

"Sure. That's one way. But there are other approaches. End runs. Just like you're doing with Cornu. Tell you what, you go to Sacramento and search all that paper out. Good experience for you. I'll visit some of the taverns on the coast and dig for background. Harvest the prevailing scuttlebutt on Castello. Let's dial all that in before anyone goes out there. Both of us will learn what to ask about. That's key, since the only real power reporters have is a license to pose questions. And sometimes you only get to do that once, so you have to make it good.

"After research and preparations, we should meet to swap our intel. Just like in the movies! Agreed?"

Palmer shifted from ham to ham in his chair. "Let's think about it," he said.

I beamed at him. "It'll be fun."

I watched Palmer weigh accepting me as a mentor. I found out later, the lad did feel bothered about his lack of real-world experience in facing down interviewees. The idea of trying to pull off confrontations with Cornu Point managers or board or club members made him fret. He guessed—correctly—that such encounters would be crucial junctures where his investigative project might either shoot ahead or stall.

If I could display such reportorial skills, I'd be an asset. Sure, ol' MacCay could act the ass. But part of that performance was I came across as defiant and assured. Were I to display that attitude in a professional setting, perhaps I could reveal a thing or three about how to engineer a confrontation.

"All right," he said quietly. "I'll go to Sacramento tomorrow. Do your part, like you proposed. We can meet over the weekend."

"Very good. I approve of this plan."

"Should we start talking to Cornu Point guys soon?"

"Why not? But put them in a position where they have to respond."

"We do have a chance to, you know, surprise them," Palmer gushed. His hunger to see this probe get somewhere grew apparent. "Maybe sooner than we'd like. Or not. But here it is. A memorial service for Beverly Bancroft is set for Sunday at 9 a.m. The public gets to enter the gate at 8:00. We can mingle in at 8:30 or so. Soon as that service ends, we could ambush some of the principals. Bet you that Eiger guy will be master of ceremonies. We should have some questions ready for him."

"Perfect, young man! Call me on Saturday." I pulled a business card from my shirt pocket, scribbled my home number, handed it to him. "We'll compare notes, conjure some questions. Then go beard the rascals in their lair. Nail them down on their schemes for our precious coast. Demand they prove hostile horses make a smarter fit for a public shore than beatific bird watchers. I'll meet you at that gate on Sunday, 8:30 sharp."

I could see Palmer's eyes narrow. He thought I was making fun of his story. In a way, that was true. But it was en route to something else. I felt I had bigger salmon to grill. I had been professionally humiliated by seeing my column, hence my public identity in The City, snatched away without warning or apology. I was now being further humiliated, finding myself hobbled to this determined naïf just so I could draw my pay stub. Hence it felt incumbent upon me to push back on the cosmos, to push down on Palmer, and so once again make my status apparent to all—most especially to myself. To accomplish that, I reached for a different sort of tool, this one quite well polished: bombast.

But first, I had to extract myself from this chair. How in heck did porkmeister Davis get out of this thing? I braced my hands on its chrome armrests, shoved down hard. As I lurched upward, I seized one edge of the cubicle wall with a death grip, and hauled on it with all my might. That wall quivered, and Palmer's desk and the computer upon it lifted slightly. For one second, my fate hung in the balance. Would I tumble over onto my back, taking Palmer's work station down with me? Or would its flimsy mass win the day, and let me ultimately rise to my hind legs? The latter. Palmer's eyes had widened amid this battle, as he experienced a different sort of apprehension. Finally I could straighten my knees. Then I turned, and thrust my free hand out to him.

"Please. From now on, just call me Mac," I said grandly.

He shook my hand, and I could tell from his grip that he was saying, *this better be for real, buddy... but I seriously doubt it.* Oh, yes, my bombast. Probably not the best moment to deploy it. But if you think about it, when is a good time, really? You just sort of have to seize the day. Before taking my leave, I raised a pontifical forefinger. I gave him my best lines from the period back when I taught night classes at City College. Back when I had believed in this mission, with much of my mind, soul, heart, and strength.

"In any news piece, don't let words get in the way of ideas. Do not let ideas get in the way of information. Do not let information get in the way of the story. And never, ever let storytelling obscure the truth. Which is to say, if you manage to spade up any truth."

That's a brief rendition of my encounter with Palmer. But only from the lip of my abyss.

One hundred yards down the mineshaft and accelerating—where I found myself located mere seconds after our meeting—it looked more like this: As I walked off, any notion that I had put something over on Palmer, let alone the cosmos, vanished. He'd emerged looking much better than I had. The young man was trying to get something done. I was snatching at straws, simply trying to delay my plunge. Hoping that some stray wisp might prove a hawser.

Once, Palmer had been me. Or more accurately, I had been him. I had possessed his fire in my belly, that socially concerned, knight-errant spirit. I could have mounted up a crusade in various ways. But for me, incarnated as the dashing young MacCay during that bygone period, a pen seemed by far the sharpest lance. The impact of a good story hitting the news racks at the right moment was a marvelous thing. From boyhood on, I had been an ardent reader of newspapers. The city's top reporters and commentators became my heroes. Every hard-hitting yarn they filed became an episode in their sagas, and I wanted the glory of igniting such spectacular detonations.

Only now, in retrospect, do I recognize the impurity of my motives. I did believe in the mission, yet performing the journalism task itself was not my highest priority. What I lusted for most was the fame, the status of a top scrivener. Which was why Palmer struck me as the better man. Presently, he cared much more about digging up an original story, even in this dark hour, as print journalism tended toward eclipse. Its star certainly was not on the uproarious upswing, as it had been for me. Palmer was facing far more obstacles—including institutional inertia—than I had, but he was prepared to make his own light. A spark had been struck, and he was reaching for a candle.

You have to take your hat off to him, you really do. As for me, I went home, sat before the shrine of the Immortal Beloved, my lost and lamented Anna, then poured a triple shot of Jameson over ice.

Let's call that particular tipple my true tipping point. Imagine something you've been doing for most of your days. Drinking, say, which would certainly be true in my case. You never think that a time will come when you tilt a glass and it will be a fatally wrong occasion upon which to do so. Big drinking moments existed for you before, so many that they all spin by in a swirling blur, a violet, violent mental whirlwind—if you feel ambitious enough to attempt to recall them. Yet an element common to all these moments was that you did eventually emerge, safe or at least intact, on the other side of 'em.

Not this time.

———

Well, here and now, I suppose I should impart some background. A few basics. We'll elaborate more as it grows necessary.

I've been fortunate enough to inhabit the marvels of America and enchanted San Francisco most of my days, but I'm no native son of this bohemian burg. I was born in Lahinch, County Clare, Ireland, in the 1950s. My mum, Lily, died when I was four, and my dad, whose name was Brian but who went by Da with us—and even with his friends, right from the moment when his sons were born—then brought me and my older brother, Connor, to the States where Da found steady work as a house painter. For a while, the man was even the proud proprietor of his own company.

Da zeroed in on San Francisco as our destination due to its cool Gaelic mists and robust ex-pat Irish community. He bought a two-story house out in the Sunset District. Connor and I attended high school at Riordan. I majored in English and then journalism at San Francisco State, down near Lake Merced. Connor studied poetry and theology with the Jesuits up on a hill at the University of San Francisco. I boxed Golden Gloves with the Irish and Russian youths of the Sunset and Outer Richmond neighborhoods. Connor published a thin chapbook of his works with Ferlinghetti, and started hanging around North Beach cafes and the City Lights bookstore.

Meanwhile, fascinated by his own cultural explorations, Da amused himself in a far different neighborhood—the Castro. He went gay. I'm not kidding. And that happened smack amid the flamboyant heyday of the early 1970s. Da had the misfortune to be numbered among that boisterous cadre of bathhouse lumberjacks in unbuttoned flannel shirts with rolled-up sleeves. The rampant infection that killed him remained a mystery to the doctors who tried to treat him, but was probably hepatitis C complicated by bacterial problems and his use of cocaine and amphetamines. This was almost a decade before the onslaught of AIDS, long before anyone understood the nature of that plague. Even so, the rapid progress of Da's decline seemed remarkably similar to AIDS in its early years.

After the funeral and burial of our Da, Connor went into the seminary, came out a diocesan priest, quit that, signed up with the Benedictines, then joined a contemplative crew at a monastery down in Big Sur, the spiritual sanitarium where he has chosen to remain sequestered ever since. I call him Brother Brother.

Me, I fled the local scene by signing on for a two-year hitch in the navy—a move that bore a trace of logic, since my draft number was perilously low. I felt so crazed by my family's recent history, my own rampaging emotions and youthful hormones, that I even volunteered for the UDT commandos, now famed as SEALs. Since

I speedily flunked out of that tough program, I ended up on the crew of a guided missile frigate during the waning days of Vietnam. But I never saw any action—unless you count a month of frenetic activity in the red-light district at Subic Bay.

Once I got back to town, I finished up a journalism degree with high honors, then devoted myself to apprenticeships at rags in one-horse burgs that ranged from Cardiff-by-the-Sea to Crescent City. Finally earning a "rep" due to reporting awards won at these regional papers, I scored a summons to join the "investigative team" (a crew of young turks) at the *San Francisco Post-Dispatch*. I pounced upon that opportunity. Riding high, I began to set the Patch's front page afire on a weekly basis. Next, I stumbled across the blessing that was Anna, and fell into an all-consuming romance. But from its pinnacle of happiness, our affair plunged toward a dire outcome. The blackest of shadows fell upon me. Of this pivotal event, I shall soon tell more.

My recovery was only partial, yet I struggled to appear whole, to continue, by next assembling my public persona as a hard-living, hot-tempered, full-throated columnist and commentator—sort of a modern-day Mencken brandishing a Left Coast gestalt. Which brings us to now, as that particular identity melted away, and I found to my dismay that there wasn't much remaining of Colm MacCay beneath it.

So, to fill that void, I sank into my overstuffed chair, swilled my Jameson, and then another and another. Since my dose so far constituted only nine shots, and I absolutely felt the need for a nightcap, I guzzled one more tumbler of three. I dozed off right then and there. I managed to shake myself awake in the mid-a.m. of Friday. A quart of water chased by a pot of coffee sobered me enough to go to work.

Unfortunately, my work assignment that day was to chat up locals in taverns. Which meant that impulse to keep drinking was easily gratified.

I completed links between public transit lines to arrive out in the shoreline town of Pacifica, and got started. A distant view of that blue sea probed by the long, tan fingers of forested ridges would prove my last lucid memory for a bad long while.

Chapter 8

Palmer stomped up to the front door of Elle and Cheryl's townhouse in Foster City at 7 a.m. on Sunday. His trip to Sacramento had left him in a foul mood. After shuttling from floor to floor in the state Resources Agency all day Friday, he'd left the capitol with a stack of stale background data, plus press releases on Cornu Point that displayed a daunting ratio of rhetoric to facts. He had managed to grab precisely one moderately useful document, plus an appointment to meet with staffers on the Assembly's Water, Parks and Wildlife Committee the following Tuesday—which would entail another long drive back to "Sacto."

On Saturday he'd tried to contact MacCay to discuss their progress on the Cornu Point probe. But the sleazy deadbeat's phone just rang and rang... not so much as an answering machine picked up.

Which was why Palmer had then called Elle, to ask if she'd be willing to accompany him to Cornu Point for the Bancroft memorial service. She might not be a reporter, but at least she'd be a companion, someone to double-check his impressions.

Elle answered his press of the doorbell button, smiled, and beckoned him inside.

"How's it going?"

"Hasn't quite made it up to 'suck' yet," Palmer groused.

"Oh."

"MacCay, my supposed partner and coach, is still out. No idea where."

The townhouse was cool, dimly lit, infused with the aroma of fresh-made coffee. Palmer noted that one wall of the entry was lined with a collection of masks, Mexican items crafted of papier-mâché, theatrical masks from Bali, and African masks carved in dark woods. Sprinkled among them were gaudy creations garnished with feathers and sequins, frail relics from Mardi Gras parades. No one mask was the centerpiece.

"C'mon. Someone I want you to meet," Elle said.

She led him toward the living room where a balcony looked out on one of the brackish lagoons that wound between the buildings a developer had plopped on mud pumped from the lower reaches of San Francisco Bay.

Just inside an open glass door that led out to the balcony, a slender black woman lay on a wooden chaise lounge. A purple bandanna was wound around her head. An afghan blanket worked in red, yellow, and green was pulled up to her chin. Lustrous, dark eyes turned toward him, studied him as he approached.

"Cheryl, this is Sebastian Palmer. The reporter I met at the gym."

The woman's full lips bowed up to jutting cheekbones. A thin hand wandered out from beneath the afghan. Palmer pressed its dry, cool fingers.

"Ah, yes, Mister Sebastian. I've heard a great many things of interest about you," the woman said.

Palmer saw a gray pallor lurked below her dark skin. She spoke slowly, not with effort, but as though she had wandered into some deep stratum that underlay ordinary day-to-day life. Although her energy seemed slight, and her voice almost faint, he sensed a steadiness about her. Her will was being channeled entirely into an effort to remain present. That narrow part of her was devoted, and strong.

"And I of you," he said.

"I understand that you have invited our Elle out to undertake discovery," Cheryl said.

"Something like that," Palmer said, befuddled by her choice of words.

"She feels drawn to any sort of investigative work," the woman said. "Look deeply into shadow. Shed light there. That is our great purpose. Relieve those who suffer. And also dissuade all the blinded ones who inflict suffering, of course. But I sense, Sebastian,

you have never been one of those. You are a well-intended soul."
She closed her eyes, and her head sank back down upon her
pillow.

"Yes," she said.

"What?" Palmer felt a bit surprised, shocked. No one had ever
dared to judge him so swiftly or so fully before.

Elle shooed him away from Cheryl, flicking her fingertips at him.
Palmer faded back toward the kitchen. On a counter, he found
a French-press pot steaming with fragrant dark roast. Two plastic travel mugs waited. He carefully filled them. Through a wide
window above the counter, he watched Elle and Cheryl murmur
to each other.

Then Elle came over to him.

"Glad you found the brew. I see you know what to do," she told
him. "Cheryl said she'd like to come along and chaperone us, but
she's too busy. Got some huge naps planned for today."

"What does she mean, like, she thinks we're on some sort of
date?"

"She's joking!"

"Oh. Well. Fine. Tell her it's not."

Elle shook her head. "You're a piece of work, Sebastian," she
said. "C'mon. Let's hit the road."

They grabbed and capped the plastic mugs, then went out the
door and down to Palmer's battered Toyota. Talking between sips
of coffee, Palmer explained his idea that if he appeared at Beverly's memorial service in a whole different set of clothes, with a
woman by his side, the cove's security service might not recognize him quickly, if at all. Then he'd be better able to pounce on
the managers and ask a few questions.

"You look like you dove into the free bin at Goodwill," Elle commented as they drove off.

"St. Vincent de Paul Society, actually," Palmer said. He wore a
khaki blazer, slightly frayed at the cuffs and elbows, his usual khaki slacks, as well as a green shirt and a plaid olive tie. His unruly
hair had been slicked down and neatly combed.

As they drove to the coast on Highway 92, Palmer brought Elle
up to speed on the problems Artie Davis had saddled him with.
Mainly, the blustery boozer he'd been assigned as coach—and all
the empty promises of said Colm MacCay.

"Just can't believe that shit!" Elle proclaimed. "You want to bring a big story to them. You'd think they'd be wowed, offer you some real help!"

"Can't explain it myself," Palmer said. "Except maybe they just don't know how seriously to take me. Or this story. What can I show them yet, except a hunch? And the dying request of a pissed-off old gal who was likely a bit of a wack-job to start with? Thing is, though, if she was right, that makes me real pissed, too. But I'm just fumbling, trying to figure out the right way to handle it. Inside the *Post-Dispatch,* it ain't much like newspapers in all the movies. It's not *The Front Page, All The President's Men, Absence of Malice,* or even *Fletch,*" Palmer said, reeling off vintage films he'd watched on DVDs while at school. "People at the paper seem way disorganized and kinda crazed."

"Shock me," Elle replied. "Nothing's like what you see in the movies."

"Can't make headway with state park people, either," Palmer said. "They like the deal with Cornu Point. They're not interested in being bothered by people with questions. In Sacramento, they handed me a bunch of fluff, and wouldn't open background archives without permission from the department director. But it took hours to work my way up to a deputy director! All he gave up was a copy of the newest Cornu Point contract, which he just happened to have on his desk. Told me that California was getting a great deal. But he said if I want the archives cracked, I need to file a FOIA request."

"What's a 'foy-ya'?"

"Freedom of Information Act request," Palmer said. "May sound simple, but it can take months to get what you're after. Years."

"Ai-yi-yi. You plan to work it that long?"

"Not hardly. I want to get at the truth, PDQ. If poor ol' Beverly Bancroft was squished on purpose, whoever did it needs to pay!"

Elle nodded. "Okay! Real close to why I want to be a cop. Something I've learned from watching Cheryl work. Justice isn't something that you find. You have to knuckle down, build it, force it to happen. Cheryl's focus is baddies who hurt kids. On the shit-head scale, I'd say people who hurt old ladies must run a close second. I want to bring justice to all those boneheads. Everybody

needs a purpose in life. Feels like I was born to kick moron butt!"
Palmer shot her a sidelong glance. "Woo, jump back!" he said.
"Avenger chick on the prowl."

Elle blushed.

"Thing is, though" he continued, "you've got to make sure it's
dialed. Otherwise you end up too much like the shitheads you
want to bring down. Detective phase comes first."

"Right," she conceded. "I need to keep myself reminded of that."

"Well, me too."

"Maybe a tattoo of some kind."

"Yep… on our trigger fingers. Well, your trigger finger. My typ-
ing fingers."

Driving down Coast Highway 1, they approached the towering Cornu Point gate with its dramatic rock pillars. Then Palmer
surprised Elle by turning off the highway to the left rather than
taking the park's entrance drive. The roadway leading left was a
narrow ribbon of crumbling asphalt that wound along the north
side of the peninsular ridge toward a high draw. Up there, they
could glimpse the vivid green crest of a redwood grove swaying
slowly, sensuously, in intermittent gusts of coastal wind.

"Where we headed?"

"We're early, so let's go check on Olivia," Palmer said. "Tried to
call her, but no answer. Got Beverly's letter right here." He patted
a side pocket of his jacket. "After Olivia sees Beverly's handwrit-
ing and signature, maybe she'll open up to us. Tell you one thing,
though: I won't let her snatch it, the way she did Beverly's glasses! Which I need to get back, by the way. Our real target is some
old Cornu Point papers Beverly said they had, some very important stuff. Hope we can score a look at those."

Palmer slowly pulled into the flat near the green guesthouse.
The red station wagon was gone, leaving an oblong of tall grass
where it had been parked. A sheet of plywood had been nailed
over the house's front door.

A huge, brown-skinned man in a Cornu Point guard uniform
strode toward them.

"Hey! Dis place all private now," he said. "Closed up. You must
turn around and leave here now. Ya."

Instead, Palmer shut off the engine and got out.

"Hi. So, what's happening with Olivia Bancroft? She home?"

"De old gal dat live here? Oh, dey take her away. She screechin' and floppin' aroun' like de fish, ya." The man grinned. "Real fonny show! But in de end, dey put her in de ambulance, and off she go."

"Where'd they take her?"

He shrugged. "It no matter. Not for you. Someplace bettah fo' dat. But you leave now, hey?"

Palmer didn't answer. He glanced around at the site. He saw a pair of yellow loaders and earth movers parked under the shadow of the trees. Then he observed, amazed, that the jutting chimneys of the old mansion had been completely knocked over, and the building's foundation had been pushed up into a heap of rubble.

"What's going on here?"

"You go now." The man stopped smiling. He plopped a weighty hand on Palmer's shoulder, gave him a slight shove. Elle jumped out of the car.

"Stop that! Leave him alone!" she warned.

The man scowled, turned to her.

"Elle, no!" Palmer said. "C'mon. It's useless. Place is probably already cleaned out." He looked at the guard. "Bye, big guy. Have yourself a fine day."

"Ya," the man said. "Soon as you gone!"

As Palmer drove them away, Elle turned her head to watch the guard through the rear window. She saw him reach into his shirt pocket, tug out a notebook. It looked like he was jotting down their car's tag number. Just before they rounded a turn, she saw him pluck a black Motorola radio from a belt holster. She told Palmer. He nodded, and grimaced.

"Might get famous around here, sooner than we want," he said.

—

Parking areas within and without the Cornu Point main gate had begun to fill at 8 a.m. The cars primarily disgorged people of middle age or older, Bay Area locals who had known the Bancroft sisters as local characters, or remembered family holidays spent playing in the shoreline park before it began to shift to operation as a fancy equestrian resort.

Palmer drove up at 8:15, and selected a space for the Toyota, well away from the guard shack. He topped off his ersatz disguise by now adding a black-and-orange cap with the SF Giants logo, and dark glasses. He and Elle loitered beside the car. Palmer hoped MacCay might astound them by fulfilling a commitment and actually showing up according to their original plan.

Finally, at 8:40, Palmer grabbed Elle's elbow.

"C'mon! MacCay's flaked on me again, for sure. We gotta go in or we'll be late!"

"You positive?"

"That loser didn't answer his phone all day yesterday! And he said he'd wait for my call. He claimed I could totally rely on him being here this morning. Goddammit, what a miserable excuse for a mentor! He's my *tor*mentor. I swear, I'm writing that alky off. If he's what the *Dispatch* sees as a partner, I don't want one. I'll do it all by myself!"

Elle eyed him. "Never seen you this riled before."

"Well surprise, surprise. I get upset too."

"Don't worry about this, Sebastian. I'll buddy you on it," she said, her voice firm and assured. "Hell, I don't know how to help write a story, but we sure can dig around together until we figure out what's happening."

Palmer eyed her, then nodded curtly.

As they hurried through the gate, a guard silently handed them a one-page map to the memorial site, a designated route marked on it in yellow highlighter.

"Thing is, I wanted a boost from a journalism pro who knew all the tricks. Now we just have to wing it," Palmer fumed.

"Well, go ahead!" Elle urged. "Anyone who redpoints a 5.10 should be able to pull off this easy crap."

Beyond the main gate, the Cornu Point Park entrance road curved sedately through a double line of stately eucalyptus. In the far distance, trim horses galloped to and fro on a green polo field as smooth as an ice-skating rink. More horses and riders were gathered under the red tile roof of a sheltered dressage area. A parking lot nearby was jammed with huge trucks and horse trailers. The faint, garbled voice of an announcer on a PA system drifted up to them.

"Well, well. Whaddya know," Palmer said, checking the map. "They picked the same trail for people to go up that I came down on last week! Kinda brazen." He pointed to a post at a trailhead to their left. A signboard tacked on it that read, TEMPORARY PEDESTRIAN ROUTE. TO BANCROFT MEMORIAL. NO HORSE USE ON SUNDAY UNTIL NOON.

They walked uphill through a forest of oak and Bishop pine until they reached the bend in the path where Palmer had seen the disturbed earth. Now that site was fully reworked. Young trees had been planted in tilled ground, with protective wire cages placed around them to keep the deer from nibbling off tender bark and leaves.

"So, here's your real Bancroft memorial grove," Palmer said somberly. "All tidied up. Can't hardly tell anything happened. Over there is where I found her glasses."

He and Elle at length hiked up to the broad equestrian trail that overlooked the sea. A reviewing stand had been erected there, draped in black-and-green bunting. A small crowd was collecting around it. A man in a black shirt and minister's collar stood on this dais. With him were two Cornu bosses Palmer remembered from the Channel 8 video, and Erik Eiger, too, preening, standing tall, massive chest puffed out. His skin and hair glowed in orange shades that looked somewhat toxic in direct sunlight.

The paunchy Cornu Point security chief stood near Eiger, speaking quietly to him. This time the guard wore a black suit and black tie, not a uniform. But he still had a brass nametag. Palmer edged closer until he could read it: D. Prichard. Palmer nudged Elle, pointed him out.

"That's the guy," he whispered. "Saw him up here, morning after Beverly died. He was trying to get a deputy to believe that she died on a horse trail. He wanted to make it sound like it was all her fault."

Elle stared at Prichard.

"Why's he wear a wig?" she asked.

"Hmm?"

Palmer studied the security chief. It was true. Prichard's longish russet locks had a stiff quality. They had been styled and combed to conceal the edges of the hairpiece. It looked expensive, made of real human hair. But after a moment's study, you could spot it for a rug.

Two uniformed guards stood in the background. Beside them bulked a large, tarpaulin-covered lump.

Eiger went to the microphone. "People? People? It's time. We should start," he said. "Padre?"

The minister stepped to the mike to beseech the blessing of some anonymous "higher power." He noted that all flesh is grass and our time under the sun is fleeting, hence we should all perform good works and seek to love one another. Then Bates, or perhaps it was Wheeler, ran through a list of Beverly Bancroft's accomplishments, not least of which was ensuring that Cornu Point's natural beauty would be saved for future generations to enjoy.

Then it was time for the star's turn.

"Dis here is a big, solemn occasion," Eiger said. "One of our own is fallen." He lifted his chin, and his stern gaze searched the audience members. "Yes! But Beverly Bancroft is not truly gone. If each of us picks up the torch her hands have dropped, and carries dat onward, we can light up dis small, green, most eggsallent corner of the world."

Eiger then explained how the funds the state gained by transforming Cornu Point into a private resort would help the California Department of Parks and Recreation keep other units open. Although access to Cornu Point now had to be restricted, to preserve human safety and protect wildlife, the net result would be improved outdoor access for more people all across the state—just in different locations.

"Bottom line, dat's eggsactly what Beverly Bancroft desires for us," Eiger said. He signaled the uniformed security guards. They hauled the tarp off a sculpted wooden bench with a shiny bronze plaque bolted to its back. A ripple of applause spread through the crowd.

"We now present the Beverly Bancroft Memorial Bench," Eiger said. "And we pray dat all who sit down upon it enjoy dis great beauty here, and feel Beverly's spirit, and some of her fantastic inspiration."

His lips spread in a grin, displaying glistening rows of perfectly capped teeth.

"And so, tank you all so very much for coming," Eiger said. "We have been pleased to have you here. And now, I announce, dis ceremony has ended. And so, it is time for all of you to leave."

Sebastian Palmer had wormed his way up to the edge of the stage. "Mr. Eiger!" he said, waving his hand. "I'm Sebastian Palmer, from the *San Francisco Post-Dispatch*. Our readers have missed seeing you appear in films. Any new movie projects you can talk about?"

Eiger's hefty eyebrows jammed together, but the smile broadened on his face.

"Oh, yah, I read scripts. But dere are not so many good ones. None I would choose. Maybe, I have to write one? I should do dat! Erik Eiger save the world, one last time. But save always the Word file first, yah."

A titter of laughter rippled through the remaining watchers. Many had already obediently begun to plod back down to the parking lot.

"And that horse, the one that you called Franz," Palmer said. "The one you rode when it kicked out, and its hoof killed Miss Bancroft, what's happened to him? Where's that horse now?"

Eiger's smile vanished as if wiped off with an eraser.

"Franz has been gone. I do not know where. Seeing him would now make me sad, so he is sold to a place where dere is perhaps not so many people. All so much better for everyone dat way, you see? It is what we all should want."

D. Prichard, the security honcho, looked annoyed when the anonymous reporter asked his first question. At the second question, he frowned. He had suddenly recognized Palmer as the interloper he'd met on this very site the morning after Bancroft's murder. And that jogged another memory: footprints he had found veering off the pedestrian trail later on that morning, which showed the intruder from Florida had managed to poke around the actual death scene—despite Prichard's early effort to groom it back to respectability.

Prichard stepped forward briskly, palm up to halt the questioning. With his other hand, he beckoned the uniformed security guards.

"Cornu Point apparently took Beverly Bancroft's sister, Olivia, out of the house where they lived together," Palmer persisted. "Where is she now?"

Eiger grinned, shrugged. "Don't know a ting about dat."

Prichard moved up to Palmer, rudely thrust his paunch against him, pushing him back from the low stage.

"No more questions!" Prichard said. "This is not a press conference! You insult Miss Bancroft's memory with this behavior." His brown eyes, with black pinprick pupils, locked on Palmer. "I could arrest you for disturbing the peace!"

"You won't answer questions from the press? On what grounds?"

"On *our* grounds." One of the Cornu Point bosses, the one without the black glasses, but equipped with substantial smoker's breath, suddenly appeared by Palmer's elbow. "You're on private property. Miss Bancroft's memorial will not become a media circus. We'll answer questions in due course, but only if you inquire through proper channels. Make an appointment! Right now, I'm afraid we must ask you to leave."

"Take lil' Snoopy here down to the gate," Prichard told the pair of guards. "Make sure it's a quick trip." The guards nodded. Flanking him, they gripped Palmer by the elbows.

Elle rushed toward them, her gray eyes ignited, her face fierce. Palmer feared the impending explosion. He felt amazed that he was able to deflect it simply by giving Elle a sharp warning stare and a firm shake of his head.

Maybe she recognized the big picture, too.

—

"Those morons completely gave you the bum's rush!" Elle was steamed. "Why did you stop me? I wanted to take 'em both out!"

"Which would have made our situation better? Come on! It's cool. They're just telling us they do have something to hide," Palmer said. "Maybe, lots of stuff."

He drove his rusty white Corolla northward on the Highway 1. They cruised past the sweeping arc of Cornu Cove, where long lines of ocean swells formed a swath of blue corduroy unfurling to a misty horizon.

"Stunning!" Palmer said. "What do you think an acre out here is going for now?"

"Hey! There's the driveway to Castello." Elle pointed at a

nondescript dirt track that bent westward off the highway. "No sign. They tear it down whenever CalTrans tries to stick one up."

"Let's go look!"

Palmer swung the wheel. The car jolted over the rough road. Out the side windows, broad draws appeared where small farmhouses stood beside dusty fields of artichokes and strawberries. Elle pointed out an overlook that was the last safe place for surfers to park. They finally reached a dirt lot that held a mélange of cars and pickups. These well-worn vehicles were parked at an angle against a sagging wire fence supported by sledged-in lengths of rusted rebar.

Signs on the fence broadcast warnings in red and black paint: KEEP OUT! THIS MEANS YOU!; CASTELLO RESIDENTS ONLY; DI MASTINI RULES; and WANT TO LOSE YOUR CAR? PARK IT HERE.

A sagging gate, draped with barbed wire, creaked in the ocean breeze. Beyond it, a footpath writhed out to sea over the undulating terrain. A wooden bridge across an erosion gulch was visible, then the path took a sharp bend and vanished.

Palmer chuckled. "Wow. The Beta version of Cornu Point." He looked about as the Toyota's engine idled. "Seems kinda dead, though."

"Walk down that trail," Elle said. "I guarantee, in about a minute, someone will pop out of the bushes and demand you explain why you're there."

"Introductions are no problem? Well, I don't think I'll try it. Not quite yet. But my car looks like it belongs. Eh, Blanca? See any old buddies?" He patted the dashboard. "I need to get you back home, Elle. Let's not make Cheryl mad—she might kick my ass."

Elle shot him an amused look. Palmer turned the car, and bounced back out to the road. As they continued north to the Highway 92 junction, Elle glanced back through the rear window.

"I'm thinking we're being followed," Elle said. "A black SUV turned off the highway when we did. Then it disappeared. Now here it is behind us again."

"Hmm! Dudes from Cornu Point?"

"That would be my guess."

"Well, we can't let 'em tail us all the way back to your place!

They don't know who you are. Should stay that way, so let's lose 'em. Seatbelt on?"

"Sebastian! This is a crappy old Toyota! What can you do?"

"We'll see."

"Don't try anything stupid."

"What if I'm tired of trying to be smart?"

Elle set her jaw and shook her head.

As they neared Half Moon Bay, the highway broadened to four lanes. A traffic light ahead of them flicked to yellow. Palmer checked his mirrors, then suddenly swerved into the left-hand lane as the light went red. An unhappy driver behind them leaned on his horn. Now the trailing SUV was two cars back and over in the right-hand lane. Palmer studied his mirrors. The SUV's windshield was too darkly tinted to make out any details about the person behind the wheel.

The light went green. Bumping over the low concrete divider, Palmer whipped his car into an illegal U-turn into the southbound lanes. Horns blared from a new set of pissed-off drivers. The black SUV surged forward, seeking to force its way over into the left lane to follow suit. Instead, it sideswiped the car that had been just behind Palmer.

A cacophony of horns and shouts faded behind them as they drove away.

Elle colored slightly. "Okay, I admit that was kinda cool," she said.

He held out his fist. She bopped it with her own, top and bottom.

Chapter 9

C ornu Point's security chief enjoyed a home perched high on the bluffs at the ocean end of the resort. Only Bates, the general manager, and Wheeler, the resort director, boasted better views from their houses.

Behind glass slab windows that looked out onto a broad deck of weathered teak, Dick Prichard began to wind down from the day's aggravations. He had plopped his russet wig on the cranium of a plastic display head, and had unstrapped his paunch — a quality prosthesis made of foam latex — from his sweaty torso and tossed it on a couch.

Garbed now in a tank top, loose shorts, and leather sandals, Prichard stood revealed as a tall, lean, hard-muscled man of indeterminate age — perhaps in his mid-forties. His shaved head was round, with a smooth, domed forehead. But tiny, pointed ears that flattened against his skull tilted him toward a somewhat feral appearance, as if a line of red fox DNA had burrowed into his genome.

Prichard held a slim crystal glass containing a purple bulb of cabernet in one hand, an open wine bottle in his other. He advanced to pour into the upraised glass of Erik Eiger, who sprawled on the couch next to Prichard's phony belly. Eiger was dapperly dressed in an ecru linen suit. Although indoors, he kept his sunglasses on.

"Something I learned over my years with the DEA," Prichard said. "Once you get scum on the run, never ease up. Keep drivin' hard. Set the agenda. Keep surprisin' 'em. That way, they never get a chance to surprise you."

"Ah. So. You do things to drive Mr. Bates?" Eiger cocked his head, struck a pose, acting like he'd said something clever. Prichard decided to let him think so.

Eiger dumped a substantial amount of wine over his lower lip, gulped it.

"Sure. Why not?" Prichard said. "If Bates has to smack away buzzing shit-flies while he tries to wrestle his deals closed for 3CD, he's got less time to speculate on what Velocity Trader might be up to in his neighborhood. But no. Mainly, we've got to shove hard on Snoopy, that pup reporter. Maybe we count ourselves lucky we just got one media hound doggin' us. And he ain't nothin' but a rank upstart. I checked. Out to make a name for himself. We gotta give him sumpin' else to think about."

Eiger turned his square head. The dark bulge of his glasses aimed at Prichard. "You told me Bancroft would be our last big problem."

Prichard's eyes narrowed. "I do recall mentioning 'big.'" He aimed a forefinger at Eiger. "Only a damn fool ever says 'last.'"

"Our sale must go through," Eiger stated flatly. "You promise me dat."

"You need to relax."

"Relax?" Corners of Eiger's thin-lipped mouth quirked. "With what?"

"Percocet okay?"

Eiger lifted a languid, indifferent shoulder.

Prichard tugged open a drawer in the side of a black lacquer coffee table that sat before the couch, extracted a small brown envelope. He shook out a pair of white pills, dropped them into Eiger's extended mitt. The muscleman caught them, casually pitched them into his mouth, rinsed them down his throat with the last swallow of wine in his glass.

"What else dere, in dat treasure box?" he asked.

"Not much," Prichard admitted. "But, any lil' thing your heart desires, I can get you, reasonably quick and damned cheap. Dilaudid-Atropin? Alfentanyl? Diprivan? Just ask. My boys are connoisseurs."

"Your boys are common sewers," Eiger repeated dreamily.

Prichard ignored that. He pulled a black ladder-back chair up in front of the couch, sat, and refilled their wineglasses.

"Here's what you need to focus on," he said.

"Focus-pocus," Eiger said.

"Everybody for miles around here is wild to move real estate. Except for me and you. We're positioned to sell options. Might not make as much dough, but in the short run we can yank our nuts out of the fire, relatively speaking, with lightning speed, then get a move on. Some roadblock or judicial finding or embarrassing document comes to light, it's not our problem. We've cashed out."

Eiger mimed working the handle on a one-armed bandit, and seeing three sprigs of cherries click into place.

"Ka-ching ka-ching ka-ching," he said.

"Exactly. Now, our top-drawer options, we scored off the dirtbag farmers around Castello. So our trigger has to be when the state finally lurches into action and evicts those deadbeat squatters at the village. Which my Sacto contacts tell me *is* in the works! All we need is one more little shove. The wops go, then the farmers go. Next, the heavens open, clouds part, a shower of gold pours on the north end of Cornu Cove, and we stand under it with a wheelbarrow. We could sell to 3CD, to the association Realtors, or shit, just hold ourselves a wild-ass Internet auction.

"Then, it's *hasta le vista!* We make out like bandidos, then gallop outta town like bandidos. Let Velocity's office space in Bermuda die a natural death, and baby, we are clean gone!

"But we need to make an extra move, right now. Something that will accomplish multiple goals. Like a pin or skewer in chess. Got to get that reporter back on the bench. Also, need us a strongly negatory PR hit on those Castello bozos, to prod the state to get that eviction underway. What should that move be? Well, I guess I'll throw the floor open for ideas."

Prichard rubbed his chin, glanced at Eiger, and realized he'd been talking to himself. The big man's impassive face was inclined toward the floor. A backlit tree outside cast a wavering shadow upon the rough tiles. Eiger stared down at this gently shifting pattern as though hypnotized.

"Ah, what a shitload of help you are. Sure you earn your twenty percent?"

Eiger's shades rotated to peer opaquely at Prichard, like the blank eyes of a large, inquisitive insect.

"Always I have done what you've ask. And always I do only what you ask," Eiger said. "What's dat worth?"

Prichard seemed startled.

"Right," he said. "Absolutely correct, Erik. If I hand you a script, you're spot on by shooting day. You hit all your marks, you never drop a line."

"Dat is damn correct! I am professional."

"You are a star. I do app—"

WHAPP!

A thump of astounding volume reverberated off the tall glass windows. Outside, a large white shape fell and thrashed about on the deck.

"Jesus!" Prichard shouted. "What the fuck?!"

He jumped to his feet. One of the glass slabs formed a door that led out onto the deck, and Prichard shoved it open. A bloody heap of white feathers, extended wings, a clacking yellow bill… a California gull lay there, quivering atop the silvery wooden boards, its neck broken, life ebbing. Against the wall, below the window, a small glittering fish humped and flipped.

Prichard looked out over the ocean. To his right, dots of white light glittered off a rumpled quilt of wings that beat frantically northward. To his left, a smaller sheet of dark wings beat at a somewhat slower rhythm, but all those birds were clearly running off. To flee what? He looked up.

Something big flew up high; he could see its shape flutter against the edge of a cloud.

Eiger stepped through the door, and his eyes followed the direction of Prichard's gaze.

"What the hell is that?" Prichard said, pointing. "You make it out? Osprey? Eagle?"

"Look, up in da sky," Eiger intoned. "Faster den a speeding pullet…"

Prichard snickered. "Crazier'n a hoot owl, aincha? Erik. Listen! Here's your take-away, all right? Bad boys rule. Whatever scared that bird lyin' there, it was bad-ass enough to make him fly straight into a wall. That's what I'm sayin'. That's what we need to do! It's our sign from heaven. We're completely on the right track."

Monday morning found Palmer back at the *Post-Dispatch*. He whipped through his obligatory scut work for the Travel section, then scouted around for Sally Sartoris. But aside from its vivid knickknacks and decorations, her cubicle stood empty. So he headed up to the newsroom to try to locate his next choice for a journalism consultant, Kurt Vreeland.

Vreeland's desk in Metro stood against windows looking out on Mission Street. A berth on that row of desks could only be acquired by persistence, i.e., seniority, i.e., longevity, i.e., abundant merit, i.e., many front-page bylines, preferably laid out in the paper's most valuable "real estate," below big headlines and up above the fold.

Palmer did not see why window desks were so prized. Sure, natural light might fall upon your work, instead of a monotonic fluorescent glow. However, views outside weren't much to write home about. Fluttering pigeons, bike messengers weaving among rumbling buses, darting cars stopping in fender benders, hooded tweakers breaking the windows of parked tradesman vans, drug deals going down or going sour, drunks shifting imprints of sidewalk concrete from their faces to their butts, the glitter of a flouncing hooker, a grimy street troll shaking a turd out of a pant leg, ambulances and cop cruisers and fire engines flashing past with whirling lights and wailing sirens—the eternally recycled, sooty commotion of downtown.

He found the inside of Vreeland's cubicle more attractive. Or, at least, easier to grasp. Hanging from the edge of the shelves, pinned-up photos showed Vreeland flying aboard a World War II-era bomber, standing on the sail of a nuclear submarine, atop the bridge of a Liberty ship, and wearing a flight helmet and a grin as he sat behind a pilot of the Blue Angels flying team.

Palmer dragged a swivel chair over from the empty religion reporter's desk, and sat down in front of Vreeland.

"Hi, Kurt. Spare a second?"

Vreeland offered a noncommittal grunt. Palmer decided that meant yes.

"Can you please tell me, if you know, why the Patch's star

ex-columnist, Mister MacCay, is such a complete, total, unre-deemed loser?" Palmer asked.

Vreeland appraised the earnestness of Palmer's question. He cleared his throat. He looked as if he longed to pull a cigar out of his mouth before he spoke. A shabby stub did happen to sit in a big glass ashtray near his keyboard. Vreeland saw Palmer glance at it.

"That's just a reminder. We used to be able to smoke in this fucking place," Vreeland muttered. "Tell me, what's ol' nasty and rasty Colm MacCay gone and done now?"

"Actually, it's what he hasn't done! Brotmann told him to coach me on a story. But he blew off a meeting to help me score key interviews. Had to handle it by myself. If it wasn't for MacCay tak-ing up space on the assignment, I could've gotten real help from a real reporter—and be way further along."

"No good." Vreeland shook his head. "Don't blame you, being upset."

"Why's he so lame? Why's MacCay even still here at the paper? Is there any way to wake him up? If not, how do I drop him? I need to team up with a real reporter. Like Sally. Or you!"

Vreeland looked down at his keyboard. Then he looked up at Palmer.

"Want to go grab some lunch?"

"You saying we must leave the office to talk about this?"

"Not exactly. Just need to show you a place where something happened."

—

Vreeland's Alfa Romeo roared out of the company lot. They thrummed east up Bryant, reached the broad bay-front boule-vard called the Embarcadero. Vreeland swept in to the curb, and pointed across the boulevard to a spot between the piers where a big white sign atop a small yellow building proclaimed RED'S JAVA HOUSE.

"Go grab us some burgers," Vreeland growled. "Single cheese. They come on split sourdough rolls, with lots of mustard and chopped onions. Tell 'em if you don't want any of that. And two cups of joe to go. Make mine black."

Vreeland rolled up onto a hip so he could get at a pocket, pulled out a crumpled twenty, and thrust it at Palmer. "My treat," he said. Palmer jogged across the Embarcadero against the light. He remembered to look out for autos, but was surprised when an electric trolley silently slid close on rails in the median, and he was forced to sprint. Inside Red's, he gave the order to a laconic counterman, then looked the place over.

Through a plate-glass window flecked with old seagull poop, he saw a mint-green bar to the north called the "Hidive," next the vaulted entrance to Pier 28, then the gray arch of the Bay Bridge as it lifted from the city and aimed for Oakland. The erector-set trusses on the structure's bottom stood in stark contrast to the long, graceful swoop of suspensor cables on top.

"Order up!" the counterman bawled, as he dropped two cheese-burgers wrapped in waxed paper into a paper sack. He handed Palmer two cardboard cups, and wordlessly pointed at a coffee urn.

On his way out the front door, Palmer saw a pinned-up photo of an ecstatic angler named Bonny Almeida holding up the head of a thirteen-foot sturgeon. Beneath it was a card from the city's department of Health Services, announcing that Red's joint had scored a 92 on its last inspection. Palmer glanced around the dingy interior, and smiled. Maybe that was out of a possible 1,000.

He made his way back to Vreeland's Alfa with more care.

"Stick 'em behind the seat," Vreeland said. "We'll eat in a minute. After we return to the paper, I want you to be able to say I took you out to lunch up on Nob Hill."

They zoomed south on the Embarcadero, went right on Brannan, then up Third Street and over Market, where the name changed to Kearny. Left on California, and the sports-car engine whined as they climbed up steep pavement. Near the summit, two lanes squeezed down to one. Here they fell behind a slow cable car laden with a gaggle of tourists holding cameras that pointed in all directions, like the guns of safari participants poised to repel leopards. Vreeland revved the car to vroom around the clattering rig at the next intersection. At Mason, they shot right, passed the Fairmont Hotel with its set of international flags fluttering above the grand entrance. Then he turned left on Sacramento, saw an open space, whipped the Alfa into it, and switched off the ignition.

"Welcome to the crown of The City," Vreeland said. "Nob Hill. A throne room for our bay's robber barons and its capital kings. Got built up for the gentry right after the Gold Rush, and it remains their bastion today. Never call it Snob Hill, though. Wouldn't be far wrong, but it's still too easy.

"Over there to the south, that huge pile of bricks is The Mark Hopkins. At the end of the block, the Huntington Hotel," Vreeland said. "Huntington and Hopkins were two members of a grand cabal. To see how their game worked, Google those guys up sometime. They were called The Big Four: Collis Huntington, Charles Crocker, Mark Hopkins, and Leland Stanford. They ran the first continental railroad into California. Then they proceeded to run most of the state."

"What's that place?" Palmer said. "Their clubhouse?"

He pointed at a cubical building of chocolate-brown stone at the very center of the hill's crest. It stood next to a small park with extremely tidy landscaping.

"Not a bad guess! That's the Pacific-Union Club. You got a billion, and you're about 200 years old, you can join. You also have to pee standing up—I think it's still guys-only. Now, take a gander over there." Vreeland pointed west.

Palmer saw a graceful, gothic-style cathedral that looked, improbably, as if made of poured concrete. To either side, this church stood flanked by square-cornered, glass-slab apartment buildings ranging from ten to twenty stories in height. Almost every unit boasted an iron-railed balcony that looked out on grand views of either The City or the bay.

"The church?"

"Grace Cathedral? No."

"What should I look for?"

"That blue apartment building. Pale blue, almost gray. Now, see the balcony up by the penthouse? Right near the top."

"Yep. Got it."

"Picture this. A summer evening about thirty years ago. Very clear, calm night, with that gorgeous, pale flare of sunset still holding at 9 p.m. in the sky above the Golden Gate bridge, just like you see on any fogless summer evening. Might look that way tonight, as a matter of fact... .

"Suddenly you see a woman. Her white clothes flutter like mad in the breeze, because she's falling. She goes off that balcony, straight down onto the pavement. Her name is Mrs. Anna Gardiner. She's the lovely young wife of William Gardiner, our ambassador to the Philippines. A moment later, Bill Gardiner flies off that same balcony, with all the style and poise of an Olympic diver, which is actually what he once was. Then he smacks down right in the middle of his wife's splotch."

Palmer looked pale. "Okay, double suicide. Or murder-suicide. So what's it mean?"

"Anna Gardiner was Colm MacCay's lover."

Vreeland unwrapped his burger, bit into it. Then he took a gulp of his coffee.

—

Palmer didn't speak at all as Vreeland wheeled the Alfa back down to the *Post-Dispatch* lot. From time to time Vreeland cocked a sidelong glance at him, and saw that Palmer's mind was churning over his revelation of MacCay's sad past.

Vreeland felt he'd shared all that was necessary. He decided to leave the young reporter alone with his thoughts, let him draw conclusions. But maybe he should've asked Palmer whether he planned to make another move on his own in the Cornu Point probe. Because six hours later, Palmer went out to Castello, that tiny village of coastal renegades perched at the north end of a windswept, rocky crescent on the Pacific Ocean shore.

—

Palmer pulled into the dirt lot. Late sun slipped behind the gray clouds that lay on the sea, pale orange light fanned out above them. Strong breezes blew fitfully off the ocean. Devils of dust twirled around the fleet of rusty vehicles. One particularly strong blast made the garish plywood signs flap on the ragged fence.

Palmer stepped from his car, looked around. The place seemed deserted, just as on his previous visit. He zipped up his nylon flight jacket — another thrift store acquisition — checked to ensure a notebook and pens were tucked in his pocket, then strolled past the warning signs and through the gate without a second's hesitation.

As he ambled down the winding path, not a scrap of litter could be seen, no paper wrappers, no plastic bags, nary a can nor bottle. It was amusing to think that constant wind off the sea had whacked all trash eastward, a half mile across the highway. But he guessed the real reason was that the residents regularly patrolled their site, kept it picked up. Despite its general air of desolation, some pride in place must hold sway out here.

He traveled around several bends in the path, finally reached a point where he could see Castello's houses. Thirty or forty pastel cubes sat on broad terraces reinforced with masonry retaining walls. This shoreline vista prompted memories of photos Palmer had seen recently of the village of Riomaggiore, at Cinque Terre, Italy. It looked almost that picturesque, especially in this soft late-afternoon light.

"Hey! Where you going?"

It occurred exactly the way that Elle had described. A rough voice came from behind him. Palmer swung around to see two men standing a few yards away on the trail. Their hands remained out of sight, curled in their jacket pockets, but their stiff bodies broadcast an air of menace. He couldn't figure out how those guys had managed to materialize behind him so silently.

"Hi... um, I'm a reporter," Palmer told them. "From the Patch—I mean, the *San Francisco Post-Dispatch*. I came out here to talk to folks in Castello."

The men glanced at each other. Palmer guessed them to be in their late thirties. Both had short-cropped black hair and olive skin. One was exactly Palmer's size, one a bit taller. They had a rough, weathered look, like people who had spent many days out in the elements, squinting into bright sunshine, faces whipped by salt spray.

"Nobody does that without permission," the shorter one said.

"Well. Guess I should start by asking for it, then," Palmer replied.

"*Pensi davvero che sia un giornalista?*" one curtly asked the other.

"*Forse, oppure appartiene a Cornu Point.*"

"Say you work for the paper, huh?" the taller one said, his tone disbelieving. "So you must carry some press ID. Let's see it."

Palmer hauled out his magnetic card key, used at the Patch front door and to activate the building's elevators. It bore his photo and name and the paper's logo.

"Sorry. This is all I've got. My business cards and my press pass haven't been delivered yet. I began to work there just a little while ago."

"Wonderful. Major shit comes down at Cornu Point. So the paper sends out a rookie."

The tall one grabbed the card key and scrutinized it. Palmer saw his hand was covered in rough skin, callused and split, grime worked into the cracks.

"What makes this real?" he demanded. "You could just be another Cornu clown trying to figure a way to dick with us!"

"And if I'm not?" Palmer demanded. "Come on! Who are you? How do I know you've got any real say in stopping me? Maybe *you're* from Cornu Point, and you just want to keep the press from speaking to Castello folks."

The small guy's eyes went cold. "We are Di Mastini, buddy. Don't mess with us. Ask anyone on the coast."

"Look," Palmer said. "I know Cornu Point Association is snatching up land around here, not just grabbing the park. They won't stop at much. They might even have murdered old Beverly Bancroft when it looked as though she wanted to block their plans. Of course they're after Castello, too. Probably have a fantasy about making a zillion by sticking McMansions out there. If you people hope to fight, and you've got a story to tell, guess what—it's time to speak up!"

The men had glanced at each other as Palmer called Beverly Bancroft's death a potential murder. Now their combative demeanor softened.

"Forse sa' quello che succede."

"E' meglio riferirlo a Pietro."

The tall one handed back Palmer's card. "All right," he said. "Maybe Mister Pete will want to talk to you. Give us your phone number. He'll decide."

Palmer scribbled his cell-phone number on a sheet of paper in his notebook, tore it out, and handed it over.

"So, can I go out there now? Just look around?"

They shook their heads.

"No. Wait at your car. We'll tell Mister Pete. If he's interested he'll call you. You don't hear from him in about twenty minutes, that means he isn't. So then you clear out. Take off. Got it?"

⌒

As Palmer trudged several hundred yards back to the dusty lot, the sunlight faded precipitously. The sea wind had acquired a frigid bite. He saw a dark SUV parked out on a curve of the dirt access road, but he thought little of it. That turnout was at the head of a path that went all the way down to the shore. Elle had pointed it out as the last parking spot surfers could use at the cove with no harassment from the good citizens of Castello.

Palmer hopped into his car, tossed his cell phone on the Toyota's cracked and peeling gray dash. He pulled a notebook from his pocket, clicked a pen, began to jot notes.

"Di Masatinni," he wrote, guessing at spelling of the phrase. "Which means...?"

The rock that burst open his driver's-side window in an explosion of shards took Palmer utterly by surprise. So did the gloved fist that gripped him by his shirtfront and collar and hauled him out through the jagged fringe of cobwebbed glass. Palmer shouted, kicked, twisted his body as he was hoisted up into the air by a towering figure in a hooded black sweatshirt. Then the giant's other arm came down on him, and clubbed him to the ground.

Stunned by the sudden attack, Palmer scrabbled clumsily backward on his hands and knees. He saw the booted foot coming at his head, and managed to dodge just enough so that the boot glanced off his shoulder and whacked into the car.

"*Kefe!* Bitch!" A low voice cursed.

"Stop! Stop! Who are you? What do you want?" Palmer panted. "You want my money, take it! I'll give it to you!"

"*Ai poki.* I get it anyhow!" A guttural laugh.

Palmer put a hand on the rear bumper and tried to rise, then saw a bunched fist coming at him, and fell over backward to escape the blow. Instinctively he kicked out with both feet as the man loomed over him. One foot bounced off the man's knee, but the other hit him squarely in the crotch. Breath whooshed out of the assailant. A brief pause came in the attack, as he stood crouched over, wide-legged, a hand braced on each thigh.

Palmer scrambled to his feet and tried to run, terrified, unsure of what direction to take. He found himself facing the gate in the fence, so that was the way he went. Heavy footsteps pounded relentlessly behind him. Suddenly, Palmer found himself seized by his collar and flung into the fence. He grabbed the closest post, a long, rusty length of rebar, and clung to it to keep from falling. The rough steel shaft wobbled in his hands. It felt loose. Palmer swiftly yanked it up out of the hoops of fence wire, like a man pulling a sword from a sheath. He turned to confront his attacker.

The big man showed he expected Palmer to swing the rod at him by the way he raised up his arms in a wedge-shape to block the blow. Instead, Palmer lunged forward and stabbed the end of the bar under the arms and up into the flesh of the man's throat. His attacker uttered a choking cry, fell back. Palmer desperately pressed this brief advantage. He shifted his hands to grip the long steel bar like a baseball bat, and swung it at the man's forehead, but the man dropped low. Palmer missed entirely, and momentum of the swing twirled him around.

A powerful hand then grabbed onto the steel. The bar was roughly snatched out of Palmer's grip, shredding skin off his fingers. Now forced to the defensive, it was Palmer's turn to try to duck, and shield himself with his arms. But the attacker's aim was unerring. The steel rod whistled through the air to shatter the bones in Palmer's right forearm, while the tip whipped into one side of his skull. Palmer collapsed in the dust.

Breathing hoarsely, grunting with each blow, the man proceeded to pound Palmer's prone body again and again. Because the rebar hit the ground at the same time, the rod began to bend into an unwieldy shape. The man cast it aside, then kicked Palmer heavily in the ribs with his booted feet.

"You like dis' back now, eh? *Fafa!* Ya," he panted. The attacker paused to gaze down at his handiwork. A red bib of blood soaked his shirt, seeping from his wounded throat. The man bent, yanked Palmer's wallet from his hip pocket, extracted its thin sheaf of cash, then tossed the billfold to the ground.

The man's satisfaction was now almost complete. He unzipped his pants, tugged out a thick penis, and spewed a stream of urine all over Palmer's body. When his bladder was empty, the large man sauntered over to the fence to peer at the signs. He selected one, wrenched it free of its rusty wire moorings, carried it back, then pitched it onto Palmer's limp form.

He walked away.

At a distance, an automobile engine started up. Tires ground into dirt. Then all was silent, except for the unending, sibilant whisper of the wind off the sea.

Palmer's arms jerked once, twice, spasmodically against the dirt of the lot. Then he fell entirely still. Threads of his bright blood drifted across the blotch of urine. The mingled fluids soaked downward into a dark and thirsty earth.

Chapter 10

Slouched in my easy chair, I watched through bleary eyes as old movies unspooled on TV. Then as Tuesday got underway, at the ungodly hour 3 a.m., my telephone rang.

A half day earlier, I'd begun my customary ritual for tapering off from a long bender. I started by e-mailing in a "sick" plea to my supervisor at the Patch, a deputy editor in Metro. Next I indulged in a long series of naps, alternating with short waking periods wherein I guzzled quarts of coffee and pints of water. I had just awakened to finish the last pot of coffee, and was meditating on whether to go in to the Patch during Tuesday's regular working hours or call in sick once again. Well, what had I been working on? Couldn't have been too important, since I didn't remember. Oh, yeah, wait—I'd been assigned as big brother to our new recruit, that skinny youth what's-his-name, down in Travel.

On my TV, Gregory Peck, the too-cool-for-school squadron commander in *Twelve O'Clock High,* had just reached his famous breakdown moment. He balked at swinging up into the cockpit of a B-17 bomber as it prepared to depart on a mission over France. Instead, bewildered, he just stood there and spasmed. Well, I knew I could do quite a bit better than that! I punched the TV remote's MUTE button, staggered over to the phone in its wall alcove. I managed to snatch the receiver off the cradle on only my second grab.

"Yesh?"

A crisp female voice spoke. "Do you happen to know a man by the name of Sebastian Palmer?"

"Yes." I frowned, sought to focus. Why would some gal ring me up at such a ridiculous hour to chitchat about the freshman?

"This is the Palo Alto Trauma Center. Mr. Palmer has been admitted to our hospital. He's been seriously injured. He's in our ICU."

"He...what?"

"Are you a friend, or a member of his family?"

"Wha'?! I? A fren'. From the workplace. I am Colm MacCay. "

"Ah. Well, we also need to find out what sort of insurance Mr. Palmer might have."

"Afraid I can—no idee..."

"What?"

"We work at the Posh-Dishpaste. Newpaper. They musht insure. Hold on."

I pressed fingers against my throbbing temples. By sheer force of will, I sought to transport blood and fresh oxygen to the speech centers of my brain, and sharpen the consonants that sloshed around on my tongue.

Two questions also whirled madly in my head. I fought to disentangle them, see each one clearly. What did our union say about how long a new hire had to work before he won any medical benefits? And what on earth had Palmer done to get himself trundled on a stretcher into an intensive care unit?

"Please, tell me what happened."

"Mr. Palmer has been badly injured. That's all I can say right now. My name is Leslie Schmitt. I work at Palo Alto Trauma. Mr. Palmer is now in our care. He's listed in critical condition. We're ringing up everyone we could find on his cell-phone list of recent calls. We especially need to locate family members. Do you have a contact for them?"

"No. Human Resources, at our paper, would. But they're closed."

"We know that."

"Of course."

My mind flailed, trying to grasp something I could say that wouldn't sound abysmally stupid.

"Anything at all I can do to help young Palmer?"

"Well, if you're a friend of his, you may wish to come down. I have to tell you, it is possible that he might not make it through the night. We're at 2001 Apricot Avenue, just off 101. Goodbye, Mr. MacCay."

Click.

⸺

Eyes rheumy and bloodshot, cheeks fuzzed by gray stubble, my rumpled clothing unevenly buttoned and—I'm sorry to say—not quite fully zipped, I hove unsteadily into the Palo Alto Trauma Center one hour later. The taxi ride from my place in the Richmond District down there cost me seventy dollars. Upon arrival, I vigorously held up my end of a scream-fest with the cabbie for my failure to bestow so much as one more buck for his tip. I excoriated him as a bum driver and worse navigator whose poor choices had resulted in extra miles and road time. A hangover had begun to ravage me in earnest by then. I was in no mood to be slanged by some uppity hack.

After a visit to the front desk, I went on to the famed medical center's neurologic ICU. That end of a long hall was deathly quiet. The ward broadcast the antiseptic-medicine-plastic aroma of all hospitals, but there was a notable lack of bustle. A supervisor directed me to Palmer's room, the last in a row of four. It was lit softly, filled with a barely audible hum of machinery and monitors along one wall.

A slender nurse with lank brown hair sat in a plastic chair near a window that gave her a view of both this room and the one next door. As I entered, she rose, stepped up, and introduced herself as Marty.

I told her that I was Palmer's coworker. I blanched at using the word "partner" or "teammate," and—growing more sober by the minute now—had realized use of the term "friend" would also be inaccurate. I said the hospital had called, and I'd rushed over to see if there was anything I could do to help.

Marty nodded, and took me to Palmer's bedside.

Palmer looked shrunken, much smaller than I remembered, almost the size of a tall child. IV tubes ran into both his arms, a ventilator puffed oxygen into a "trach" tube in his throat. His breathing sounded rapid and shallow.

Except for purple, bruised rings around his eyes, Palmer's skin was as white as new parchment. Where his head was not swathed in bandages, I could see his hair had been shaved off. I had expected that he would look badly hurt, and he definitely did. But I was completely unready for the wave of deep sadness that swept over me as I gazed down upon him.

"Sebastian has a depressed skull fracture on the side of his head," Marty said quietly. "Other breaks too, mostly ribs, and his right forearm. Many contusions. His head injury is the most serious. The surgeon got the bone chips out—they weren't driven too deep. We're trying to reduce swelling in the brain with an osmotic diuretic, that's one drip. And fend off seizures with Dilantin. His blood pressure's pretty bad, 140 over 40. The good news is that both his pupils still respond to light, so we're hopeful. But he is comatose. On the Glasgow scale, we're rating it at about six."

"What's that mean?"

"You and me, we'd hit about fifteen on the scale," the nurse said. "That chair over there is a three."

I felt aghast. "That's your good news? He's got twice the awareness of a piece of furniture?!"

"Sebastian must be tough. He wasn't found until several hours after the attack. Could've died. In fact, it's kind of amazing that he didn't."

"You said, 'attack.' What occurred?"

"Lay terms?" Marty shook her head. "Some thug beat the crap out of him. Cops say the attacker used a steel rod. About a five-foot-long hunk of rebar."

"Where did it happen?"

"You know that little coast town near Cornu Point?"

"Castello?"

"Sounds right."

"Shit!" I spat it out.

"What's wrong?"

"That place is... hooked to a story... Palmer was working on."

"He's a reporter. You both are."

"Yes." I uttered this half-truth with meager conviction.

Marty didn't seem to be a woman who let much get by. Her chin came up and she eyed me.

"So, you know anyone in his family?" she asked.

I shook my head. "He's from Florida. Met him barely over a week ago. But you know, as I told your Miss Schmitt, I can get the contacts you need after the *San Francisco Post-Dispatch* offices open."

"Actually, we have reached his parents. Same way we found you—off his cell phone. They're divorced, but both said they'll land at SFO sometime today."

A flurry of shuffling footsteps sounded at the door. I turned to see a red-haired girl with a strong face come into the room like she owned the place. She was oddly garbed in a purple down jacket, white flannel pajama bottoms, and black flip-flop slippers.

"Sebastian! Where is he?" Elle Jatobá demanded.

The nurse bristled. "Are you a relative?"

"I'm his friend! That's him?!" Elle moved swiftly toward the bed. "Omigod, Sebastian! What did they do to you?"

She reached out to touch his hand, but Marty interposed her slender body and shoved Elle back.

"No!" the nurse said. "Don't touch him!"

"Okay, all right, I'm sorry."

"Who are you?" I asked her.

"Elle Jatobá. His friend. I was helping Sebastian. Who're you?"

"I'm Colm MacCay." I held out my hand to her. "I happen to work with him."

A sudden look of disgust contorted her face. She glanced at my outstretched hand as if I'd just offered her a dripping glob of garbage.

"MacCay! You? Why bother to show up now? You piece of shit! Sebastian told me all about you. You were supposed to help him, you useless drunk. Now look what's happened! Where were you? Some partner!"

My face burned as if she'd slapped me. Actually, I would have vastly preferred a blow across the snout. Elle had just punched my most sensitive switch with precision. Yet she could not know how deep within me the detonation wires ran. I could neither speak nor move.

Nurse Marty abruptly took command.

"We will not have scenes in this ward!" the nurse said firmly. "Ma'am, I want you out of here. I mean now!"

Elle's strong jaw stuck out belligerently. "You can't throw me out!"

"You bet your ass I can," Marty said. "All it takes me is one call. Will you leave on your own, or do I need to pick up the phone?"

"Tell me how he is first," Elle said. "Then I'll go."

Marty sprinted through a clipped version what she had just told me.

"Thank you," Elle said stiffly. Another gray laser blast hit me from her eyes. She flung a pitying glance in Palmer's direction. Then Typhoon Elle stormed out.

"Whew!" Marty said. "We don't need any of that."

Then she studied me. "All right. So you and Sebastian write the news. You were reporting, researching some kind of story together?"

I could feel muscles in my face work, a sort of random twitching. I wondered how it looked from the outside. I fought to regain composure, to focus on the mission.

"Yes," I said. "Exactly. Like that. So, I don't suppose... you didn't find... was there any digital recorder or camera or notebook found with Palmer?"

"We found a notebook and his cell. Plus his billfold, all the money removed. But the police said they had to take everything for evidence. Deputies, I mean. San Mateo County Sheriff's Department. We pulled the recent calls off his phone just before they took it."

I produced a business card from my shirt pocket. Luckily, a last one did rattle around in there. With a ballpoint, I scribbled, handed it to her.

"That's my home phone. Business line and e-mail's on the front. Kindly tell me of any change in Sebastian's condition. Also, call if you remember any more details of the attack. Or if Sebastian revives, happens to say anything. Thanks. I know you'll do your best for him."

The nurse fingered my card thoughtfully, put it in her pocket.

"Well, there's one thing."

"What?"

"Cops said he got beaten with that metal rod. But as I cleaned him up just now, I found rust and dirt on the palms of his hands, torn skin. Sebastian might've gripped that bar himself, or another one, to use as a weapon. He wasn't only a victim."

I pondered that.

"Thank you," I told her.

—

You might think I had just coped rather well—for a middle-aged lout coming off a multi-day bender. But in my own humble opinion, my competence was marginal. By the time I exited the hospital, my odyssey through rosy inebriation had jolted to a rough end. I resumed flight toward my primary destination, plunging down into the abyss with renewed velocity. Such plunges are accompanied by a sound that can rise or fall in volume, but never goes silent entirely: a voice, suspiciously like my own, that pronounces accusations and curses.

What terms does this voice use? Elle Jatobá actually managed some close guesses. "Useless?" Certainly. "Drunk?" Absolutely, though I much prefer the term "substance abuser." "Piece of shit?" Well, that's merely a putty knife loaded with blue-collar, conversational Spackle. The term Elle didn't use, but which she might as well have shouted, was "coward." It's a verbal club I've used to beat my mind to mush for lo these many years.

I gnawed my knuckles like a rabid mutt during the long cab ride back home. With a different driver, of course. Him, I did tip. I had no energy for another wrangle. Could barely wait until I was through my front door before I shucked off clothes. Then I stepped into the grimy shower and cranked the cold knob to full blast. You see, the heat of shame had started to bubble up like lava from my core. I knew I had to cool the system, or another breakdown might occur, one that could render me paralytic for weeks.

I've endured two such episodes during my life, and now desperately fear another. During each breakdown, retaining sanity, even clinging to survival, had been a nip-and-tuck campaign. So, I stood for a long time under the gushing nozzle, sought to chill my brain and calm my rampaging thoughts.

Finally, after a half hour beneath the frigid waterfall, my mental frenzy had cooled down to the low simmer of neurosis, blame, and despondence that constitutes my ordinary condition.

I emerged, toweled off, then stood at the sink to shave. There was a three-day growth of stubble to deal with. I felt grateful for this mundane, practical problem. One of my affectations—and believe me, a huge array of habits is required to glue my botch of a personality together—is use of an old-fashioned shaving mug and brush. I'd add a stropping strap and a straight razor to this kit, but a potent urge to make a Sweeney Todd move across my own throat might prove irresistible.

I got through most of the shave. Then I made the colossal error of glancing at the wrong spot in the mirror. I looked far too deeply into my own eyes. Suddenly I bashed the glass into smithereens with the shaving mug. Hurtling splinters of ceramic and glass gashed my right hand.

Luckily, the sting of those cuts focused me, took me further away from the volcano in my mind, brought me closer to the physical present. I now had a task, this one with a near deadline. I needed to stanch the red ribbons trickling down into the sink. With my good hand, I rummaged through the medicine cabinet, found old gauze and tape, a tube of antiseptic. Using my mouth and teeth to open the packages, I bound up my wounds. Then I finished the shave, rinsed, lubricated.

High time, then, to go to my ultimate place of refuge: Anna's Shrine.

Before I met Anna, and in all years since, I've dwelt in the same apartment, an "in-law." A type common in the Outer Richmond neighborhood, an in-law is usually a small suite of rooms located behind the garage, on the lower floor of a two- or three-story house. Typically, the family living upstairs will stash a single, usually older, relative in such a space.

My landlords, a prosperous Chinese couple, didn't need the apartment for familial purposes, and had chosen to rent it to me. They overlooked my idiosyncrasies. I never groused about their all-night Mahjongg parties.

Another factor nurturing our arrangement: the Changs never inspected my digs. Lacking that, and with no visitors to prepare for, my place stayed mostly, well, let's call it untidy. Nevertheless, one spot remains invariably spic, span, and well-dusted: a claw-footed, walnut table. It's the place where Anna and I last dined.

Just before I drove her up to Nob Hill, so she could inform her husband that she was leaving him.

I keep Anna's picture atop that table. A photo snapped just prior to our last supper. A glorious walk on Ocean Beach. The brim of her broad straw hat is bent by the sea breeze; she clutches the flimsy thing upon her black curls with one hand to keep it from flying off. She laughs at me and straight into the camera. There's Anna's wide, red, succulent mouth, extravagantly lashed dark eyes, that silky skin.

Tucked behind the frame of her photograph is a diamond ring. Which I never quite had the chance to bestow upon her.

Here, I sit for chats with my Anna. I light candles, as we so often did to dine. Pour two drinks. Toss mine down, sip hers. In that amiable glow comes a moment when I summon Anna's voice. I speak, hear her reply.

No, I'm not so far gone that I believe I can hold a séance! Still, this is a phenomenon akin. We enjoyed such affinity, Anna and I, a rare ability to complete each other's thoughts or share them without speech, that I feel our communion had to endure. This ritual is as close as I can come to being with her, to produce echoes of the splendid creature that we were.

On this desperate morn, as faint grays of sunrise filtered in through shabby curtains, I sat to talk with her.

"So, where's my drink?" Anna said.

"Not today, dear," I told her. "A boy's been badly hurt. Afraid it's my fault. It's all so greatly sobering. I mean, at least, I think I must be sober to face it."

She waited, knowing I'd bring her the full story.

"I'm on the cusp... of something," I said. "A pail of icy brine has been heaved in my face. I awaken to find that I'm standing high up, on a slippery rail. All around, and below, is darkness. One misstep, even the slightest, I'll be lost for good and all."

"Colm," she reproved. "Dramatizing, aren't you?"

"That is my forte."

Came again to me the blessing of her laugh—ripe, hearty, musical. "Don't I know it!" she said.

"The game reached much grander stakes while my attention was diverted," I told her. "Don't mind suffering, myself. In fact, I've gotten good at it. But I mightily loathe being the cause of suffering in others. As Brother Brother might say, such a sin may occur due to omission as well as commission."

Anna knew I referred to my elder sibling Connor. When I visit Brother Brother at the Benedictine monastery at Big Sur, he reproves my lost faith. I tease him about feeding on delusions. Anna had observed several such sessions. She liked to amuse herself by taking alternate sides of our argument, at whim.

"When those WestWorld idiots took away my column, it felt like a catastrophe! Naturally, I went into a massive sulk. But now a genuine calamity has cropped up. Which has adjusted my perspective."

"You look cute when you pout. Makes you seem more kissable."

"Well, don't wonder who's kissing me now. Nobody."

"Get out more, Colm! You always were the life of any party. If you lost a little weight, did something to improve that awful wardrobe —"

"Anna! Let's not go into that. We have to deal with something far more serious."

"All right. I'll be good."

"Don't forget! Okay, what I missed was that the gods had given me an opportunity. A slim chance, yet a decent one. Still, I casually disregarded it. I was like Doc Manette from 'A Tale of Two Cities,' recalled to life. But instead of walking out of the Bastille, I just reeled round and toddled on back into my prison cell."

"I'm not understanding."

"Well, I used to be a decent reporter."

"You were amazing, actually. A young lion. We all thought so."

"I started out assigned to the night police beat —"

"Then moved on to state and local politics. I remember."

"Yes. Well, all those laboriously assembled tools now lie coated in rust. I like to imagine I still know how to use them. Evidence indicates otherwise. I was assigned to mentor that cub Sebastian Palmer. Should've taken it seriously, should've brought those skills back up then and there, joined him on the probe, guided him on the path. Instead..."

I could not finish that sentence. Heat rose, that lava of shame and fear, thickening in my throat, blocking speech. Then I could feel Anna's touch, her cool fingers patting my hand.

"Cut to the chase, Colm. What's to be done?"

Ah, Anna. Her sharp dart, zinging right into the bulls-eye.

"Too late. Poor kid is in the hospital. He's got tubes stuck—"

"It's not too late! You're just letting yourself stagger back into a cell, like you said. Come on, Colm! You're better than that. Don't disappoint me!"

"Don't disappoint you?!" I was shocked.

Yet I also felt aroused, in some neoteric way. It was the last thing Anna had to tell me before she faded back into her picture. Her gaze of concern, with that tiny cleft between her brows, became once again the laughing eyes and grin she'd worn during our final walk on Ocean Beach.

Chapter 11

S hould have moved out of that dim in-law apartment long ago, I suppose. But couldn't stand to leave my ocean and my fog, and my table and bed, and links to my most precious memories of Anna. But because I stayed out in "the Avenues," as we City homeboys say, my commute to work at the *Post-Dispatch* was a bit on the long side.

I walked down toward the old Golden Gate Park windmills to catch the Number 5 Fulton, then rode the jolting, wheezing Muni streetcar for a half hour before jumping off to walk a block and a half south of Market. Ordinarily, I would spend that time leafing through the *New York Times* and *Wall Street Journal*, or my *New Yorker* or *Smithsonian* or *Atlantic* or *Economist*, or mentally assembling my next column and scrawling notes on a legal pad.

But my usual habits had been booted into a cocked hat by the assault on Palmer—my colleague whom I'd so fecklessly abandoned to a bloody fate. So, on this trip downtown, I tugged on my chin, ran fingers through my hair, stared balefully out the streetcar window, and went over and over all I knew about Cornu Point and Castello.

At that point my knowledge made a pretty small heap. Not much beyond what Palmer and I had discussed. And yet I had kept part of my promise to discover more, had in fact managed to visit taverns in Pacifica and Half Moon Bay to tug on coats and score a bit of the skinny from locals.

In a Pacifica pub, I'd scored my modest jackpot, finding a scrawny old soul named Pat Mulcahy from Pescadero who told me that he was tight with a few Castello residents. After I donated a libation or two, Mulcahy yacked about the raw deal his pals were getting from the swells at Cornu Point.

"See, tha ting is, they don't have title to tha land," he had told me. "They been payin' oot a teeny lease far tha park, but tha state's been tryin' to knock 'em offen it for years 'n' years. They got 'stenshin after extenshin, but tha string's aboot run oot! Now, they're jus' alive on borrowed time, and tha's tha trooth!"

I turned that last bit over in my mind that morning as I headed in to the Patch, plodding along a stained (please don't ask by what) stretch of SoMa sidewalk. If denizens of Castello were terrified of losing their homes, getting up in arms, I could see them growing paranoid, adding to their already combative and ornery profile.

Yet why jump on Palmer? Especially if he started off—as he should have—by identifying himself as a reporter? Brutal greetings had been meted out in the past to intruders at Castello, but nothing as bad as this. The assault on Palmer was so completely over the top, it could only bring down on the village too much attention of the worst sort. It made no sense to summon it.

Maybe there was no logical explanation. What if the attack on Palmer was random, had zero to do with Castello or Cornu Point? Thugs on drugs pop up in lots of places. Maybe some coastal gang-banger, tweaked out on meth or PCP or both, had seen Palmer as a target of convenience. What began as a simple robbery then went horribly wrong.

That was as much ratiocination as my alcohol-deprived brain could produce. I had by then gone almost an entire day without so much as a dram. I sighed as I made my way up to Palmer's desk in Travel, on the off chance that he'd left some notes or background material lying about. To my surprise, I found Dewayne Frost, our short, plump, good-natured chap from the mailroom, boxing up the contents of Palmer's desk.

"What's going on?" I asked.

"Oh, Brotmann wants all this stuff," Dewayne said. "Did you hear? That new guy Palmer got beat up, pretty bad! He's in the hos—"

I waved him silent. "I know, I know! Already seen him in a Palo

Alto ICU. And yes, he's in bad shape. Why does Brotmann want his stuff?"

"Says he has to look it over. Then he'll give it to the guys working on the story."

"That would be me."

"Well, maybe," Dewayne said cautiously. "Mr. Brotmann just sent Mr. Stein out to Castello, and Mr. Ericson down to the hospital. I think that's who he meant."

Old pain, plus new confusion and anger, swirled for a moment in my brain. Anger won. And then I deployed it, with a degree of residual craftiness.

"Initially, I was the one assigned to work with Palmer," I said. "Say, know what you ought to do, Dewayne? Go get mail from the Travel slot, so we can add it to your box. May be some important stuff that Palmer had coming in. I'll help you sort through it, and we'll see."

Bless the hearts of the innocent. Dewayne toddled off. As he disappeared, I plunged my arms up to the elbows in his carton. Didn't find what I expected, flash drives or CDs that might hold backups of Palmer's notes from his laptop or desktop computer. Instead, I was startled to discover four plain, cardboard-covered reporter's notebooks, a rubber band snapped round them. I slipped the band off and riffled their pages—they were dense with writing. Good find! Accessing the hard drive of Palmer's desktop computer was out of the question for me; systems guys were likely already vacuuming his electronic files. These notebooks would have to do. I shoved them in my coat pocket.

Then I jogged—or what now passes for a jog with me—to the office supply locker at the end of the hall. Here I snatched four blank notebooks, then ran back to the cubicle. I got the band snapped on them and crammed them in the box just as Dewayne puffed back around the corner, his arms stuffed full of Travel Section effluvia.

"On second thought, you'd better just drop all that in, Dewayne," I told him. "No telling what Mr. Brotmann might think is important!"

"Okay," he agreed, and dumped his load, which raised the box contents to its brim.

"Say, I saw Mr. Brotmann on his way to his office. I told him you were here. He wants you to come and speak with him."

"That would be my pleasure," I replied.

———

Dewayne and I entered the august person's presence together. Dewayne set his box gently on Brotmann's desk, then backed out, almost doing obeisance. I stood before Brotmann, awaiting his notice. He looked up.

"MacCay. How are you?" he asked. I was surprised—and instantly rendered wary—by his benign tone.

"Breathing."

"What happened to your hand, there?"

I lifted my bandaged right paw. "Oh. I cut myself. You know, shaving."

Disbelief flitted across Brotmann's face.

"Haven't been in any bar brawls, now, have you?"

"No," I told him. I almost added, "not since last month," but saw no gain in boosting his level of suspicion.

Brotmann steepled his hands. "So. We have a situation."

"I'd say."

"What was Palmer doing out at Castello?"

"Researching our Cornu Point story. That's my guess."

"Arthur Davis says that Palmer had already worked a full shift on Monday, and hadn't requested overtime. So there's a question of whether Palmer was working for the paper, or out at that cove on a private jaunt of some sort."

"Why do you need to figure that out now?" I was puzzled.

"Palmer's medical bills will be sky-high. He had to work here a month before getting covered on insurance. If he wasn't actually on the job…"

Brotmann let his inference hang.

"Your concern is touching," I said.

Brotmann twitched. His facial expression grew more hostile. The man resembled a mannequin shriveled by a heat gun, but I saw that some genuine feeling still vibrated below his crinkled surface.

"Our main source of information should be you, MacCay!" he

snapped. "You were his assigned coach! What was Palmer up to?"

"On Sunday he planned to attend a memorial service at Cornu Point for Beverly Bancroft, that woman who died on the horse path. My plan was to look into the situation at Castello. Palmer and I were to meet this week and compare notes."

"Why did Palmer go out to Castello last night?"

"I don't know," I lied. Seemed like the wrong moment to confess that I'd lost the weekend and all of Monday in a boozy haze, and had completely forgotten about my meeting with Palmer. The kid had likely given up on me, and decided he had to go do his work, and mine, too.

"What have you learned about Castello?"

"Oh, it's preliminary. Land underneath that village may not actually belong to the villagers. The Cornu Point Association wants to acquire it. All shoreline property out there is becoming more valuable, due to that new tunnel on Highway 1."

One of Brotmann's slim hands had toyed with a sharp pencil as he spoke. Now he tapped the eraser on his desk, and stared at me.

"That Castello land is owned by the state, and leased to Cornu Point along with most everything else out there," Brotmann said. "The residents have skated by, as sub-lessees, paying low fees, almost forever. The state has tried to boot those deadbeats out for ten, twenty years. But the Legislature, under urging from a few local politicians, managed to pass bills for two lease extensions. However, the final one expires this year. Did you know that?"

I shook my head. "Not those particular details, no."

"How is it, MacCay, you've been on this story for five days, but I already understand more about it than you?"

Brotmann had me flatfooted. I didn't know what to say. Brotmann nodded to himself, then tapped his chin with the eraser.

"A *Post-Dispatch* reporter has been assaulted in the line of duty," he said. "A team of Metro beat reporters are writing an A-1 story, to run tomorrow. As for you, MacCay, further efforts are not required. You may return to your broom closet and do whatever it is that you do."

I felt anger well up, my face went hot. But Brotmann had gotten under my skin once before, and I thought I knew how to scrape away his little stinger.

"Might do that. Or I might not," I told him. "I happen to feel a bit under the weather. I may go on sick leave."

Brotmann glanced up, as though surprised that I had not yet left his office.

"If you stay out more than three days, we'll need a doctor's note," he said casually. "It's a new rule."

I leaned onto his desk. "I've lived in San Francisco for forty years," I said. "In one hour, I can get you a half dozen doctor's notes. Just pick whichever one you happen to like best."

Then I stalked out.

Actually, I'd been messing with him. I fully intended to stay on the job. And the only notes that held any interest for me were Palmer's. I patted the coat pocket where his notebooks were tucked. I felt eager to crack them open. I'd no idea why a new-tech weenie would scribble so much on paper, but was delighted he had. If I was to make headway, outflank Ken Stein and Tod Ericson—the I-team that Brotmann had assigned to Cornu Point—I needed to score a boost from Palmer.

Before I left the building to move on to that, I had one other chore. I went back downstairs to Travel, and saw that that corrupt toad Artie Davis had finally come in. He sat at his desk, his ample posterior crammed into his sagging swivel chair.

"Why did you tell Brotmann that Palmer wasn't on the job when he went to Castello?" I demanded, without preliminary.

Davis looked up at me pop-eyed, his jowly face sagging—the nearest thing to a bloated, human-Pekingese hybrid you could imagine. "Palmer didn't say he was going out there, or even ask to go," Davis hedged. "I'm his boss."

"You're the boss of shit," I informed him. "You gave management a huge opening to deny responsibility. Palmer or his family could get socked with a giant bill for his care."

Davis' eyes shifted nervously about in his round skull.

"He had to have my permission to take overtime," he insisted. "That's policy."

"Policy, shmolicy. I don't care why you want to screw Palmer. I'm just telling you it won't work," I said. "Brotmann plans to make a hero of our brave young reporter, struck down in the line of duty. Which means that he, in fact, was on duty. So now you can remember it differently."

"Palmer is a snot-nose punk!" Davis said. "He must've finally smarted off to the wrong guy! He deserved to get the crap pounded—"

A few neurons clunked together behind that self-important face. Davis realized he had gone too far. His little eyes widened in fear, like he thought I was about to punch him.

Actually, Davis knew it a split-second before I did. Since my right hand was still swollen and sore from the cuts acquired at my bathroom mirror, I shuffled my feet (a bit of Golden Gloves was left to me), stepped forward, pulled back my left shoulder, then threw that shoulder and arm in a hook. My onrushing fist tagged him in the kisser, right on those loose, pulpy lips. Davis' swivel chair flipped over, and he tumbled into a heap against his cubicle wall. His burdened desk shuddered, then disgorged an avalanche of paper down onto him.

For one shining moment, as I left the building, I felt fabulous. Maybe I had turned my anger inward for far too long. Be careful, though, I warned myself, about sending more squirts of magma outward. No matter how bad things are, you can always make them worse.

"Hope I'm not disappointing you now," I thought at Anna, and blew her a kiss.

Next, I thought about Brotmann. He would shortly hear that I had just slugged Davis. Hard to see how that might play in my favor. Still, it could. Now he'd have no idea what I might try next. Perhaps it was now his turn to be careful around me.

An oft-repeated saying of my auld Da drifted through my mind. "Might as well be hanged for a goat as a sheep." Absolutely.

———

Cab rides had already cost me a frickin' fortune. And if the Patch now considered me to be on med leave, I'd be unable to expense them. But there was no other way for me to get around fast after I departed the zone of regular mass transit. You see, I haven't owned a car since that day I'd sat staring out a windshield as Anna died.

What Vreeland had told Palmer during their jaunt up to Nob

Hill was true, as far as it went. But there are other parts to the story no living being knows, except for me.

For example, after Anna decided to tell Bill Gardiner their marriage was over, and I drove her up to Nob Hill, the notion she'd go all alone up to their suite to announce it—well, that idea was mine. Brilliant, eh? To me, it seemed a fair, considerate, even civilized gesture. She'd tell him, he'd politely consider, then accept her decision, and that would be that.

After all, Bill himself had not exactly been Mr. Faithful—far from it. The State Department's golden boy had diddled a long parade of society beauties of all ages and both sexes. He wasn't particularly picky, nor was he discreet.

Why did I never consider that Bill Gardiner might blow? Three decades on, I still beat myself up over my willful blindness, my rank stupidity. On some evil and haunted days, I conduct this assault on myself hourly.

The frequent and ruinous explanation I conjure is that I was a fool and a coward. I'd whiffed on assisting Anna in this most serious confrontation. With me at her side—or at minimum, standing just outside in the hall—I might have had a fighting chance to protect her.

But I sat alone in my car on Nob Hill, more or less where Vreeland had parked his Alfa. I scratched my chin, puffed on a Viceroy, considering what pub I'd take Anna to for a celebration of her new freedom and our life together. Instead, I witnessed a fathomless horror—her fall and death. Then her murderer's leap.

No, I did not go over there to survey their crumpled bodies, nor did I offer any testimony to the police. Instead, I lurched from my car and stumbled like a zombie all the way out to Land's End and the Golden Gate Bridge. After that, I staggered back to my apartment in the Richmond. My brain reeled between trying to deny what I had seen and seeking to comprehend it. That's when my place became a hermit's cave, as I went into a complete breakdown. I did not emerge for days.

Eventually, my car was ticketed and towed off Nob Hill. Eventually, I did have to talk to the DA's office, then the coroner. Eventually, I heard from the city that the impounded car would soon be sold at auction unless I paid fees and storage. I never bothered to reply.

And I've not touched a steering wheel since. That's the long way around to why I had to engage another cab for the long haul back down to Pescadero, instead of simply renting a vehicle.

My strong hunch was that Castello would now be buttoned up tight, both by its residents and the cops. Any entry to talk to the people out there would have to come courtesy of an insider. Pat Mulcahy, that windy old Irishman from Pescadero, might be my key. I had to find him.

As my taxi took the long and winding Highway 1 southward, I occupied myself by studying Palmer's notebooks. I was startled to see how methodical they were. His writing wasn't a reporter's typical, hurried cursive or shorthand scrawl. My own hand would defeat the most astute cryptologist. But Palmer's notebook pages displayed the neat, blocky print of a true anal personality. Who knew? Not a trait I would have picked for him.

I grew fascinated, reading Palmer's account of the first phone call from Beverly Bancroft, his surprise at hearing of her death two days later, his plucky solo foray out to Cornu Point park. Next, his discovery of the glasses and the probable deception surrounding her murder. His spontaneous partnership and growing bond with his new friend Elle—which helped explain her angry tirade at the hospital.

Reading about the letter from Bancroft to Palmer was the core revelation in the notebooks. Its content cut through the murk like a bright blade. Where was that letter located now? In the box Dewayne had taken to Brotmann? I regretted that Palmer had confided none of this to me. Had he done so, would it have made a difference? I'd like to think it would, but honesty compels me to admit: probably not.

It took a shock on the scale of the assault on Palmer to whack me out of my stupor.

And just a short time prior, my skull had been placed on the driving-range tee by the lesser surprise of losing my column. That had been a form of professional life support, letting me substitute rhetoric for actual work. Much as I hate to say it, even now, Brotmann had actually done me a favor by prying me out of that rancid little niche.

The cabbie turned left at Pescadero Creek Road, and we rambled two miles inland from the sea, passing a wide brackish marsh, black-soiled fields freshly plowed, a collection of clapboard houses, and finally the Stage Road—which is what passes for a main drag in Pescadero. (The name of the town, if you're not up on your Spanish, means "a place for fishermen.")

Right at the corner was Duarte's, a dark-red barn-like structure holding a restaurant and bar. I especially liked its sign, with a pink neon cocktail glass perched atop the name of the place in neon green, and LIQUOR announced below in red. It was all aglow, even though it was not yet noon. I gave the cabbie six twenties for the fare, and showed him the hundred I would pay if he waited an hour. Then I went inside.

The tavern, launched in 1894 by Frank Duarte with a barrel of whisky, still used the crude and battered wooden counter where that barrel had once stood. The place had a glowing jukebox by the door, deer heads and antlers on the walls, and portraits of some very canny dogs cheating their way through poker. Mulcahy had mentioned that this roadhouse was one of his favored hangouts.

That sign awakened in me a mighty thirst, but I knew I had to meter myself, so I shunned the cocktails for mere pints of beer. While nursing them, I chatted up the barkeep. As I had anticipated, he knew Pat Mulcahy well. He said Mulcahy commonly drove his battered Ford Bronco down from his hut in the woods to lubricate his innards about an hour before lunchtime. If I kept sucking up beer, I knew I'd blunt my effectiveness, so I went outside, ambled up the street, and installed myself on a green bus bench by the Arcangeli grocery.

Down the street came an old Ford Bronco of faded blue and gray. I recognized the driver, and stood in the street to wave Mulcahy down. When he stopped, I told him who I actually was and what I was really up to. He blinked, but he took it all in.

"As it happens," he said, "I do know that Castello wants some outside help, since tha young fella got hurt. My friend, Mister Pete Savante, called me just this mornin' to consult. I'm on my way there now."

"Will you take me with you, Pat?"

He considered. "Aye. But tha fog is comin' in heavy on tha coast, y'know, just now."

I'd grown so absorbed in reading Palmer's notebooks on my ride down that I had failed to notice.

"So?"

"We'd do well to insulate ourselves with a wee drop of fog-cutter afore we go," he said.

And we did that very thing, downing double shots of Maker's Mark neat at Duarte's. Before we went in, I paid off the hack who'd been waiting on me.

After our libation, Mulcahy and I wended north in his shuddering Ford. Even with my window rolled down, the ride was a hardship. The air inside Mulcahy's rolling wreck was redolent with the mingled aromas of rotted seat stuffing and old, damp, incontinent dog.

The pooch himself, thank God, had been left at home. Either that or he had passed on a few days earlier, and now lay interred below the rear seat cushion.

Chapter 12

Mulcahy drove his shaky rig up the highway through swirling fog, past a pair of pillars. I could dimly make out fat spiders of construction workers swarming on a web of scaffolding. A new sign for the equestrian resort already hung from a frame of welded steel. CORNU POINT floated in the mist.

"Y'know… if the big-dollar boys score their heart's desire out here, Pescadero itself could go under their blade soon after," I said.

"Aye. I know," Mulcahy said glumly.

The road bent in a long sweep around the bay. Suddenly Mulcahy braked hard, steered the Bronco off the shoulder to the right. Then he twisted the wheel further. We bounced down a rough dirt track until we were far below the level of the highway. The Bronco lurched to a halt. I peered out the window. We were parked in a narrow gulch upholstered in dripping vegetation. There was not one sign of human habitation.

"What the hell?" I asked.

Mulcahy laughed.

"Let's say, in tha old days, ya had consarns aboot infernal revenooers an' all. Need a clandestine way in. Or, out! Na, would ya not?"

We hopped out of the little truck. Mulcahy led me down a weedy slope. A rusty iron grid blocked the mouth of a tall culvert that ran under the highway. I saw that the grid was actually a gate. Two locks of corroded brass hung on its sliding bolt. Mulcahy twirled the dial on one to the proper numbers. He winked as he pulled the ponderous gate open.

I followed him down the corrugated steel tube. We kept as high as we could on its sloping walls, to avoid a muddy ribbon of water rippling along the base of the pipe.

On the west side of the highway, we clambered out into an ectoplasm of gray light that washed down through thickly interwoven tree branches.

I did not see a path. Mulcahy pointed out a faint track that led up through a tangle of brush and vines. We trod through that, thorns snatching at my socks and cuffs, to finally attain a narrow, rocky ledge.

Mulcahy capered on, agile as a goat. I did my best to follow. We made our way over rough terrain, around a few bony points of land that jutted like accusatory fingers out into the sea. Unseen waves made hollow, percussive booms against the cliff beneath our feet.

The dull silver light hovering all around us began to take on a hotter and tawnier hue.

"And thar she be!" Mulcahy proclaimed. "Castello!"

I peered in the direction my guide pointed, just as the fog shredded and began to whisk away. Coming into view on the slope just ahead of us were strips of colorful houses painted in bright pastels and arrayed on broad terraces. These narrow manmade plateaus stood buttressed by walls of stacked rock slabs wedded together by thin lines of mossy mortar. Most of the homes had wind turbines on poles that poked up from their backyards. As we drew closer, I could discern glass greenhouses on the south sides of many.

Overall, Castello bore the raw, rough look of a tiny frontier town. With warm, unfiltered sunlight now showering down, I began to see the charm of living on this stretch of rugged shore. Yet it was also evident the place had taken it on the chin from mighty storms. The only trees were wind-crippled Monterey cypresses. Everything appeared weathered, even the gravelly soil underfoot. To dwell here, you had to endure whatever the North Pacific might decide to hurl at you.

We were noticed. People waved to Mulcahy and gawked at me. Being with him seemed to provide me with a visa—I passed unchallenged. He led me down to the village plaza. Paved with uneven cobbles, it lay at the focal point for the arc of the lowest terrace. Benches of stone, concrete, and driftwood slabs were scattered about in no discernible pattern. Near the center of the plaza, a cement plinth exalted the bust of a mustachioed, bearded figure with flowing hair. I guessed this hero to be Garibaldi.

Present leadership seemed to be in the grip of a stout chap wearing a white shirt and blue overalls, both forearms tucked inside the bib. He sat in the plaza on a wooden bench shaded by a pale pink wall, where he spoke to a half dozen supplicants.

Mulcahy led me in. As we got close, I noted the man wore a porkpie hat, brim turned up, and plastic tortoise-shell glasses. A bristling Wilford Brimley mustache flourished on his upper lip. A quid of chewing tobacco made his cheek bulge as if he were trying to hide a walnut. Between his work-booted feet lay a Chihuahua clad in a multihued hand-knit sweater.

"Mister Pete!"

"Mulcahy! And how might you be?" The capo pulled an arm free from his overalls, thrust a thick-fingered hand out to my guide.

"Never better."

"Wish we could say the same."

Behind lenses of milky plastic, unwavering brown eyes studied me.

"Who's this person? Why do you smuggle him to Castello?"

"Man's a writer, from tha *Post-Dispatch*."

Mister Pete made a disgusted downward sweep with one arm. "Reporters! Far too many showed up today! We stopped 'em all at the gate. Why bring this one in?"

"Well, his name is Colm MacCay. Seems a right sort. And he did ask me quite properly for tha favor. Sound like he wants to help. Y'did say you wanted to locate a reporter with sense, one that you could trust. Y'know, MacCay's had tha opinion column named after him, ran in tha paper fer years."

Pete's interest flickered faintly. "Recall your byline. Regular chickenshit, mostly. But sometimes good."

"Thank you," I said.

He reached behind a leg of his bench, hauled out a coffee can, spat a copious gout of reeking brown fluid into it, then wiped droplets off his mustache with the hairy back of his hand.

"You were sharp enough to charm Mulcahy, so to you I grant our first statement," Pete said. "We were just now discussing how and when to do that. Here it is. We feel sorry your paper's reporter was injured. Despite what others may claim, no one at Castello had a thing to do with the attack on that young man. There. All right. Now, you can go. Di Mastini guys will escort you out."

Three robust-looking gents regarded me intently. They did not smile.

Since I didn't have much to lose, and no other move sprang to mind, I decided to shake a few particles out my meager sack of Garibaldi lore.

"Lovely refuge you've got here," I said. "A secret fort. What are you? The lost tribe of redshirts? Trying to make a Rome where you are?"

Pete's interest ratcheted up half a notch.

"*Qui si fa l'Italia, o si muore,*" he said.

I had zero idea what that meant. Tourist phrase-book Italian only took me so far. I remained quiet and kept a poker face.

Pete scratched a whiskery jaw with his stained fingernail, stared at me hard.

"Anyone who values democracy and freedom should also have an interest in truth," Pete said. "Please see to it that our message gets out."

"Love to. I'm glad to hear you had no involvement in the assault on Sebastian Palmer."

"Media types always seem to leap to conclusions," Pete said. "They particularly like to lay blame. Already, it happens on radio and TV. Generating harm to us, and giving a boost to Cornu Point."

"Might see that again tomorrow. On the *Post-Dispatch* front page."

"You work there, right? Why not do something?"

"I am doing something. I'm warning you."

"But will you stop it? Change it?"

"No."

Mister Pete shot a glance at Mulcahy.

"I like how this guy sweet-talks me."

Mulcahy shrugged his thin shoulders. I could see he had second thoughts about bringing me out here.

"Maybe, instead, I help you build a competing story," I offered.

"Meaning what?" Mister Pete said.

"Dueling narratives," I said. "How the world does business.

Quite often, all it comes down to is this: may the best yarn win."

I had his full attention now.

"I want to expose the truth," he said.

"Sure. Make truth your friend. A story that crumbles to dust soon as anyone gives it a hard look, that can't be good," I replied. "The more truth you can pour into your story to help it stick together the better."

Pete smiled despite himself. The can stood by his boot. He directed another goopy streak of juice down into it, taking care not to splash the Chihuahua. Then his eyes fastened on me again.

"A story-building session such as you describe, how does it start?"

"Exactly like a hand of poker. You lay down your cards, and I lay down mine."

"All right. You first."

That suggestion looked strongly seconded in the gaze of the burly guys and only slightly less robust women scattered around me.

"Okay! My draw. Beverly Bancroft was killed," I offered. "Then her body was moved to make it seem as if it was an accident. And all her fault."

Mister Pete's eyes narrowed. "That is true," he said. "She was kicked by Eiger's horse on a pedestrian-only trail. Afterward, Miss Bancroft's body was moved up to a horses-only trail. Things got tidied up fast at that first spot, then messed up in the other, to make it appear the opposite."

"How do you know that?"

"How do *you* know it?" he countered gruffly.

"I don't. Or I didn't, not until you just backed it up! Sebastian Palmer first suspected it. I just read it in his notebooks. Palmer made a visit out to Cornu Point the morning after her death. Even found her eyeglasses near a bend of that footpath."

Pete paused. Nodded.

"There's an animal, very small." He held his thumb and forefinger two inches apart. "You do not often notice this fellow, since he lives so quietly below ground. But on and on he digs, then pops up in unexpected spots to take a look. We say, '*cieco come una talpa*,' to be blind like that. Still, he sees everything he needs to see."

"A mole, you mean."

He nodded again. I felt a stab of intuition. He wasn't only talking about Palmer.

"You have a mole at Cornu Point," I guessed.

"More than one. Why not? A big place like Cornu needs stable hands, kitchen help, groundskeepers, lots of staff. People, even at low levels, always hear things, see things. Put two and two together. They give me their best stuff. I make a story, like you say. Still, it's best to keep thoughtful. Put out your story in the wrong way, or at the wrong moment, then all you end up with is people losing their jobs."

"Mm-hm," I said. "Tell me, what else have your moles found?"

"No. It is your turn."

"I already dealt and bid. You only anteed. Why not raise?"

Mister Pete smiled at Mulcahy, but he jerked his thumb toward me. "He is kind of fun," he said. "I think I'll tell a story."

He folded his arms comfortably into the bib of his overalls, leaned back against the wall. The half-dozen denizens clustered around Mister Pete, who'd been chattering away as we initially approached, now took up postures to watch him perform. I guessed how Mister Pete came by his authority: he was the most entertaining guy they had.

"All that we possess here is due to a deep and abiding friendship. Max Bancroft, a retired banker, was best pals with Rudy Wyatt, the silent-screen cowboy. They might have been old in years, but still showed a zest for fun. During Prohibition, and at the time of the Great Depression, fun was sometimes hard to find. Out here at Castello, we had plenty. We enjoyed great vintages and blue-ribbon booze, we had fabulous food, we had music. Also, we had women who enjoyed having fun.

"Max and Rudy came here often. They got to be friends with my grandfather, with everyone, and so eventually tried to help us deal with a problem. I should tell you, our town of Castello was founded in 1874. A schooner, the *Cornu Arietis,* ran aground at this spot in a heavy fog.

"Must've turned sunny a minute later, just as it did for us a moment ago. Because many *paisanos* off the wreck decided to settle down right here, become coastal fishermen. They were weary of captains, maybe never wanted to be under another boss. Anyway, these seaman-squatters basically founded our Castello.

"Coastal farmers gradually settled the land around us. Maybe we should have figured out a way to get a genuine title back then. But it was not seen as necessary. The farmers couldn't grow crops out here, and they liked having us around, just as Max and Rudy did—and for the same reasons.

"In 1932, Max and Rudy bought land at Cornu Point, put those riding trails in all over. They'd railroad their Hollywood playmates up, then stagecoach 'em out to Cornu for pack rides and horse camps, barbecues, and so forth. Some came to Castello for extra entertainment. Max and Rudy decided to buy title to this horn of land from a few farmers who imagined they owned it—just to be sure—then donated everything to the state.

"Their idea was that we would be allowed to stay on, paying a lease set at 1933 prices. They didn't grant us title outright, so individuals here would not be able to sell the land again. Castello could be broken up, lost that way. Frank and Rudy nursed a romantic notion that our village should stay the same, more or less as they knew it."

"Net result, you're an Indian reservation," I said. "I mean, except for being Italian."

Pete inclined his head.

"We went on, dumb and happy, not seeing a second mistake. Never got the park's founding documents. As it grew more powerful, Cornu Point Association made trouble. Tinkered with the lease, got the Legislature to pass a law putting in a sunset clause. Max and Rudy were long dead. We had access to a few politicians, and for Castello we won two extensions. Still, our feet have been on banana peels for years."

"Those original founding documents might still exist," I told him. "Beverly Bancroft claimed that she had notarized copies. Her lawyer thought they would hold sway. She planned to show them to Palmer."

Pete nodded. He looked sad. "Beverly's lawyer was Simon Winger. She recommended him to us, and we consulted with him. Yesterday, we hear Mr. Winger has a new job. He's become lead counsel for Cornu Point Association."

"Ouch!"

"Exactly."

"And that sister, Olivia?"

"Quite frail. I'm not sure how many marbles are left in her bag."

"Palmer said Olivia was grabbed, put away somewhere."

"She resides now in Desert Buttes-Sunset Estates. A giant rest home in Vegas, also owned by 3CD Corporation. Where the horse also is."

"They put a horse in a rest home?"

"Don't be stupid. I mean, the horse also is in Las Vegas. The big one—trained to kick on command—the one that killed Miss Bancroft. Let me finish by saying 3CD bought controlling interest in Cornu Point Association after it changed from nonprofit status. Mr. Bates and Mr. Wheeler came from the offices in Vegas to oversee new development."

My head felt close to exploding. I would say Mister Pete had fanned out a royal flush of hot tips to produce precisely that effect on me. He crossed his legs, tugged his arms from his overalls, and laced blunt fingers across his knees. The Chihuahua lifted its head as if expecting a pat, but was ignored. With a minuscule sigh, it laid its chin back down upon its teeny crossed paws.

"You and I should begin to negotiate seriously," Mister Pete said.

———

From a coat pocket, I whipped out the last of Palmer's notebooks, the fourth, which had a few blank pages left. I began to scrawl notes right where his neat lines left off, as Mister Pete and an abruptly talkative chorus of his cohorts filled me in.

They figured the attack on Palmer had been staged at their doorstep with malice aforethought. It was a setup, and they didn't like it, but their reputation as tough guys was not going to help. Particularly since it had been earned. During Prohibition, Castello men acted like Chicago gangsters to keep their cut of the smugglers' pie. They formed a fraternity of firstborn sons called *Una Banda di Mastini,* the band of mastiffs, or guard dogs. They were *uomini d'onore,* men of honor, enforcers. That gang outlived its original purpose. Di Mastini still functioned as perimeter guards—preventing their village from being overrun by tourists and other idiots. Gradually, though, they had grown to reject physical violence. Now, they focused on intimidation, backed up by stints of vandalism. Given their rep, that worked well enough.

The firstborn of either sex tended to stick around, that was the tradition. But it grew harder for younger sibs to stay in Castello. Outside, there was the lure of faster pace and better jobs. But even after they departed, loyalty to this place and their families endured. Consequently, Mister Pete accessed a network of blue-collar intelligence, woven into the warp and woof of life at Cornu Point, and indeed much of the Bay Area.

Before he tossed me keys to his kingdom, Pete wanted my oath that I would do my utmost to publish a truthful story about their long struggle, first with Cornu Point Association, now 3CD. No half measures or shallow sensationalism would suffice. He figured they had one good shot to set the record straight.

I readily agreed. I wished to exact payback for what had been done to Palmer. Beyond that, I felt a revived zeal for the original mission: squish some bad guys. And I had to admit, revving up to take on these tasks might do me a world of good.

"I do not yet know how far reach of the association may go," Mister Pete said. "Into courts? Into our county offices? Into the Sheriff's Department? State government? Even some media?" He shrugged, palms upward. "I'm not saying our good citizens of the coast don't want to do the right thing. But a strong news story often helps them *see* the right thing, *capisci?*"

"I have long nurtured that same hope," I said.

Soon Pete gave me contacts for Lt. Rafael Flores, the sheriff's detective handling the Palmer assault; the address of Desert Buttes Rest Home in Vegas and a number for Patricia Delicato, who worked there as receptionist. Of even greater interest, he offered the name and location of the stallion that had lofted Beverly Bancroft into the hereafter.

It was not "Franz," a name Erik Eiger gave the stable crew at Cornu Point after they had settled and groomed that big horse. Eiger claimed Franz was a Russian Orlov. But they'd already learned different from the truck driver. Eiger had tried to conceal this horse's origin by having it first delivered to Santa Rosa, then having a second truck bring it to Cornu Point. But this arrangement had not gone strictly according to plan. Arrival of these trucks had accidently overlapped.The first driver came late, the second was early. These drivers had gossiped, and the gist of their communication eventually reached Pete's sources at Cornu. Turned out the stallion's actual name was Mephisto Medea XII, and he was the star of an equine circus gig at Big Top Casino.

Immediately after Bancroft's death, Mephisto was shipped back to Vegas. Eiger shed a crocodile tear, sniveling that he could not stand to throw a leg over "Franz" anymore. For him, horseback riding was ruined, perhaps forever. Meanwhile, the sheriff's investigator was fed a red herring about Franz being sold to a broker in Mexico—a tall tale accompanied by a photocopied receipt. And good luck to the detective in deciphering those scribbled contact numbers if he hoped to try tracking down Franz in Chiapas.

"'Franz' was no Orlov," Pete said. "Actually, I think he's like a Lipizzaner, a show horse trained to kick out hard on orders of a rider."

I cudgeled my brain. "You mean those horses in the old Disney movie?"

"Less cute. This stallion does not show any 'L' brand on his cheek, as is usual. He does have similar breeding, and those moves. Maybe he was a dropout from the training. But he knows plenty, all of those tricks they figured out, centuries ago, I think, for mounted cavaliers to use. Moves of great help when you must fight foot soldiers."

"I'd say," I replied.

"One thing more. A huge, young Samoan man was on the Cornu Point security force, name of Aiano Tuato. He just flew back home to Samoa today, on emergency leave, due to family troubles, I am told. Yet Sunday, a coworker heard Tuato rant about this little punk haole who apparently made a big complaint about Tuato at the Cornu front office. This haole kid supposedly called Tuato 'a fat, ugly, nigger bastard rent-a-cop.'"

This left a bad taste. "Doesn't sound like Palmer," I said.

"Doesn't have to," Mister Pete told me. "It got fed to Tuato anyhow."

"So, this Sheriff's Department detective, Rafe Flores, does he look to you like he wants to do a good job?"

Pete spread his hands. "With county sheriffs, I have to say we have the uneasy truce. Sometimes, a *coglione* from either side tests the limits. Not often. Flores annoys me by acting as if he's already got this figured out. When I know he does not."

"Make him your friend," I suggested. "Give Flores your intel on this Tuato. And here's something else he can use." I repeated what Marty the nurse had said about the steel rod, and the rust and torn skin on Palmer's hands. "Ask him to check that rebar, see what blood it's got on it besides what spurted out of Palmer."

"Next they see if anyone looking like Tuato entered a Bay Area ER to get a wound treated," Pete said. "Eventually they get a DNA sample from Tuato, or a close relative, then try for a match."

"Eureka!" I applauded. Mister Pete was not only clever but well-read.

"See, here's my thought on Flores," I said. "Put him on the scent now, maybe you wind up with him on your side. That would be a good sign. And a big deal. Cops can pull off stuff that you and I can't. Then, down the line, maybe he gives you something back. That's fair, eh?"

"All right," Pete said.

"So, who's your top pick for the chief bad dude out at Cornu?"

"All of them! Follow the money. Most of these bastards plan to get rich on our backs!"

I shook my head. "Sure. We'd all like a big bag of dough. Who wouldn't? But nobody can hatch a plot to make somebody dead, then welcome all comers. That kind of project has to be closely held."

"Eiger knows. He has to know."

"Sure. But it can't just be Eiger. Also, it can't be everyone. Let's narrow the field. Who riled up Tuato, then pointed him at Palmer? If we can't answer that, more digging at Cornu Point is needed."

"Cornu was hounded by many reporters today. Even as we were. They are on alert, defenses up."

"All right. If I go there to poke and pry, maybe I'm not a reporter."

"What, then?"

"I'll think of something," I said, sounding wiser than I felt.

"*Grazie a lei,*" Pete said, nodding. "Are we done?"

"For now," I told him. "I think we are."

Mister Pete spat carefully one last time, grabbed his vat of sepia effluent, rose to his feet.

"C'mon, Shorty."

The tiny dog jumped up and began to trot, leading the way to a nearby house.

"I'll do my best," I said.

"Yes! Your very best. No less!" Pete peered back at me through thick, scratched glasses. "Or I'll sic Di Mastini on you." He winked. "And if that don't scare you enough, watch out! After them comes Shorty."

Chapter 13

I asked Mulcahy to bring me to Half Moon Bay, then took a cab back up to The City. I needed fuel, didn't have a great deal of time, so I gobbled Dungeness crab cakes, sweet pepper soup, and seafood linguini Provençal at the Beach Chalet. From the bistro's salt-streaked second-floor windows, I gazed out upon the broad, wrinkled slate of the sea. Then I walked the sidewalks back to my place.

Finally—a moment to catch my breath.

It had been astonishing to feel the old newsman instincts rear up and surge back to life, blasting out of a mental mausoleum where they'd feigned death for so long. Years spent developing and deploying those skills had neither been wasted nor lost. Having them back was a bit like finding out that I'd been reincarnated as myself, without all the bother involved in actually having to die, then somehow acquire a new body.

Drives linked with the journalistic mission of unfettered inquiry spread through my mind once again, weaving together a new net of fibers from old materials. Maybe here was my real safety line, the thing that could halt my plunge, sustain me above the beckoning depths of the abyss.

Back home, I decided Anna had been right about my wardrobe. Nothing was the matter with it that squandering a king's ransom at Wilkes Bashford couldn't cure. But no time to shop for a touch of class. Maybe I could take a déclassé shortcut. At a Tevis Cup endurance ride in the High Sierra, I'd once interviewed financier Warren Hellman. Absolutely zero about the tattered horseman's outfit that Hellman wore had shouted, or even whispered, "billionaire."

I picked out a clean white shirt, old Wrangler jeans, and a ranger vest of faded canvas. (Don't know if you've seen a classic ranger vest, but modern photographers' vests are modeled on them. The ranger model has a large, square pouch pocket that extends the length of the back panel. Designed to hold a professional forester's gear for timber cruises, all his maps and whatnot, such a vest is great for toting legal pads, or hands-free carry of a laptop.) A pair of scuffed Wellington boots added another outdoor touch. Also, as an Irish expat in good standing, I owned many visored caps in varying shades of tartan plaid, and picked one out.

But Cinderfella also needed a coach that wouldn't make him look like a bumpkin pulling up to the curb in a pumpkin. I got on the horn to an old friend of Da's who ran a Financial District limo service. Well, a nephew now owned the show, and the kid did recall my name. Due to that bygone connection, he was willing to hire out a brand-new Lincoln Town Car that had no transport service license stickers pasted on it yet, plus a live chauffeur in a traditional suit, for a fee that was only moderately exorbitant.

Soon, perched on the pillow-soft, fragrant leathers of the big bench seat in the back of the Lincoln, I glided back down the Coast Highway. I had the driver put KCBS on the stereo, in case the station's 24-hour news offered any details on something I intended to use as one of my talking points. It did me just fine by airing a bulletin that covered the attack on Palmer.

I pondered the act I was about to try to pull off for the Cornu Point swells. Making a strong impression would be more than half my battle.

We pulled up right in front of the main office. I had the driver get out and walk around to open my door. No reporters seemed to be loitering about at the moment, which was perfect. Might have made my routine harder to maintain.

The building looked like a Henrik Bull design for an Alpine ski resort—robustly thrusting skyward with a macho prow made of roughhewn timber, native stone, and smoky glass. Inside I found a young receptionist with dark hair swept up in a French braid. She also looked well built, but along far more feminine lines.

"Good afternoon," I said, deploying my plummiest tone. "We're on the hunt for an equestrian resort, my family and I, to use during the summers we stay in California. Thought we'd take a peek at your place! Mr. Bates in?"

"Oh! Well, would you like to meet with our membership concierge? She can tell you everything about Cornu Point, even take you on a tour. I think she's available right now... ."

I let my face sink into a moue of dissatisfaction.

"I came to see Bates," I grated.

"Oh." She hesitated. "Is he expecting you?"

"Well, damn! I should hope so."

"Ah. I'll tell him you are here. Mr.—?"

"Call me Ishmael," I said grandly. "Howie Ishmael. Thanks. That's lovely." And I flashed a patently insincere grin.

"Do you have a card?"

"No! Don't use 'em. Never give, nor accept, cards. Transmit germs, y'know."

"Um," she said. Then, "I'll be right back. Excuse me."

I lingered in the lobby, admiring the modern artwork on display. I wondered whether these paintings were hung right-side up. I decided that it didn't matter.

An average-sized chap with a pleasant face, black hair moussed and combed back from his forehead, and square-rimmed glasses with thick black frames approached, walking a pace behind the nymph of reception.

"Mr. Ishmael!" he said. "Don Bates. So! I hear you may want to join us out here at Cornu Point. Welcome." He reached out to pump my hand. He looked disconcerted when my arms remained resolutely by my sides.

"Sorry," I said. "I have special needs in the realm of hygiene."

"Er," he said. He and the receptionist swapped a glance, but took care to keep their faces devoid of any expression.

"Well. Please, come into my office. Let's visit a bit, get to know one another."

He was about to put a hand on my back and give me a steer, but suddenly thought better of it and just held his palm hovering above my shoulder for a few seconds.

"For some reason you didn't make it into my appointment book," he said. "I do apologize for that."

"Yes, hmm, well." I responded.

He planted me on one side of a sleek mahogany desk, installed himself in a plush swivel chair, and flipped open a glossy cardboard binder with colorful brochures tucked in its pockets. With his fingertips, he twisted the material around so it faced me, then slid it across the desk.

"All one might need to know about investing in a wonderful future at Cornu Point can be found right there," he said smoothly.

In a pig's eye, I thought.

"Can I get you something to drink?"

The fantasy of ordering a Bombay sapphire martini with three almond-stuffed olives in a frosted cocktail glass crossed my mind. Then the same thought wheeled around to sashay past again, eyeing me like a flirtatious streetwalker. But I demurred.

"Ishmael. Now, that's a fairly unusual name," Bates said, attempting to lead the witness.

"Yep." I declined to be led.

"What's your line?"

"I'm retired. Mostly. A few clients did insist I stay with them."

"And your field?"

"Oh, wealth management, mainly."

The general manager of Cornu Point Resort deftly managed to avoid licking his lips. I saw how badly he wanted to do it. I felt tempted to prolong the moment. But, time to move on. I had to take control of the interview.

"We're looking for a good place on the West Coast to stable and train our horses," I told him. "I and several friends. We all have a thing for Irish hunters."

"Hunters," he repeated, nodding his head, yet still looking mystified.

"You know, jumpers," I encouraged. "Does Cornu Point have a steeplechase course? Or hurdles of any sort?"

"Ah!" Bates said. "No, not at present. But certainly it's the sort of facility we could establish to serve the right set of clients! We do have the polo field, dressage ring, many riding trails, and what *Horse & Rider* rated as the top stables on the West Coast. Our lodge, restaurant, spa, and tennis courts have all been built to exceptionally luxurious standards.

"And there's more to come. A few exclusive homes will be built at prime sites overlooking the sea. And on tracts around Cornu Point, fine estates are being planned as we speak, each with its own stable and pasture and trails that connect to our system. Probably, I shouldn't even mention this because it's still in the permit process." He lowered his voice, arched his eyebrows, leaned forward. "But I can't resist! Two words, all right?" he whispered. "Air strip!"

Then he leaned back, an expression of triumph on his face.

"Interesting," I said. I had always thought airstrip was a single word. "But one thing bothers me."

"What?" he inquired. But I'll bet you he already knew.

"Well, on my way here, I overheard a radio reporter talk about an assault or attempted murder at — what's it called — some town nearby, Castle-something...?"

"Castello. Yes. A tragic story. But what I can tell you, Mr. Ishmael, is our problem at Castello is *this* close to being resolved." He held tips of his index fingers a quarter-inch apart. "The state is preparing to evict the people who live on that land illegally. This unfortunate assault provides all the impetus they need to act. I don't wish to call the people at Castello bums or thugs. Let's just say they aren't fully civilized — or even civil, for that matter! But their free ride is about to come to an end. Meantime, our security chief guarantees no Castello problems spill over to our grounds. He's got a fantastic background in the military and law enforcement, our Mr. Prichard. He can deal with such types."

"Once that area's finally cleared, will shoreline estates be built?"

"Oh, yes! Castello has splendid views — its only redeeming feature, at the moment."

Bates chuckled.

"And the valleys, just inland?"

"Uh-huh, yes, the little farms." Bates bobbed his head, folded his hands. "Well, Cornu Point has possession of the Castello site. Those surrounding farms are optioned to another entity. But frankly? We're not too impressed with their financing. I won't bore you with details on our maneuvers. I will say, in all likelihood, that that acreage should be in the Cornu Point portfolio soon. Do those sites particularly interest you?"

So it went. Bates invited me to dine at the resort restaurant.

And he wished to provide a tour of facilities. Unfortunately, I could not meet Erik Eiger, since the star was back in Beverly Hills. But wasn't it fabulous how Cornu Point, founded by famed actor Rudy Wyatt, was able to keep that glam' Hollywood link going by getting Erik Eiger to act as its ambassador?

"Wonderful," I said. However, sorry, I needed to sprint off. I was scheduled to meet soon in San Francisco with the famed financiers, Mr. Hellman and Mr. Buffet.

I watched Don Bates almost inhale his own larynx.

My rented chauffeur wafted me northward aboard the plush Town Car suspension. I reviewed what I'd just learned. The development scheme had been made clear. But Bates was merely a real estate flack. His knowledge and feel for horse culture constituted a paltry add-on. Bates did not have the soul of a killer. Whether he possessed a soul, well, that was a question for another day. But if I hoped to locate an evil genius at Cornu Point, I had to keep looking.

—

Once back at my sad little pad, I threw my keys into an empty cigar box on the desk, waved hello at Anna, and went for the liquor cabinet. Chivas Regal seemed a good bet for tonight. I brought the bottle and a pair of shot glasses to the walnut table.

"Here's how," I told Anna, and threw hers down.

She wavered to life, slowly shaking her head, while I sipped mine.

"You need to slow this sozzling down some, chum," she said. "You overdo."

"Aw, merely taking a wee drop to oil me gears," I told her. "And when did you start to tee-total? Don't you want one? Who'll drink for you if not I? And if not now, when?"

"Time for me to set an example. You're drowning in it! You told me just this morning you had to stay sober to avoid more missteps. That was you, wasn't it?"

"Eh? Did I happen to use the 'S' word? Well, I did fine work today! I deserve a little R&R. Or J&B, as the case may be. "

"Yes," she conceded. "Good work. Reminiscent of the old Mac-Cay. But what of tomorrow?"

"My drinking is precisely calibrated."

"Sure, sure. But where can it take you? Or more important, why can't you ever stop? See, I worry about you."

"The journey is all. 'To travel hopefully is better than to arrive.' Stevenson said that. Or some bit quite a bit like it."

"See? Now, you're blathering."

"Perhaps."

"What of that young man in the hospital? You let him down. You've admitted as much. Now you're supposed to be making up for it. What you have not admitted, even to yourself, is the high degree of discipline such a battle will demand. Have you?"

"Yes. I would even say, 'Yes, of course!' Let me pose a question back to you. Planning to become a nag in your old age?"

"No worries, there. I can't age. Not anymore! That's your job."

"So unfair!"

She did not answer. Ring and rattle of our conversational epees faded. She began to dim, too.

"Stop! Come back. I'm sorry! You're right."

But Anna returned to her photograph. Still, unmoving, eternal.

Well! A full four fingers were left in my fifth of Chivas. Nearly enough for a decent nightcap. I sourly slurped it down. Just to prove I could.

Chapter 14

My knockout drops of Chivas fully functioned for two hours. After that, I floated in a groggy zone, mired on the threshold of dreams. I kept circling around to a vision of Palmer's bandaged body supine on a hospital bed, hooked to a spaghetti of tubes and colored wires.

Yet sometimes that shape was mine. So I stared out at a bleak ICU through Palmer's heavy-lidded, unmoving eyes. I saw the face of Marty the nurse gaze down with all her fierce professional pity—except Marty occasionally turned into Anna, who also regarded me in that same thoughtful, unsentimental manner.

Unsettling. Enough to make me want to snatch the cork out of a fresh bottle, and guzzle myself back into a stupor. But Anna had already called my number on the nonproductive nature of that evasive maneuver. I needed to not disappoint her again.

The result of this struggle was that I rose at about the same second the sun did, feeling utterly frazzled. I flung on the same urban cowpoke outfit I'd worn the previous day. Walked over to the Seal Rock Inn to get an omelet. En route, I hit the news racks for fresh copies of the Patch and Comicle, then scanned both over breakfast. The *San Francisco Chronicle* crammed a short about the assault on Palmer on an inside page. A brief covering the basics. About what I would have assigned were I editor at a competing paper.

The *Post-Dispatch* splashed it above the fold on A-1, just as Brotmann had promised. It had Palmer's employee foto and a few lede grafs out front, then went to a jump. Gist was, Palmer had boldly put himself in a dangerous position by traveling alone to a known high-crime area. He was young and inexperienced, albeit an idealistic reporter, and so forth.

Identity of assailant unknown. Strong implication? A thug from Castello. Body of the story plundered the morgue, dredging up decades-old reports to paint this village as a last outpost of the Bay Area's wild, woolly Barbary Coast era.

Quotes from Palmer's shocked parents, from a Palmer college professor. The trauma center vacuously hedged about Palmer's condition and prognosis.

Cornu Point provided a quote from Larry Wheeler, executive director, lamenting lawless ways of "a few isolated places on this incredible shore," while promising the resort would never let a savage crime alter its plans to improve the environment, offer responsible development, provide high-quality recreation, blah-blah-blah.

Yet the story held no response or defense from Castello. No onsite, real-time, first-person accounts of the place. So Mr. Pete had held firm, and I still enjoyed my "exclu" entry out there, and access to all that the villagers knew.

Ericson and Stein were better reporters than this piece indicated. Our vaunted I-team had been treading water. Odds were this respite wouldn't last. To stay out in front of my own paper — let alone many other Bay Area news outlets — I needed to keep moving. Since there was now not only an "accidental" death, but also a vicious assault to wring their hands over, reporters would soon begin to swarm around this story like crows on roadkill.

I put my elbows to either side of the sticky remains of my breakfast, propped my head in my hands, closed my eyes, and thought hard. Number one priority: nailing the lead bad guy by figuring out his (or her) means and motivation. I had to follow the evidence where it led, while eliminating other suspects. I needed to load up fast with deeper intel so I could assemble both goads and incisive questions.

In the arena, preparing to face all the bull sure to be hurled at you, one should heed the Matador Rule: A suit of lights may be optional, but a sword and cape are mandatory. The cape distracts the opponent, the sword provides that useful surprise.

A logical first step would be to grill the farmers around Castello, find contacts for the entity who had bought up options on their land, and backtrack from there. However, if that seemed logical to me, it would swiftly occur to others. No telling when that info pathway would be prioritized, or by whom, or how fast it might grow clogged by competitive inquisitors. My instincts told me that whoever had engineered the arrangement likely had taken great care to cover his tracks. Unraveling such a trail might take days, and require the type of data-bank mining for which I had scant patience. Especially now.

Fortunately, there were two other targets of opportunity: Sacramento, where I could try to locate genuine dope on the founding of Cornu Point, or discover who had a strong interest in concealing it. And Vegas, the desert playpen that held Olivia Bancroft as well as Mephisto, the magic pony. Finding out the truth about either could provide a shortcut into the meat of the story—and potentially give me a fast way of ushering my initial hit into print.

All right. Course set. But first I had to pay a call on Miss Elle Jatobá, the damsel who'd reamed me a new one at the Palo Alto ICU. She was not only Palmer's confidante, but his notes implied she also had witnessed Larry Wheeler and Aiano Tuato perform bits of their act. Before leaving town, I had to find out what she knew. Given the amiability Elle had displayed at our first meeting, I certainly looked forward to seeing her. What fresh insults might lie in store?

Whew! Already, I was trying to move quicker than I had in years. And I knew that the pace was bound to only increase from here.

Back at my flat, I packed a small duffel that included toiletries, a change of clothes, and my camera gear. I slipped legal pads and laptop into the broad back pouch of the ranger vest. Next I caught the Fulton 51 downtown, grabbed a BART commuter train to Millbrae, and took a taxi from there to Foster City.

The cabbie swerved along streets that wound past lagoons and canals, until he found the address that Palmer had helpfully filed in his notebooks.

We're all temporary sojourners on the planet. Foster City underscores that merry maxim to the nth. In the 1960s, Jack Foster had the bright idea of taking a dairy farm on a former salt marsh, bolstering its levees, then pumping out water while pumping in more sand and mud. Next, he laid out streets, homes, and parks to serve some 30,000 residents.

Buyers crowded in and soon faced a swarm of problems, including skyrocketing taxes and pollution flowing through their scenic lagoons. These investors revolted, incorporated, and threw off the developer's yoke. They won a soupçon of independence. But I see them as plowing on through deficits of the original concept, including, but not limited to, land subsidence, levees pummeled by rising sea levels, and the sad datum that the ground most prone to rumba like a slab of tapioca during an earthquake is—you guessed it—mud and sand.

And Mister Pete thought he lived with his feet on banana peels!

What sorts of bravehearts dwelt here? The cabbie dropped me before a townhouse where a faded rainbow flag flapped languidly on a pole. I looked up at it, speculated on its meaning. I rang the doorbell. After a minute, rang again.

I hadn't called ahead. Didn't want Elle to fume, build up a head of steam. Thought I should just pop in on her. Ambush can help you set an agenda. As it turned out, I got to be the one surprised. Right after the door swung open.

"Yes?"

I was nonplused. A tall, slender black woman in a blue turban and fluffy robe of yellow terry cloth stood before me. Despite the outlandish outfit, she had an elegant bearing and a gentle, patrician way of speaking.

"I am here to see Miss Elle Jatobá," I said. "Is she in?"

"And who might you be?"

"Colm MacCay. I'm a reporter for the *San Francisco Post-Dispatch*."

"Ah."

In that single syllable, she conveyed that she knew a helluva lot more about me than I did about her. Yet she proved willing to share.

"I am Cheryl Bullock, Elle's partner," she said. "Elle should return shortly. Would you like to come in and wait for her?"

"Certainly. Thank you."

She held open the door, then I followed her down a short hallway, past a wall-mounted collection of exotic masks. My brain busily processed the twin revelations that (A) Elle was gay, and (B) this older black woman was her main squeeze. I hadn't gotten either out of Palmer's notes. Cheryl moved with an eerie grace. She seemed potent and self-contained, yet somehow fragile.

"I was just making tea. Would you care for some?"

"Yes. If it's no trouble."

"None at all... It will be chamomile, to settle my stomach. You see, I've not been well."

We took our mugs out to a balcony that opened onto the lagoon. Across the band of gleaming water, some kids goofed around on a muddy beach. They pushed small pirate ships made of milk cartons, complete with Popsicle-stick masts. Cheryl settled down on the thick mattress of a wooden chaise lounge. Leaning back with a sigh, she patted a matching chair beside her. I sat without putting my feet up.

"Elle went to visit Sebastian," she said. Those large, dark, fathomless eyes turned toward me.

"He is constantly in my thoughts," I said.

"It's tragic, what happened. Not only to him. Also Miss Bancroft."

"Yes. I'd like to see this whole situation become a good deal less tragic."

"Have you any plans to assist the process?"

"I'm working on it."

"As a reporter?"

"Exactly." I held both hands out, palms up. "It's all I've got."

"You may be surprised by this, but I myself know some ways of doing that type of work." Cheryl's chuckle was an alto throb, rising from deep within her lean chest. She saw my questioning look, and her smile broadened.

"True! You know, they say you need to pick your fights. Well, my fight picked me, and did so early in my life. But I was really only able to begin battling back four years ago. That's when I founded a group based in Oakland called C.A.P., Campaign Against Pedophilia. I and my staff track child-abuse perpetrators and their networks, figure out how they sell and share their information, pictures, and videos. Then we turn tips and background data over to local cops, the FBI, even Interpol."

I stared at her. Into the mystery that radiated out under Cheryl's placid surface.

"I have not been able to exert myself much for my group in

recent months," she said. "Still, I often consult with those in our office. And I always take an interest when I hear about any sort of good investigation underway. Like Sebastian's and Elle's. Yours..."

"The key trait a reporter or a detective must have, I would say, is curiosity. Seems as though you have some," I said.

"More than a little." Full lips curved up. For a second, her eyes sparked with vitality. "Perhaps a trait the four of us share. You and I, Sebastian and Elle. They are both young warriors. You know, her heart's desire is to become a cop someday."

"Yikes!" That just slipped out of me.

"What makes you say that?" Hint of a frown rippled that marble brow.

"Oh... it's only that... I think she would be, um, formidable."

"I certainly hope so."

Cheryl's look probed me. I had the uneasy sensation that, with much less background to draw on, she somehow saw into me about as well as Anna ever had.

"Elle has many sides, much capability. Beyond what she showed during your tiff at the hospital."

"You know about that."

"Naturally. Elle and I discuss everything. Including the inquiry she helped Sebastian start. Since you now work on it too, I imagine that the actor who shills for Cornu Point, Erik Eiger, is a person in whom you also take interest. If that is so, then I have a useful tip for you. Certain rumors about him have come my way through C.A.P."

Cheryl saw my reporter's ears prick up. She gave another low chuckle.

"Many think Eiger's just a washed-up Hollywood muscle boy, with his last big hit twenty years in the past. His career did go into a nosedive after Schwarzenegger got picked for *Conan the Barbarian*. But Eiger had already enjoyed a good career in film in America, and before that in Europe. And what I hear is, long before he got famous, while very young, he began his work before the camera by appearing in fairly dicey 16-millimeter porn shoots."

"Well, holy crap!" I whispered. A sordid history like that probably didn't have much, if anything, to do with recent events at

Cornu Point, but it sure as heck could sell newspapers. If prov-
able, it was a gift. I told Cheryl as much.

"Can you track that down? Let me know what you discover?
Could be the juicy bit that rivets public attention. Wrongdoing in
high places works perfectly fine as a story theme, but add some
tawdry sex and you've got a brew that'll make readers bring their
cups back to your counter for refills. Salted popcorn is not even
necessary."

Cheryl laughed a bit ruefully, shook her head. "I will do it," she
said. "I will help however I can."

We chatted on. Cheryl broadcast an almost mystic serenity. When
we first met, I knew no details of the medical horrors she'd endured. After I heard of them, her demeanor made sense. Month
after month, Cheryl had faced a near prospect of death. She fought
back toward life with no guarantee she'd make it. Dwelling in
that limbo between earthly presence and absence, she made her
peace with existential uncertainty. This granted her an elevated
perspective. She saw deeply, celebrated life's possibilities, yet was
not overly or even overtly attached to them. She knew all could
vanish in a snap of the fingers, with a mere wave of fate's wand.

On that day, I merely found myself envying her philosophic
mood, wishing I owned even a particle of it.

Abruptly, the front door banged open. Elle Jatobá swept in like
a gust of storm wind. She started to sing out a greeting to Cheryl,
but that died on her lips as soon as she caught sight of me.

"What the fuck is this meathead doing here?" she demanded.

Ah. I wasn't a piece of shit anymore. I had come up in the world.

"Colm and I were discussing the Cornu Point story," Cheryl
said to Elle.

"I found your address in one of Sebastian's notebooks," I added.

Elle's indignation was unrelieved. "Oh. Finally figured you'd do
some work?" she said. "Well, I just came back from the hospital.
Sebastian's still in a coma."

"Elle, I do care about Palmer. Don't try to suggest I do not," I
said. "Following the assault, I reached his bedside before you did."

Cheryl glanced at me, then Elle. "Now, children," she reproved.

"How is he?" I asked.

"Still no response. His parents are there now," Elle reported.

She stalked past us, out to the farthest corner of the balcony. She turned to lean the small of her back and elbows on the rail and faced us. Elle wore black tights under a short denim skirt, a black top, and a denim jacket with a yellow bandanna casually knotted above one elbow. Her flaming hair was tied back in a ponytail. It was a fetching look.

"What are his folks like?"

"His mom's tubby and hysterical. His dad's tall and silent, stringy and knobby. They love him. But they don't really care for each other. Just like you and me."

"Elle. All right. You and I had a bad start. Call that my fault, I won't argue. But if we stay at odds, that doesn't help a goddamn thing. I'm serious about solving this. I want to find the person who beat up Sebastian. I want to figure out who killed Beverly. And I want to stop this greed-head hijacking of a stretch of California coast.

"You partnered with Sebastian, you can confirm certain things. You might even add to what I found in his notes. Whether you help out or not, I plan to continue. If you hate me, so be it, I understand. But what I need to know right now is can you put that aside, for even a moment?"

Pale lashes lowered, Elle's eyes narrowed to slits, and her long jaw worked. It amazed me how someone could be so expressive without even opening her mouth.

"Your turn, girl," Cheryl advised.

Elle spun around. She gripped the railing with both hands as she stared out over the lagoon. A lone snowy egret glided out over that long beam of flat water. A shadowy, upside-down egret mirrored its every move from beneath.

Cheryl glanced over at me, flexing her eyebrows as if wanting to communicate something. I had absolutely no idea what she was trying to tell me.

After a long pause, Elle turned around again. She stepped toward me and thrust out her hand. "Okay, let's start over," she said simply.

I was floored. I took her hand, found her grip strong and sincere. "Ah. Well. Good," I said, at a loss for other words.

Then we went over Elle's trip with Sebastian out to Cornu Point, beginning with her description of the security guard who had confronted them at the Bancroft house. When I asked if the guard might have been Samoan, she said it was possible. Then she stared at me, wondering how I had guessed.

Elle couldn't resist a dig about the time wasted, as she and Palmer had waited and waited for me at the Cornu Point lot. I focused on her description of that over-the-top eviction of Palmer at the end of Beverly's service. Plus an SUV tail put on them after they left? Ludicrous! These dudes didn't act like they had much to fear. "Brazen" was their default mode. They must have potent friends in high places, or a bankroll with the heft of a black hole.

When Elle mentioned the name on the security chief's name-tag, Dick Prichard, a tiny alarm rang in my head. So, his full name was *Richard Prichard*? Sounded like an alias picked by a person who considered himself smarter than everyone else. His small joke. Like a reporter introducing himself as a character from Melville.... I made a mental note to check out this security chief. And he was Tuato's immediate boss? Loads of opportunity for influence.

For Elle and Cheryl, I ran down my visit to Castello. As I told my tales of Mephisto, then Aiano Tuato, Elle saw where it all led. Her freckles vanished into the deepening flush on her face.

"Damn!" she said. "Good I don't own a shotgun, or I'd go to Cornu Point and clean house!"

"Won't need one," I said. "Actually, the *Post-Dispatch* owns a howitzer. With the right story, we blow a tunnel through their little balloon. And they crater. No problem."

Elle eyed me. "What will you do?"

"First move? Same as I promoted to Palmer. Root through every document, all the paper I can find. That's what made Izzy Stone and Jack Anderson so great. Might sift a ton of straw, but you sometimes discover golden needles that can sew a case shut. Palmer got stalled, but I have a special contact, a navy yeoman who wound up working as an auditor in the state controller's office. If old Henry's still around, maybe I can put him up to some of his old tricks."

"And if he's not?"

"Figure another angle. My motto is 'Try all doors!' Actually, the hard part won't be Sacramento, but Vegas. That's where I go next, to find that horse. I also plan to drop in on Olivia."

Finally, it seemed I'd impressed Elle. I mean, in a good way. Her mood, decidedly hostile when she arrived, had shifted toward suspicion. Now, it looked as though I'd won a wary acceptance. Even that felt like a big score.

Cheryl levered herself out of the chaise lounge. "Can I interest you guys in a sandwich? More tea?" she asked.

"How about a phone? Can I use yours?"

We went inside. Cheryl pointed to an end table. I snatched up the receiver. An information operator gave me the controller's office. I tugged Hank's old extension number from memory. It didn't work. I got myself routed to a receptionist, offered her Hank's name and former job title, she sent me to his new berth. To my mild shock and immense relief, my old shipmate picked up. I recognized his Texas twang immediately.

"Front and center, swabbie!" I bellowed into the mouthpiece.

"Hey. Who's this?" Hank asked, cautious, unbelieving.

"You know damn well who. It's Colm."

"Mm-hm. Been awhile."

"Can't say it hasn't, mate."

Henry Frist and I go back to our service aboard the USS *Fox*. We ran the shipboard chess tournaments, and occasionally climbed high up the mast to smoke a joint, well above the whiffing range of senior officers. After our navy stints, he went into accounting and law, and I—well, you know about me. Although it had been at least ten years since I'd last spoken to Hank, we still dropped immediately into our shared lingo, half navy slang and half political reporter's shorthand, with a fifty-cent word sometimes fired off for effect.

I ran down the situation at Cornu Point.

"Fascinating," Hank said. "I'll do what I can. When will you be here?"

I looked at my watch, calculated the time it would take me to summon a cab and then haul my carcass to Sacramento. I knew I didn't have time for a bus or train. Inwardly, I flinched at the cost. After Sacto, I supposed, I could catch a flight to Vegas, and gad about there in yet more taxis.

"How about four-thirty?" I said.

"Okay, meet you down in that building cafeteria, on the first floor. Still there, our same old spot."

We rang off. I looked up to see Elle staring at me.

"I want to go along," she said.

"What?" I was astonished.

Cheryl, perhaps, was a little less so. She stood at the entry to the kitchen with a plate of sandwiches.

"Hm. You'd be back in a real investigation, the kind of thing you've always said you wanted to do," she said.

"And nail those shits who beat up Sebastian," Elle replied.

"Well, I think you should, sweetie," Cheryl concluded.

Once Elle's mind was made up, frank determination wrote itself all across her face. And it didn't look like it would be easy to erase.

"I'll help you out on this, MacCay. Under one condition only." Elle held up a stern index finger. "No booze. None. You don't even gulp so much as a beer as long as I'm around. Understood?"

I must have gaped at her. I didn't recall having invited her along. Meanwhile, my rampaging alcoholic urges and my new-found impetus for restraint chased each other around my skull like the boarhound and the boar. It was one thing to negotiate a settlement with myself; it was entirely another to accept an out-side chaperone—who wasn't Anna. By my own estimate, I'd been doing splendidly. Alcohol in liberal quantities had been banned from my system for much longer than normal. Why, I'd attained nearly two full days of moderation!

I don't know what expression I wore while I conducted this meditation. But when I snapped out of it, Elle and Cheryl smiled as if they'd just enjoyed a laugh at my expense.

"What?!" I said. "Well, all right. No tippling. I'm already more than halfway there. Completing this story comes first and fore-most. Afterward, though, all bets are off."

Some of their hilarity drained away.

"And I have a stipulation!" I insisted. "You come, you pick up half of all cab fare. Otherwise, I'm ruined."

Cheryl put down her tray, reached into a ceramic bowl that held sets of keys, and pulled out a bunch decorated with a fob of wo-ven horsehair. She held out the keys to Elle.

"Why don't you just take Ruby?" she said.

Chapter 15

Which is how, an hour later, I came to be speeding along at a steady 80—a mere 15 mph over the interstate limit—in Elle and Cheryl's burgundy Chrysler Crossfire. Elle sat at the wheel, I in the passenger seat with a cucumber and tuna on whole wheat sandwich wrapped in a paper towel beside me on the console. I had pulled my laptop out of the back pocket of my ranger vest, and propped it on the glove compartment door.

Once our decision had been made, Elle packed her overnight bag in mere minutes. In terms of rapid travel preparation, it was the most incredible female performance I'd seen. Then we hit the road—a much odder couple than Jack Lemmon and Walter Matthau ever played.

We didn't talk at first. I think we felt stunned to find ourselves shackled in each other's company. A form of buyer's remorse set in. That decision to scoot off together on assignment suddenly seemed a bit hasty. Even a tad mad.

Elle isolated herself under iPod earbuds and wraparound sunglasses. She tapped out rhythms from her tunes on the steering wheel, using her severely trimmed—perhaps chewed—and entirely paintless fingernails. I typed, fiddled with notes, tried to organize what I knew, see where it led, prioritize the stuff I needed to find out.

The Crossfire hurtled out onto the Sacramento River Causeway. Sacramento skyscrapers jutted out of the Central Valley plains like the spires of Oz. Elle shut down her music, lowered her shades to the bridge of her nose, turned toward me.

"Don't get me wrong, I love charging at things," she said. "But why do we need to get all this done in one go?"

"Deadlines," I said.

First, I told her, any investigation resembles chess play. A game starts. Suddenly, there's a rush to probe and discover on one side, to block or conceal on the other. A constantly shifting, morphing deadline. To win, you must adhere to the battlefield rule once uttered by General Nathan Bedford Forrest: "Git thar fustest with the mostest." The easiest and smartest way to do that is to attack at a place where the opposition does not expect you.

Hence our little trip.

Other deadlines crop up during the reporting phase. For a story to enjoy highest value, one must beat the other media to it. Win, and you gain place of pride in the profession, your outlet becomes a go-to place for coverage. Such fights grew more intense with the advent of the Internet. Harder now for newspapers to break news. Most of the time, they beat out their own paper editions by launching stories on the Web—just so no competitor will beat them to the punch.

More deadlines come from society at large. Be first to publish a narrative on any major topic, then all other players must react. Sometimes you keep them on their heels. When a more powerful and alternative reading beats yours onto the street, you're the one forced to respond. After a narrative gets established, making the public mind reassess it is like trying to throw a battleship into reverse.

Senator John Kerry's 2004 presidential campaign was my main case in point. Notions he was a spineless flip-flopper on the issues, and a bogus war hero, got traction through the well-financed "swift-boating" strategy. Kerry let those stories build in the public mind without a timely riposte. And he was left on the ropes for the rest of his campaign.

A similar thing was occurring with Cornu Point. Beverly Bancroft's death had been cast as an unfortunate accident, one that underscored a need to keep horses and hikers separate. Also, the story of the assault on Palmer fingered denizens of Castello as suspects, a strategy evidently designed to make it easier to evict them.

From now on, I assured Elle, media-savvy hands would push both angles. PR firms hired by Cornu Point and 3CD Corp. would work to make public sentiment go their way. The ploy of throwing arms around the deceased Beverly Bancroft, co-opting local concern and grief, was an example of the sort of cynical manipulations they'd try to pull.

But if we set off a truth-bomb, we might blow such lies to smithereens before they became entrenched. That was another deadline.

I realized that I was delivering an oration, perhaps even a rant. I looked at Elle to see if she felt annoyed. On the contrary, she looked entertained. Which was *so* endearing... .

All this leads to ultimate moments of truth, daily deadlines, I said. The megillah is that put-it-to-bed instant when your A-1 front page centerpiece must be laid in the paper's five-star edition. Reporters are told copy must come in by 6:00 p.m., which they strive to do. But they and editors know space can be held, deadlines bent, and a story inserted into the paper by 7:30 or even 9:00 p.m. But to do that, it's gotta be hot. Or hottest. If something occurs on the scale of a presidential assassination, urban disaster, or terrorist attack, some of the press run is held back until the reporting is done. Readers who live in zones far from The City don't read the same headlines as those in town. Ink on metropolitan papers can steam a bit more.

Elle nodded, returned her full attention to delivering us to the state capitol.

I let my mind rummage on through my journalistic past.

I sat once more at my first scarred desk, on the fourth floor of the *Post-Dispatch*. I was twenty-six, just a few years older than Palmer. I felt that massive building tremble as shudders from iron presses cranking up in the basement were transmitted from the foundation beams up through thick concrete pillars.

I ran down the stairs, yanked a door, shouldered past a cranky, ink-stained pressman. I stood by gantries of blackened machinery to observe front pages whisk past on the rollers of a conveyor. Gaping, I whooped with ineffable joy at seeing my first A-1 story whip by over and over again. Black-and-white photos of a state senator emerging in handcuffs from a high-stakes gambling den in Stockton were barely recognizable. My byline was a blur. But those freshly minted pages would arrow out into the world and change things.

On the loading docks, men heaved bound bundles of newsprint into vans, for delivery to stands, coin boxes, and doorsteps. Soon my story would be unfolded alongside breakfasts across California. Life would not be the same, for me or that senator. His bill to restrict Indian gaming would lose all resonance.

And there were personal deadlines, for people, I reflected. I faced a big one. Bad stuff, even terrible stuff, comes to everyone. The trick is to not let it pull you down, not allow your existence to be about constantly reliving a tragic moment. To defeat this loop, you must commit to possibilities. Insist on not learning it? Opportunities to learn shall steadily erode.

I knew I'd gone far past the lip of that drop. Below? A bleak vacuum at the core of my abyss. What might retrieval look like…? What I was doing now. Somewhere, Anna nodded her head, smiled. It was a realization she'd tried to sell me on for years.

"So where do I turn? What exit?" Elle said. We closed in on the Highway 50, I-80 interchange. Sacramento's downtown skyscrapers loomed.

"Take 50, then I-5 north, then the Capitol exit," I announced, purely from reflex. "Park soon as you can. It's right there, on Third."

—

Elle stood watch outside, sitting at the wheel of the Crossfire, which was parked in a yellow zone. I pushed through the swinging glass doors of the bureaucrat cafeteria. Not much movement around the scratched Formica tables. Food service folks had shut down their steel hot-food bins. Just one person remained, behind the cash register. You could still buy a soggy sandwich, sticky pastry, wilted fruit, or boiled coffee. I went for a weary-looking raspberry Danish and a nasty cup of joe.

Hank entered five minutes later, right on schedule. He was a paunchier, wearier, relatively hairless version of the robust young salt who'd accompanied me on romps around Subic Bay. Hank looked around, smiled when he saw me. He grabbed a cup of that grim coffee for himself, sat down. He raised his right hand to sip from his cup, pushed a folded newspaper across the table with his left. I saw a thick manila envelope tucked inside the newspaper.

"Ahoy," he said. "Nice to see you again, Colm. How've you been?"

"Bilge to masthead and back," I told him. "They busted me down to grunt reporter. I'm trying to make it work."

"Wondered what happened to you. Thought I'd pissed you off somehow."

"Nah," I said. "Just mired in my own muck. Sorry, I won't let that much time go by again. What sort of present did you bring me?"

"Sad to relate, all founding documents, letters, and memoranda for Cornu Point have been sucked clean out of the archives," Hank said. "Resource Agency lawyers requested them for analysis. They never came back."

"Who requested the stuff? Who signed for it? Who has it now?"

"All good questions. I'll find out what I can, send it along. Meantime, here's your next best. State audit from 1989. Fully legit; I knew the guy who did it. In the executive summary, you'll see some key provisions of those documents summarized by bullet points."

"Not as good as having the originals," I guessed. "But—?"

"Still, an approved, authorized, and accepted state document," Hank finished. "Also, you get a copy of the current contract with Cornu Point, and an in-house memo showing how the terms of the state contract evolved, shall we say, over the years."

"Okay, fifty words or less, now. What's your take?"

"Given the state's budget woes, the parks department is desperate for operating funds, so they made a deal with the devil. They call Cornu Point a hundred-year lease, but have no control. So it walks and quacks like a sale. They get back about half a million a year, no matter how much 3CD or the association or anyone else manages to make."

"Castello?"

"It's history. Highway Patrol plus all available rangers will arrive in force to boot out the residents next week."

"Lovely," I said. I pulled the paper to me, extracted the envelope, and raised my eyes. "And? How are you?"

"Personally? Joyful. Since I'm set to retire," Hank said. "My thirty years are up by December."

"And then?"

"The art of gardening shall achieve its apotheosis," Hank said. We have always talked like that.

"After we exit the lists, whence will the heroes of the republic arise?" I asked.

"The answer blows about in the wind, my friend," Hank said.

"Can you testify?"

He thought it over. "Affirmative," he said. "After first of the year."

"Dig more, if you can. Ping me on what you get. Help me keep all this interesting. Nothing's worse than a hearing low on revelation. Bored legislators tend to wander off when there's no cameras or press."

"Aye-aye."

"I'll keep you informed of our progress!"

"Roger that."

—

Then Elle and I found ourselves motoring through the Owens Valley, on the east side of the Sierra. Sunset rained mauve light on the mountain ranges bracketing us. Purple shadows drained, darkening, on the pavement and shoulders of Highway 395. We aimed to make Death Valley, Beatty, and Las Vegas, in that order.

By the time we hooked a left at Lone Pine, Elle looked pooped. Daylight had disappeared. So had signals for NPR stations, which I'd been chasing around on the FM dial.

Elle turned our bulbous little coupe off the highway, onto the cracked asphalt lot of a 76 gas station and mini-mart. "You take over," she said. "I need a nap."

I looked at her, then at the steering wheel.

"Can't," I said.

"Want to be in Vegas tomorrow morning? You have to."

"You don't understand. It's been thirty years since I've driven. Any vehicle."

Elle looked at me. The lower half of her face yawned. The upper part revealed only mild interest.

"Okay, so once upon a time you drove. Here's a chance to start again. All the way to Vegas, it's straight desert highway. Almost zero cross traffic. Ruby has power steering, auto transmission. C'mon, MacCay. Don't wimp out on me!"

Even imagining wrapping my fingers around that wheel made sweat bead on my forehead.

"I don't have a license."

"Well, don't break a law! How many cops patrol out here at night? Drive like a sane person, we're cool."

I estimated length, breadth, and depth of things I would need to make Elle understand, before she actually understood.

"Okay," I said. "Want me to drive? Let me have a few beers."

Elle's jaw jutted. "Good luck hitchhiking out here!" she said. She was no longer sleepy in the slightest. Her gray eyes could've set paper aflame.

I touched her hand with a fingertip.

"I know what I agreed to. You didn't. A few beers won't make me high. I'll still be further away from drunkenness than you are right now."

"Meaning you're an addict."

"Yes."

"All right." Elle wrestled with the concept. "So you admit it?"

"Always. And never more so than right now."

"After two beers you can still drive?"

"Indubitably."

"Okay, say you pop two, and we do get pulled over by a cop. What about your beer breath?"

"My yearning corpus shall absorb every last vapor."

Elle hesitated, then finally bestowed a tiny, grudging nod.

"Make me regret this, MacCay... and you won't need to get buried. I'll pound your butt straight into the ground!"

I entered the mini-mart. I emerged with a cardboard six-pack of Miller Draft in bottles. I quaffed a pair in rapid succession, then hurled the empties out into the darkness. They made a satisfying chink and crunch against unseen rocks.

"Thou art silica," I declaimed. "And unto silica thou shalt return."

I tucked the rest of the bottles behind the front seat, then stood up straight and looked out into the night. High above, one of the Milky Way's spiral arms glittered like a plume of diamonds. Its tip trailed away into darkness. Made me recall my dreams of buying jewels I could never afford, to wrap about Anna's delicate wrists and ankles. Never even got close. The one diamond ring

I'd managed to buy Anna still lay there, desolate and unused, behind her photograph. She'd never so much as seen it. Elle had gone to the passenger seat, and reclined. I saw her eyeballs glint as she shot me one last look of doubt. Then she yawned, both eyelids aflutter. I put a hand on the roof, swung down into the driver's side. Slammed my door closed, curled my fingers around the wheel's padded vinyl. Didn't feel so bad. Maybe it wasn't such a big deal?

I looked at the shifter, studied it, pushed the knob to "D."

Chapter 16

Elle slumbered as I steered us through Death Valley. The energy that animated her taut face while awake had slackened considerably. Her lips puckered in a sweet little pout, like the mouth of a child. She made a gentle wheezing sound, almost a snore. Glancing over at her, I felt a vague stirring of a paternal impulse—something rare in the life of a fully confirmed bachelor.

Climbing out on the east side of the valley, winding through the shadows of the Armagosa Range, I experienced a compelling urge to whiz, and pulled over. Standing outside our car, I soaked a defenseless desert bush with my excess fluids. I myself bathed in the cool glow of the unsullied stars. I glanced at my watch, and realized that I probably ought to grab some sleep myself, but I was still too keyed up from the unfamiliar challenge of driving. *Should just stroll around, chill out for a bit,* I thought.

I glanced back down at Elle, innocently wheezing away. Strange fate for a man in his fifties, startled awake from a years-long stupor, like some Ripped Van Winkle, to abruptly find himself both mateless and childless.

It was not that, in the years since Anna, I had totally lacked for female companionship. Far from it! Over most of that time, however, I paid for it. I mean, in dollars. If you must get your ashes hauled, hire professionals. Keeps the rugs cleaner. On those rare occasions when the attraction between myself and an amateur happened to boil over, I swiftly pinched the relationship closed or dialed it back down to a friendship. And, of course, I could always rely on my faithful standby since junior high, Merry Palm and her five sisters.

But the net gain? A rather lonesome existence.

My family background being what it was, I also had to consider whether I was struggling to keep from discovering that I myself was gay. After mulling it over for a while, I decided in the negatory—not, as Seinfeld so memorably put it, that there was anything wrong with that. Though I must disclose that after dear Da's altogether agonized passing, I'd gone through a reaction that made me disparage gay life. I took pleasure in mocking it, especially in the late 1970s and '80s, amid the upsurge of rainbow activism when the love that dare not speak its name became the love that just wouldn't shut up.

But one could not live and write in San Francisco—or dine or shop or go to theaters, galleries, opera, ballet, or symphony—without eventually making one's peace with gay culture. So, eventually, I'd gotten there. I'd been boosted along by learning that many relationships of gays and lesbians were more "normal" or "healthy," if you will, than plenty of the bizarre configurations we heteros devised.

After that discovery, I settled upon a new operating tautology for myself: people are just people.

So I took Elle as an individual. I admired her strength, while still feeling somewhat intimidated by her impetuosity, her intensity. Well, her allowing me to make a case about my need for a brew or two showed an unexpected flexibility. All in all, I could have done worse than have Elle Jatobá at my side during this wingding. I could not expect her to perform in a calmly considered manner at every moment, but I could always trust her to be her.

I swung open the driver's door, lowered myself into the seat, reclined it. I shut my eyes, and focused on making my breathing become as sleep-like as possible, deep and slow.

—

We roused ourselves in the predawn light, stiffly extracted our cramped bodies from the seats as we exited to opposite sides of the car to take a pee. Then it was on to Beatty, turning right on

I-95 to complete the last 120 miles or so to Las Vegas. The high desert at this early hour was a rolling gray tarpaulin, rumpled by sage and brush, dotted with yuccas, and held down at its edges by gnawed beige buttes.

Suddenly, new suburbs of densely packed condos and townhouses popped up to either side, as if a wizard had conjured them from the pebbles. Far ahead, tall skyscrapers along The Strip reared up into dim haze like a thicket of giant tombstones, oddly garlanded with celebratory lights.

"Fairyland!" Elle exclaimed.

"With rather scary fairies," I replied. I pointed to a billboard sliding by on the side of the highway, announcing a live show called "Bite." It appeared to promote the tortured tale of gorgeous, be-fanged, bare-breasted vampires.

"Hey! Not our only option." Elle pointed to signs on the roadside opposite, promoting bistros to be found at the next exit. "How about hot coffee and breakfast?"

"Capital," I said.

—

Seated in a booth that was sheathed in leprous orange plastic, we forked up bits of what had seemed like the least objectionable stuff on the menu. Still, it was difficult to think that the limp green scraps in my scramble had ever been spinach. *When in Rome, I thought, one simply must dine at the vomitorium.*

Elle was talking about the reasons why she'd taken a shine to Sebastian.

"Always wanted to have a brother," she said. "Well, I've got a half brother, but he was born years after my mom remarried. And they're over on the East Coast, so I never was able to watch him grow up. Would have been so cool to have them closer, but…

"Anyway, Sebastian. He's so open and earnest, I guess. The sort of person who makes you just naturally want to help, to be his friend. And brave too… but in that quiet kind of persistent way. Not flashy. Doesn't care if you notice. Not interested in showing off."

From the moment he entered Cliffhanger Gym, Elle related, she saw that Sebastian possessed all the basic traits of a good climber. Even after his terrifying slide down that giant hump of Yosemite granite, Sebastian had mentally, emotionally, bounced right back. This type of resilience was what one needed to face down the challenges of a multi-pitch face. Which, I gathered, was Elle's way to describe a cliff.

"Hope he bounces back from that assault," I muttered.

And right then a fresh thought made hairs on my body prickle and stand at attention. Holy crap! Why hadn't I considered it before? We were chasing down people who had killed an old lady and damn near pounded a strong young man into mush. All well and good to put myself at risk, but what in hell was I thinking, letting Elle come along for this ride? Did I actually want another body on my conscience?

"What?!" Elle demanded, staring at me.

I moistened my mouth with a gulp of the restaurant's sour and murky orange juice, then let myself speak.

"Listen," I said. "I think it's best if I handle this next part myself."

"Why?" She was starting to look angry.

"Because..." No way to lie to Elle—she'd rip any deception apart like a Rottweiler attacking a sausage. "It's dangerous."

Elle's mouth quirked at the corners, then she laughed.

"MacCay," she said. "Why do you think I'm even here? To rescue your flabby white ass if you get into trouble!"

"Oh." I thought that over. "Well, what about your freckled white ass?"

"I'm pretty good at handling myself. But if things go south, I expect you'll do your best to help out. That's fair, right?"

"Well-l-l, okay," I agreed at length. "Long as you know what you're getting into."

"Do you?"

"Nope," I admitted. "But soon I hope to."

⎯

We departed the Grease-on-a-Dish Café. I snagged a city map at a nearby gas station. As Elle steered Ruby, I unfolded the map to plot a course. The stream of Vegas-bound traffic thickened, slowed, imitating a Los Angeles rush hour. The air also strongly resembled L.A.'s.

A fat streak of brown smog squatted over the desert town, full of the oily reek of diesel exhaust. I directed her to go right on I-15, then exit on Sahara. Unwittingly, I then had Elle take a side street too soon. Suddenly we were on a narrow access road, trapped behind idling dump trucks and concrete mixers. Took us a half hour to get loose. But we did score a peek at the churning frenzy behind the glittering high-rises. Palaces were being demolished at a frantic pace to permit even grander, more ornate grotesqueries.

"Growth for the sake of growth. Ideology of the cancer cell," I quoted. "Edward Abbey said that. At least, I think it was he."

"Who?"

"Desert writer, adventurer," I said. "Man! My last time through here was many years ago. Biggest thing on casino row then was a fifty-foot neon cowboy. Now that guy would be just a dwarf."

Finally, I managed to navigate us onto The Strip, heading south through a valley of gleaming towers and raucous billboards. Signs promoted dimming stars, rising comedians, and incandescent magicians. My personal favorite announced, THE ASTOUNDING LOZENZO—LUNACY, COMEDY, SORCERY.

"All right," I said. "We want The Big Top Casino. Look for a huge ringmaster wearing a red coat, top hat, and a large, curly mustache. Snidely Whiplash on steroids. And, probably, a little blow."

"Who?"

I sighed. "A cartoon character from the Stone Age. Guess I'm dating myself. But that's all right. I'm always available."

We motored slowly toward a huge pile of gilded glass on our left, and a similar gilded slab on our right, the legend, TRUMP modestly affixed to its summit.

"How do they get the glass to shine all yellow like that?" Elle wondered.

"Easy. They suck money out of visitors' pockets, exchange it for gold leaf, then spray that on buildings with a fire hose," I told her.

We came upon lagoons where pirate ships seemed poised to conduct a battle at sea. Next, we passed a niche where sculpted bronze heads with bouffant hair gazed benignly upon the parade of pedestrians slouching by on the sidewalk.

"What's that?" I aimed my finger at the sculptures. "Tomb of the Unknown Chorus Girls?"

Elle glanced. "No! Siegfried and Roy. Famous lion tamers. Or tigers. They have a big act there. At least they did until a tiger munched up Roy."

"Oh."

Another lagoon appeared. Jungle noises screeched out of vegetation bordering it. An Eiffel Tower loomed on the left. The marble columns of Caesar's Palace soared on the right. Fountains pushed gouts of water up into the sere, brown air. Then an outsize 3-D image of a motorcycle appeared to burst through a wall. In the distance, a scale model of the Empire State Building probed the smog.

"The phrase 'wretched excess,' can't even touch it," I said.

"There he is!" Elle cried.

A red-jacketed ringmaster tilted out over the boulevard. He leered at the crowd while touching the haft of his whip to the brim of his top hat. Snidely's free hand pointed at the entrance of a huge casino. Beside him, a neon seal balanced on its nose a ball of lights that bore a legend: BIG TOP CASINO — THE BEST SHOW ON EARTH!

"See any place to park?"

Elle found a narrow alley that led to FREE PARKING! We dismounted, strolled into the casino. Its lower floor held gaming tables shrouded with brown cloths from the previous night's shutdown. Remaining open for business, however, were rows of beeping, blinking machines. Weary women pumped away, hoping to stimulate their slots past endurance — at which point they'd spew coins into trays, and the bongs and dings of a Tinman spasm would echo through the early morning and the empty building.

In the very center of that floor we found a sawdust and dirt arena ringed by bleachers. Above that space, all floors opened up. This round cavern was capped by a dome painted with the broad white-and-blue stripes of a circus tent. Above the ring I saw a safety net for acrobats, and high above that a set of trapezes.

The only other folks present were a dark-skinned man who twirled the end of a white rope, and a skinny woman in a warmup suit, practicing her arabesques as she hung about forty feet off the ground. A poster looked like it might announce upcoming shows. I went over to it.

"Good news is, first act is a horse show," I told Elle. "Your other news, it won't happen for two hours. But I've got a plan."

I led the way outdoors and around to the back of the casino. There was a yard, a loading dock, and the double-door entrance to a staging area. A rotund security guy in a blue uniform drowsed on a folding chair by the gate.

"Ask you a personal question?"

Elle hesitated, then nodded suspiciously.

"When did you last flirt with a man?"

Elle's eyes hardened, her jaw protruded.

"Please allow me to rephrase that. You ever flirted with a guy?"

"No!"

"Care to start now?"

"What in hell you jiving about, MacCay?"

"Within that staging area, there must be horses. Also, stable hands. Let's say you walk up, seem avidly interested, sound them out on their horses, their work. And their phone numbers, availability for dates. You might then discover whether their star stallion, Mr. Mephisto, recently took a trip. Bet you can even find out whether he went to California."

"Yuck!" Elle said.

"Got a better idea?"

"Why do I have to ask for names and phone numbers?" She was frowning.

"Later on we can produce an identified witness. Or two. Someone who can be interviewed on the record, or subpoenaed."

"Why don't *you* do it?"

"Think they give a hoot about a plug-ugly Irishman? Nope. A comely lass such as yourself has a far better chance. Also, I've already got my job. I need to distract that guard while you slip in through the gate."

Elle hemmed and hawed.

"Come on. You gonna be a cop? You've gotta learn detective work."

"Who said I wanted to be a cop?"

"Cheryl did. Look, I can buy you some hot-pink lip gloss if you think it'll help."

"Never touch the stuff."

"Well. Wanna get the guys that beat Sebastian, or not?"

Finally, and grudgingly, Elle gave way. I clapped her on the shoulder, grinned.

"Once inside, I'd say work two themes: Your love of horses, and your hope to party hearty in Vegas tonight. After you're done with them, ask how you get through the building and up to the ring for the show. I'll meet you there."

She nodded, yet her every pore leaked disdain.

I grabbed our city map out of the car, then walked up to the guard, and asked him if he knew where that neon cowboy had gone. The guard said the old cowpoke on the casino sign actually had his own name: "Vegas Vic." He once hung out at the Pioneer. Vic liked to lounge around in a museum now. The guard seemed delighted to have a chance to natter about old-time history. As we chatted, Elle strolled up to the gate from the opposite direction and she slithered through, unchallenged. After she was safely inside, I bid farewell to my new pal, wishing him a grand and lovely day. He wished me luck at the tables.

Among the bleachers that ringed the Big Top's arena, I found an electrical outlet and plugged in my laptop. But I couldn't link to any unsecured WiFi, so I couldn't check the Patch's website, to see what new stuff they'd run on Palmer, Castello, or Cornu Point. Instead, I concentrated on building my own version of the tale, cutting and pasting from notes and files to assemble the spine of my narrative.

I wondered how Mister Pete's rapprochement and strategic negotiation with San Mateo County detective Rafe Flores was proceeding.

And I utterly lost track of time—an excellent sign for a working writer. I was startled when Elle's tight little butt plopped down in the seat right next to me. I noted that she looked rather smug.

"Yes, yes, and yes," she said. "Mephisto's here. And he just got back from a quick trip to California. To perform at a show out there, they said."

I sensed that Elle held something back. "What else?"

"Oh. Horse show director's not a guy. She's a cowgirl from Arizona. Amy Blithesdale. Real nice. Here's her number and e-mail address."

Did I detect a blush on Elle's cheeks? I gave her a break by glancing down at my watch.

"Great job!" I said. "Now I need to observe this show. If Mephisto demonstrates any moves that could have squished Beverly, then I've got my lead. You mind running out to the airport, check the newsstands, grab any California papers you find? Let's see what they say about the Cornu or Castello stuff. Or Sebastian! I'll meet you out in front of this heap at noon. Next, we go find Olivia."

Elle bounded from her seat like she'd been launched from a circus cannon.

"Out front. Noon. Sharp!" she emphasized, and was gone.

I checked my digital camera. A stagehand began messing with lights. A pair of clowns guided casino customers toward seats. A man wearing a red-sequined ringmaster's coat and top hat snatched up a microphone and began to mime the swagger of the icon on the casino sign. But his act was sabotaged by the off-center wobble of the phony black mustache. His gum seemed to have lost its spirit.

"Lay-deees and gen-n-ntle-men-n-n!" he intoned.

The show opened with a pair of white horses loping around the ring, one bearing a showgirl dressed in feathers, sequin clusters, and not much else. On the other horse rode a young man with Elvis hair who had perhaps prepared for his role by cramming a pair of tennis balls into the crotch of his tights. This duo performed daring gymnastic tricks. Sometimes they vaulted back and forth between the horses. Then they scampered off.

The ringmaster next introduced the one and only Mephisto, famed stunt horse, a star on two continents, favored mount of celebrity actors, and hero of blockbusters like *Blah-blah,* and *The Son of Blah-blah*—movies I'd never heard of.

A white stallion galloped into the arena, then hit a stiff-legged hockey stop that would have done a roping horse proud. A cascade of sand fanned up and outward, sending a shower of grains into the audience. I got that shot. The rider wore a coat dripping with gold braid and a helmet with nodding plume, some producer's fever dream of a dragoon. He brandished a chromed saber in one hand, clutched the reins with his other. His mount champed at its bit.

Mephisto's own tennis balls were the size of grapefruit. But this extravagantly male beast still seemed impressively compliant, and he moved lightly, for all his bulk and power. As soundtrack music blared, the rider guided him through complex maneuvers, using mere touches of reins and heels. Mephisto pranced sideways, forelegs neatly crossing each other. The stallion reared on command, hopped. Then, a pièce de résistance: it reared, leapt entirely off the ground, and kicked out powerfully with both hind legs at once. Despite the chill that cascaded down my spine, I thought I was able to snag the picture. If that move was the one used to nail Beverly Bancroft, it astonished me that her head had remained attached to her body.

The stage dragoon made the stallion rear a final time, brandished his sword, and dashed for the exit. The next act consisted of midget clowns conducting a farcical romp with monkeys on midget horses. I'd seen enough. On my way out I found show programs in a stack. The cover photo showed Mephisto delivering his double kick. I grabbed it for backup. It would scan well enough to produce a usable news photo. Graininess and the casino logo added authenticity. I tucked it in a pocket of my vest, right beside the Amy Blithesdale contact info. Poking my hand through the armholes, turning them into a handle, I toted my vest like a satchel.

I blinked my way out into sunshine, loitered for a few minutes by the boulevard curb. Elle zoomed up in the Crossfire. Tires squeaked as the car halted at my toes. She shoved open the door, and I dropped in. She swung her arm, swatted two folded newspapers against my chest.

"You scored a Patch—and a Chron. Good goin'!"

I flapped them open, eagerly scanned the headlines.

"Where are we heading next?"

"Hang a U," I advised. "Then turn right on Tropicana and north on Nellis. When you see Lake Mead Boulevard, make another right. Let's go see if we can find Olivia."

"Aw-r-i-gh-t!"

"Oh. If you spot a pay-phone, pull over. I need to make a call, find out if a certain receptionist is on duty."

"You don't carry a cell?"

"No."

"MacCay, you are *such* a dinosaur."

"Hey! I own a laptop," I protested. "Gives off all the radiation anyone needs! You think I ought to clap some more up against my head? Look. I'm a columnist. I don't need a cell. Well, I was a columnist... ."

She plucked a slim phone from her shirt pocket, handed it to me. I studied it, flipped it open. "How do I turn it on?"

Elle rolled her eyes, held out her hand. "Oh, shit, gimme," she said.

She rang up Desert Buttes-Sunset Estates, tried to locate Patricia Delicato. I speed-read the papers. Sebastian was still in a coma. A deputy secretary of the state resource agency declared that shutting down Castello and clearing it out to enhance the future of the park remained a priority. "They've overstayed their welcome," was how he put it. But no comment from the head of State Parks. Hm. Might mean that a fix was in from the top. The resource agency deputy was a new political appointee, whereas the director of parks was a holdover from a previous administration.

Both papers carried identical quotes from a Pietro Savante of Castello. Took me a second to recall that meant Mister Pete. He had been forced to bend to media pressure, I reckoned. Still, he gave them only the gist of what he'd told me: Castello had zero to do with the attack on Palmer; and the claim of their village people to this site was fully legit. No proof offered for either, however, and nothing further.

After that, their coverage diverged. The *Chronicle* detailed Beverly Bancroft's long and frustrating crusade. The *Post-Dispatch* described budding plans for new development on the coast. It confirmed that most of the acreage around Cornu Point lay either in the hands of 3CD Corporation or investors and Realtors in the association. Around Castello, options on the farmland had been nabbed by a mysterious entity named Velocity Trader. Headquartered in Bermuda. Which made me smile. Good cess to Stein and Ericson, trying to penetrate that Atlantic fogbank!

I folded the front-page sections, pushed them into a side pocket of my vest.

Our plan to make an end run to the heart of the story still seemed like a smart bet.

Chapter 17

Lake Mead Boulevard wound east past tire stores, tacquerias, fast-food emporia, and a Wal-Mart. The real estate values appeared to rapidly escalate. Acres were occupied by fancy apartment buildings, luxury condos.

The Desert Buttes-Sunset Estates retirement home was an immense three-story structure, clad in a rock-slab façade, bordered by palm trees, and encircled by a chain-link fence. We found a parking spot near the front door.

Elle had learned that Mister Pete's contact, Miss Delicato, was out sick, so in terms of gaining access to Olivia, we would be on our own. We sat in the Crossfire, and haggled over the right approach.

"Try this," Elle said. "Let's call you my nutcase great-uncle. I need to stash you somewhere, so I can grab your fortune. And I've heard that my great-great-aunt Olivia Bancroft already lives at Desert Buttes and is doing just great, which is why I decided to check the place out. How's that?"

I made a sour face. "Why not just say I'm your dad?"

"You're too old!"

"No, I'm not!"

"Yes, you are. Plus, then I'd seem too callous, trying to shed you. Over the top."

"Well, shit!" I took a deep breath. At the moment, I couldn't think of anything better. I heaved a sigh. "All right."

Elle went over me with a critical eye. "Your clothes are perfect. Maybe we should pull out your shirttail, mess up your hair. Can you drool? Just from one side."

"Get me a picture of Grace Kelly in her prime, and I'll see what I can do."

—

We entered, stated our business, and endured a cursory tour for prospective customers. Then we were invited to meet with Desert Buttes' executive director, in her pine-paneled office on the third floor. Peggy Carson was a stout woman of indefinite age, with a short mop of tight blonde curls and the stiff countenance created by a series of ambitious facelifts.

Miss Carson said I might qualify for warehousing at Desert Buttes. Letting us visit Olivia Bancroft, however, was a tougher proposition. She called up something on her computer screen, then rose from her chair to unlock a filing cabinet. She hauled out a binder, fanned through its contents, stopped at a page, and looked up.

"The Bancroft family attorney, Mr. Winger, supplied us a list of Olivia's approved visitors," Miss Carson said. "Don't see your names on it. Sorry." Finality frosted her voice.

"Well-l-l, we are pretty distant," Elle said. "Olivia's way out on my mother's side of the family. And Mort here, he's from my dad's side." On her own, she had dreamed up Mortimer Brewer as my alias. Alas. But I played along.

"Olivia," I echoed. I let a wisp of awareness flicker over my face.

"Visitation is not recommended, anyway," Miss Carson said. "For Olivia's own protection," she added hastily. "She's in our seclusion section, for clients with dementia. We can't take a chance on agitating her, except for the most serious of reasons."

"I see," Elle said sadly. "Well, I'm glad that you protect her. What do you think, could Mort become your client? Would that seclusion section be right? We hear that Olivia receives excellent care. Mort's had a hard life. He deserves a nice rest."

Miss Carson pursed her lips. Quite a trick—since she could barely bring them together over her teeth. "Well, let's see if Mr. Brewer qualifies," she said. "We require a family total resource disclosure form, of course, to ensure that all the fiscal demands of lodging with us can be met. A full physical is also needed, naturally, which includes a mental function evaluation. A TB test is mandatory, since we can't run a risk of infection. More tests and interviews determine which of our wards, if any, may be a suitable destination."

She obviously had the Desert Buttes brochure tattooed some place where she could read it daily.

"Money is no object." Elle airily waved a hand. "Uncle Mort is loaded! He can afford the best. We want him in a nice, well-controlled institution. Not one of these cheesy rattraps you see for old people, a place he could slip away from, wander the streets, meddle in family affairs, upset things. That's been a problem."

"I see," Miss Carson said. From her tone, she clearly did. I would have bet my ranch, if I had one, that the seclusion section held a bunch of wealthy elders who needed to be under very tight control. For their own good, of course.

"Want to ask dear old Mort a few questions, get a sense of him?"

Miss Carson strutted around her desk like a pouter pigeon, roosted on its edge, faced me.

"Tell me, Mr. Brewer," she said, not unkindly. "Can you remember what you ate for breakfast this morning?"

"Eggs."

"Good!" she approved. "And for dinner last night?"

I gritted my teeth from the sheer intensity of my mental effort.

"Eggs," I said finally.

Miss Carson digested my answer. Elle had risen from her chair, gone to the window, and now leaned on its sill, gazing out over the grounds.

"Such a beautiful place," she said. "Might like to live here myself someday. But not for a good long while, of course!" she laughed.

"Thank you," Miss Carson responded. She focused her gaze on me again. "Any memory of what you used to do for a living, Mr. Brewer?"

"Eggs."

Elle slid back into her chair, chuckling. She reached over to pat my hand. "That's right!" she said. "Uncle Mort was a Petaluma chicken farmer. Very successful. Then he sold off his land for a subdivision, made a pile—a huge pile."

"Well," Miss Carson said. "I'll provide you the necessary forms. After you fill them in and return them, we can discuss welcoming

Mr. Brewer into our care. If you want to get Mr. Brewer examined by a local physician, I can provide contacts for doctors we work with regularly."

"So cool! Thanks very, very much." Elle paused. "Oh. If Mort has a little, you know, incontinence, that's not a barrier to being here, is it?"

"No. It's rather common."

"Because he's totally into Depends. Loves them. He has some on right now. Mort's favorite thing is getting himself changed and powdered. Poor man has so few pleasures left."

"All right," Miss Carson observed drily. She turned to put the binder back in the filing drawer.

I scowled at Elle. Stuck out my tongue as far as it would go.

—

Once back outside, we went to sit in the car.

"Was that really necessary?"

Elle clapped her hands, snorted and chortled. "Gotcha!"

"Can we focus? We're not much further ahead!"

She sobered slightly. "Well, your turn for a brainstorm. Right?"

At that moment, there was a movement over by the rest home entrance. Miss Carson churned out the front door. Without noticing us, she strode to a silver Porsche Cayman, hopped in, revved it up, then tore out of the parking lot.

"Hmm," I said. "Might that be a break? A gift of some sort?"

"Where's she going?"

"I can see her lusting for a nooner. Just can't imagine a partner."

"Is she going to tell someone we tried to see Olivia?"

"Why not just phone them?"

"No matter what, I'd say it is a break! Come."

Elle jumped out of the Chrysler. I emerged also, wondering. She glanced at me. "Get out your bag," she ordered. "Change your shirt. Comb your hair."

"What's up?"

"Let's go back inside."

"How?"

"You'll see!"

Minutes later, we stood in a corner of the building where its entry poked out from the main structure. Big slabs of red desert rock that clad the front walls met in a right-angle joint. A thick palm tree and several high bushes screened us from the street.

"We're right below her office," Elle whispered.

"So?"

"I unlatched her window while we were up there."

"Aha!" I liked it.

"I always, always wear approach shoes. They're formed for both hiking and climbing. So whenever I see a good wall, I can jump up on it, do some buildering. It's my hobby. This'll be a piece of cake."

"Hey," I said. "Forget law enforcement. Just go straight into espionage. That's where you'll make your reputation."

Elle grinned, wiped her hands on her short denim skirt. Then she shot straight up that thing. She bent her fingers, hooked her nails over coin-thin ripples in the rock, smeared her toes against the stone on opposing sides of the corner. She rose like she was being hoisted on a wire.

Once up to the third floor, Elle placed a palm flat against the window, slid a panel aside. Gripping the frame with one hand, she turned to display a thumbs-up gesture, then hauled herself inside. Soon, her head poked back out.

"Wait there!" she hissed.

Five minutes passed, during which time I pretended to inspect the shrubbery. See, I fantasized, I worked for Nevada "Ag." I was trying to locate damage from the state's swelling infestation of yellow-spotted leaf mites.

Then a woman in a pink and brown dress—a mash-up of something a nurse and a waitress might wear—appeared at my elbow. She wore the uniform of attendants at Desert Buttes.

"Mr. Brewer?" she said. "Come with me, please."

"Elle?" I double-took. "Where did you score that getup?"

"Laundry bin! It's wrinkled, but not too bad."

Strangled in her fist like the neck of a dead swan was a white plastic trash bag. She untwirled it to let me peek inside. Between Elle's neatly rolled regular clothes, I saw a familiar file.

"Bigger score! Boss-lady left her filing cabinet unlocked! Now we've got Olivia's binder. Also a facility map." She patted her uniform pocket. "I saw one pinned to a bulletin board."

"Consider your salary doubled," I said.

"Now, Mr. Brewer. High time we got you back to our seclusion section. You need to take your meds."

"I'm greatly looking forward to it."

Her free hand hooked me by the elbow. She led me through the entrance. Her uniform worked like a charm. Gatekeepers saw that pink and brown and waved us through.

The place evidently was so huge, and its staff turnover so constant, other women in uniforms didn't give us a second look. Unmolested, we made our way through a maze of halls. The closer we got to the seclusion section, the more I shambled, letting my head bob and loll.

The ward entrance looked like our first major obstacle. A stainless steel box awaited the swiping of a magnetic card key. I didn't think one of my old credit cards would work. But as we stared at it, the pneumatic door it controlled shushed open. A pink-and-brown attendant emerged, leading a skinny old gent with rheumy eyes and a vacant expression. Instantly, I slumped into a posture that matched his.

Elle snatched the door's leading edge with her hand, prevented it from shutting behind them.

"Thanks!" she said to the other woman, who offered us a curious look. "We're from the Reno facility," Elle informed her. "They forgot to give me a key." She pointed at me. "Transfer!" she said. Then she led me inside. The door shushed closed behind us.

The seclusion section of Desert Buttes-Sunset Estates was indeed a rarefied realm, a veritable Avalon for the aged. Its general lounge was paved in stinky all-weather carpeting, printed with a complex pattern designed to camouflage stains. Soft lighting glowed benignly upon utterly mawkish wall art. Bland elevator music tinkled from hidden speakers.

About sixty doddering elders sat in a scatter of chairs, couches, and wheelchairs. At first, it was hard to spot differences between individuals. Nearly all were crowned with white hair. They all wore identical gray slippers, green jammies, and blue bathrobes. At one table, two bored-looking male attendants, wearing short-sleeve shirts in the same color combo as Elle's uniform, played backgammon while pretending to help the elders enjoy a game.

They would each make a move, then ask their charges what they thought about it. The elders gaped, but had no opinion.

Having no clue as to Olivia's appearance, I despaired of identifying her among this shriveled crew.

Trust Elle to cut to the chase: she cupped her hands to her mouth, then hollered, "Olivia!"

Startled faces turned toward us. One held a glint of hopeful recognition. Beside it, a skeletal hand tentatively poked up. Elle led me over there rapidly—to keep up I had to jettison my stumblebum act.

"Olivia Bancroft!" Elle said. "Is that you?"

Shy and forlorn, Olivia sat on a leatherette easy chair, her slippered feet propped up on a leatherette hassock. I'd seen pictures of Beverly. Now I realized that Olivia was simply a more ancient variation on the Bancroft theme. Her eyes, magnified by wide-frame glasses, shone with an intense, tremulous look that mixed fear and hope.

"Who are you?" She quavered. "Are you here to save me?"

"Yes! Absolutely!" Elle asserted. "Olivia, how have you been?"

"I don't like this place!" Olivia said. "Take me home!"

Elle knelt by Olivia's side, stroked her thin arm.

I had an abrupt inspiration. The Patch's story about Cornu Point, with a reprint of Sebastian Palmer's employee photo, still lay folded in my vest pocket. I pulled it out, smoothed the paper open at his picture, showed it to Olivia.

"Olivia!" I said. "Remember this young man? He came to your house on the coast a few days ago. The house where you lived with Beverly."

Olivia clutched at the newspaper, peered at it. "Yes..." she said. "And he gave me Beverly's glasses." She began to snuffle. A liver-spotted hand crept down to a pocket of her bathrobe, and plucked out green plastic eyeglasses with a black keeper chain wrapped around the folded earpieces.

Olivia glanced around furtively. "It's all I have left," she said. "They don't know! I told them these were my spares."

"Olivia, wasn't there something special you and Beverly were going to give to Sebastian? Do you know what happened to it? And those green glasses... can we bring those back to California, please?" I asked. "They might be important evidence."

"No!" Her knobby fingers closed around the glasses, shoved them back down into her pocket. "Told you, they're all I have. They took everything else, everything … ." A tear crept out of her eye and rolled down the side of her long nose.

"Olivia, we're truly here to help you!" Elle implored. "Trust us!"

"All of you say the same thing!"

"I'm a reporter from the *San Francisco Post-Dispatch*. And this is…"

"Beverly told me she spoke with someone from that newspaper!" Olivia marveled as a clear memory bobbed up through her mental chaos. "Before she… was that you?"

"No. That was Sebastian Palmer. But I work at the same newspaper. We're trying to help Sebastian. You, too."

Olivia pressed trembling fingers to her temples. "It's one thing after another! I feel so confused!" She glared at us. "I don't care what you say, I won't swallow any more pills. I won't! I'll spit them out! So help me God!"

"All right, Olivia," Elle soothed. "All right. Everything will be fine. But tell me. Were you brought here against your will?"

"Yes!" Olivia screeched like a banshee. "And I want to go home! Now!"

The male attendants looked over at us, then at each other. They got up out of their chairs and came toward us. I poked Elle with my finger, and she noted their approach.

"Olivia, maybe we can take you home. But only if you help us," I said hurriedly. "Now, as I said, I work for the newspaper—"

"I know what you really want," Olivia whispered hoarsely.

"You do?"

"Yes. The Cornu Point papers. Beverly wanted to give them to you. But she had me wear the key, for safekeeping."

A slim silver chain hung about Olivia's scrawny neck. She plucked at it with her knobby fingers. Up from her sagging bosom, she tugged the carved cameo of a Roman goddess, pure white against dark orange agate. Except it wasn't merely a medallion. It was a locket. Olivia's quivering claws found the catch, popped it open, and extracted a small brass key.

"Use this to open… use it to open…" She gestured, at a loss for words.

"What? Open what?" I said.

Elle and I both reached out for the key. Because she was young and quick, Elle got to it first.

Olivia struggled, pointing down at her feet.

"Under where…"

"Underwear?" I repeated, puzzled.

Olivia shook her head. "Sebastian gave me Beverly's!"

Suddenly, the two attendants loomed over us.

"What's going on?" asked the huskier of the two. He had thick, chimpanzee-furred forearms, and a good five o'clock shadow underway—although it was only midday.

"Oh, hi there. I'd like to introduce you to Mortimer Brewer," Elle said. "A relative from Miss Bancroft's family. Here for a visit."

"No foolin'," the man said. "What did she just give you?"

"Nothing," I and Elle said simultaneously.

The man smiled grimly. "Personal property of our residents is highly important," he said. "It all must stay right here in the facility. That's the rule."

"Sounds good." I nodded sagely.

"Who are you?" the man said, looking at Elle. "This is a restricted section. Don't recall seeing you here before."

"Just got in!" Elle said brightly. "I came over from the Reno facility."

"There is no Reno facility."

"It's new."

"Uh-huh." The man glanced at the other attendant and nodded. That one backed away, spun, strode for the door. Our interrogator folded his arms on his chest and stared hard at us. It was obvious he had not bought a penny's worth of what we'd been selling.

"What's up with you? What's your deal with Miss Bancroft?"

Elle and I looked at each other. Olivia, I noted, seemed frightened by the man. She sat silently trembling.

"Well!" I said, "Love to stay with you and yack about whatever, but we have to leave. Appointments, you know. Miles to go before we sleep, and all that."

Elle got on her feet, her silver eyes ablaze. I knew her well enough to read the danger signals. He, however, didn't.

"Both of you sit. Right now!" he barked. "Neither of you goes any-place. Not until we find out who you are and what you're up to."

"Sorry. No can do," I said. "What, you want to kidnap us, too?"

He didn't reply. Elle didn't say anything either. Instead, she dove straight at the floor, landed on her hands as if intent on perform-ing a cartwheel. Her legs whipped up, her feet smashed into the man's face. He promptly went over backwards. He tried to get up, but Elle scampered across the floor like a spider, on all fours. She looked at him between her legs, then kicked out straight, nailing him right in the chops. He fell again, tried to get up again. Elle dove forward, rolled onto her back, swung one long leg across the floor, swept his feet right out from under him. He went down across a coffee table this time. He didn't break it, but he knocked it over, scattering ancient magazines across the room.

By then, mostly recovered from my astonishment, I'd resigned myself to Elle's game plan. If you could call it a plan. I had seri-ous doubts about the degree of forethought or analysis involved. But when that hairy bugger tried to rise again, I stepped up and bashed him on the beezer with one of my patented left hooks (since my damaged right hand remained a bit on the sore side). This time, our man stayed down.

I grew aware of the sound of cheering. Looking around, I saw the whole room had erupted with geriatric hoots and gales of laugh-ter. One old gent rhythmically whapped his cane on the floor as he howled. Olivia wagged her chin from side to side and clapped in a ragged rhythm.

Elle stood, I threw my arm over her shoulders, and we made a deep bow to our appreciative audience.

"Olivia," I said. "We'll come back soon, help you escape. Don't worry—you're going home!"

She gave us a snaggle-toothed grin and bobbed her head enthusiastically.

"And yeah, don't eat any more pills if you can possibly avoid it. Always spit 'em in the john." I looked at Elle. "Now, my sugges-tion is we get the hell out of Dodge."

We sprinted for the door.

"Wait!" Elle doubled back, frantically snatched up her plas-tic cargo bag. Then we burst out into the hallway. No one was in sight. "Wait!" she yelled again, and yanked the institution map from her uniform pocket. She jabbed at the map with a forefinger. "There's a service elevator back this way. Let's go!"

We practically skidded around corners, making other attendants and patients shrink back against the walls in alarm, staring goggle-eyed at us as we charged past. We found the elevator, and took it straight down to the basement.

"What in heck were the moves you made on that guy?" I asked.

"Capoeira," she said.

"What?"

"I'll explain later."

We reached the basement. It turned out to be a garage full of pricey-looking vehicles. Plus one golf cart, piled high with laundry bags. A key—thank God—poked from its start switch. We commandeered the cart, and zipped up a ramp into the outdoor parking lot. We got to the Crossfire just as the building's main door swung open. A mob of agitated people piled out, heading our way, so I left the golf cart in DRIVE and aimed it at them while Elle bailed. Then I threw a bag of laundry on the accelerator pedal and sent the cart zooming at our pursuers. They scattered like pigeons.

Elle already had the Chrysler cranked up. I dove into the passenger seat. We burned rubber as we roared out onto the street.

—

"California, here we come!" Elle sang, then whooped. Her cheeks were flushed, her eyes sparkled. She was having the time of her life.

"Pipe down," I told her. "You don't seem to realize we just took a swan dive into deep crap. Every cop in Las Vegas will be hunting for us."

"Good!" she said. "We can tell them how Olivia was kidnapped! Those bastards even wanted to kidnap us!"

I shook my head. "Won't work. Cops will have more evidence of our mayhem than any proof that Olivia was grabbed. Maybe a kidnap charge on the Desert Buttes people can cancel out what we did, but that will take days. Time is exactly what we don't have. You are now driving a suspect vehicle. They're going to broadcast your plate number and a description of us. An APB—all points bulletin."

Elle worried her lower lip between her teeth as she considered this. "What should we do?"

"Vegas papers will love seeing a San Francisco reporter mess up on their turf. This violates my prime directive. Never be a headline in someone else's newspaper."

"All right, all right! C'mon, what's next?"

"Oh-ho! Now you want a plan?" I waited for an answer until she swung her head to incinerate me with her gaze. "Okay, let's ditch this car. We take a taxi to a car rental. We each get a new rig—something nondescript, not like this coupe. We split up, because they're looking for a pair. We go back to California by separate routes. That doubles the chances of one of us getting home with the goods, to raise some hell in the right spot."

Elle shook her head, shoved out her chin. "Uh-uh. Nonstarter! This car is Cheryl's—no way I'm going to fucking leave it in fucking Nevada!"

I saw that getting her to submit to my scheme would require, at minimum, use of a tactical nuclear device, so I shut my eyes for a moment and tried to devise something else.

"Okay, how about this," I said, opening my eyes again. "Take a left right here. Yes, now! Good. So, we're pointed at the Vegas airport. Stop as soon as you see any sort of barbershop. I'll go in, buy a high and tight—I mean, a crewcut. Then I'll catch a cab and go grab a seat on a plane. Meanwhile, you find a car wash. Get Ruby nice and wet. Then leave town; drive on the shoulder or a dirt patch somewhere until she's coated with dust. It'll make her harder to ID. But clean your windshields at a gas station, so you don't get pulled over for a minor infraction. Then go to San Francisco, but not straight. Not the way we came. Drop down to I-10, then work up and over to Morro Bay. Come back up to the Bay Area through Big Sur. That'll be your best chance."

She floored me by agreeing instantly. "Sharp, MacCay. I like it."

On the pavement in front of a barbershop, the Crossfire idled. Elle fished Olivia's little brass key out of her sock where she had wedged it. She also dug from her bag the Desert Buttes file on Olivia.

"Guess you'll know what to do with these," she said.

"The binder? Sure," I said. "But I'm scratching my head over the key. And the word salad that came with it. I mean... Sebastian gave her Beverly's underwear? Makes no damn sense."

Elle spread her hands to indicate her own incomprehension, shrugged.

"I'll call if anything occurs to me," she said.

"Leave it on my home machine."

"Right. You're the reporter without a cell phone." She bestowed a pitying look.

"Just let me know when you're back in the Bay Area. Throw a rock through my window."

"Yup."

"And don't speed."

"No, mother. Not unless I see flashing lights creep up behind me. In which case, I'll give 'em a run for the money."

"Thanks for something else to worry about."

"Take care, MacCay."

We gripped hands, eyed each other. Enjoyed a split second of good, solid, wordless contact. Then she was gone.

—

After twenty minutes under the barber's buzzing shears, I didn't look so much like myself as I had previously. To continue developing a fresh appearance, I crossed the street to a drugstore and bought wire-framed sunglasses. I tried sucking in my gut and standing up straight, shoulders back, but the paramilitary posture was too damned hard to sustain.

I hailed a cab, took it to Mandalay Bay casino, then shifted to another taxi for the ride to McCarran Airport. There I bought a seat on the next Southwest Airlines flight to San Jose, which I thought smarter than going straight for SFO. I breezed through security, then found a TexMex bar halfway down the concourse to my gate. The hostess sat me in a quiet corner where I could plug in my laptop. Between bites of a passable tostada and swigs off a pair of Dos Equis *cervezas* that carried balm to my parched brain, I worked on a draft of my Cornu Point exposé.

A show horse named Mephisto performs daily at a Las Vegas casino, delighting a crowd of gamblers, families, and kids with acrobatic tricks. But evidence from a Post-Dispatch investigation indicates this stallion was the same animal whose strong kick caused the death of activist Beverly Bancroft on a trail at the swank Cornu Point resort in California just ten days ago.

Cornu Point frontman Erik Eiger, retired actor, and other resort officials told sheriff's deputies that Bancroft's death was an unfortunate accident caused by Bancroft's decision to walk on trails closed to hikers. They claim Bancroft spooked the horse, causing it to lash out.

But the revelation that Mephisto is a horse specially trained to kick on command—using cavalry combat tactics developed centuries ago—now calls that explanation into question.

The Cornu spokesman also claimed the stallion had been sold to a broker in Mexico after Bancroft's death. As falsehoods about the use of this animal are exposed, they prompt further questions about shady and possibly criminal methods that may have been used by 3CD Corporation, owner-operator of Cornu Point, to assemble a real estate empire along the central California coast.

Among emerging revelations:

- *Post-Dispatch reporter Sebastian Palmer, while investigating the death of Bancroft, was viciously assaulted on Monday evening. He remains in a coma due to a fractured skull. Blame for the assault initially fell on residents of Castello, a small coastal village with a shady past. But now authorities say a Cornu Point security guard, rushed out of the U.S the following day, is suspected.*

- *Olivia Bancroft, 84, older sister of Beverly Bancroft, was moved, against her will, out of her home in California during the week following Beverly Bancroft's death, and is currently being held incommunicado in a "seclusion section" at Desert Buttes-Sunset Estates in Las Vegas. Both that rest home and The Big Top Casino where the circus stallion Mephisto performs, are properties of the 3CD Corporation.*

After whisking through this draft, I paused to reread. Some parts made me uncomfortable. I needed to find more proofs, and double-up on sources, so I could yank out fudge words like "may have been." And I absolutely had to get confirmation on that Tuato character from the San Mateo County mounties.

But that wasn't what was really bothering me.

A bigger worry was—once I got my piece up to pro standards—how could I be sure the *Post-Dispatch* would run it? I'd damn near burned my last bridge (and swung a wrecking ball through its tottering pilings) with Tom Brotmann, the Patch's new executive editor. His bloodhounds were already out running down other parts of the Cornu saga. Brotmann might freeze me out just to spite me and to demonstrate who was boss.

Even that wasn't the true bother.

The barbed spike twisting in my gut was that if no story ran at all, I would have let everyone down again. All my effort to change would have gone for nothing. Once upon a disaster, someone had dared to love and trust me. Even so, I had not been wise or strong or brave enough to prevent her death. Since then, I had shunned any situation that had even a remote chance of turning out in similar fashion. Until recently.

Falling on my ass in my role as Palmer's supposed partner had felt lousy enough. Now I had Elle on my hands, who'd made the trek from complete distrust to emerging faith. What did it mean if I could not follow through? For her? Or Olivia or Beverly—or even Anna, once again?

Yes, I'd managed to retrieve a few of the old tools and traits of a real reporter. But my lunge at those things had a manic quality. In attempting to fling myself into that revived identity, I sought to flee the inertia and mass of the depressed MacCay, the one who had spent years spinning out fluff for camouflage while mired in a psychological pit of his own making. That self-damned MacCay, whose essence remained dark, immobile, brooding.

Now a boat was departing the pier. I had one foot set on the rail. Instead of finishing the leap aboard, I found myself hanging back, too much aware of the weighty history that had always prevented my shipping out in the past. And directly below, a chasm of black, icy water steadily widened.

If I could not come across and deliver, consequences were hideous. The enormity of what I had promised, compared to how achievable it all really might be, tumbled down upon me like a collapsing wall. I gripped both sides of my table to prevent a sudden onslaught of dizziness from toppling me to the floor.

There was just one obvious salvation, and it hovered right before me. A tiny cocktail menu nestled in a chrome-wire stand on my table. I snatched it. My eyes roamed avidly over offerings of margaritas, martinis, cosmopolitans, rum drinks, and other lurid libations. It brightly announced I could order them by the pitcher. I imagined pouring them down in torrents, a flood that would not only wash back doubts and fears, but send the core problem itself reeling off, and perhaps let me defer dealing with it for another whole set of years.

"Colm. Colm. Colm." It was Anna's voice.

I swiveled my head, looking for her, but I could not find her. Not until I spied my own reflection, flicking a wild glance back to me from a panel of frosted glass that rose up between my table and the broad, white fluorescence of the concourse. It was strange seeing a ghost of Anna's lovely face superimposed upon my own mutt's countenance.

"Anna! What on earth are you doing here?"

"Sweetness, you know I love to travel."

"Guess so. What's your opinion of Vegas as it is now?"

A vertical line appeared between her brows, deeper than I'd ever seen it. That unusually serious frown, plus the steadiness of her gaze, scared me a little.

"Colm, you and I don't have much time left. Let's not waste any."

"What are you saying?"

"Last round of the bout, my friend. Fail to rally and you'll hit the canvas for a full count."

"I was just—"

"Gearing up for a snootful. I know the signs. Try it this time, you don't win a postponement. It'll be game over. Fall, and you fall the distance."

"Well, tell me, why is this night different from all other nights?" I said.

She knew that I sought to buy time with this gibe, a reference to the Passovers of her Russian-Jewish girlhood.

"Very funny." The cleft of severity between her eyebrows deepened further. "Your back's at the wall, buddy. You can't retreat any farther. See, you've not only been pursuing the heart of a story, you also went to the heart of your fear. People are now relying on you. Betray them, you're toast. Your big fear will finally be the main and only truth about you.

"As I see it, your sole option is to bare your teeth and come out fighting. Make the full leap over into life, instead of endlessly hanging around on the threshold to death. If you can't, or won't, you might as well finish that walk out onto the Golden Gate Bridge. The one you began on the night I died. Because, Mac, you won't be any damn use to anyone. Least of all, yourself."

"Um," I said. "Harsh."

"But you can handle it. Since you must," she said. "Let's take one more gander at that big fear. You actually never did betray our love, darling, you never did let me down. You were not a coward. Sending me up to talk to Bill on my own—yes it was your idea, but we both made the decision, remember?—that was entirely reasonable. We just couldn't imagine how unreasonable Bill was prepared to be, how much rage he'd feel. That was a shock. Perhaps he even surprised himself."

"I've tried to see it that way. I nearly got there once."

Anna regarded me straight on. The pupils of her eyes were dilated and dark. "Okay, I think I've softened you up. Ready for an uppercut?"

"Hit me with your best shot. You're only a girl. How bad could it be?"

"Colm, when you failed to follow me into death on that night, despite your vow to jump off the Golden Gate, that didn't make you a coward either."

"Oof!"

"Instead of forcing yourself to leap, you walked home. Absolutely the right call. It wasn't cowardice that stopped you. It was simply good sense."

I fought to keep from crying by my usual method—groping for a lame witticism—but I could not think of what to say. I looked down at my hands, saw that I still gripped the drink menu. I flicked it onto the restaurant floor.

Anna smiled; fetching, tiny dimples installed themselves at the corners of her mouth.

"There you go! This is your chance, this is your day. You are my lion, Colm."

"Anna. I'm only a weak, faltering, mangy beast. Who knows how many teeth are left in my jaw? But I'll try. I'll give it my very best. And I will do it for you."

Her chin lifted. "No, no, no," she said. "That's all very sweet, but it's not what I want, and it's not to the point. You have to do it for you."

My flight touched down at Mineta Airport in San Jose at 10 p.m. I was just able to catch the last CalTrain north, the 10:35. It was a local, of course, hitting every stop to collect all loose and weary wanderers of the night. I didn't reach San Francisco until midnight. Next came one more cab ride all the way out to my digs in the Richmond.

I let myself in, said hello to Anna's photograph—she didn't seem to have a word to say, not so much as a greeting—and stumbled on into my bedroom to grab some shuteye. I'd need it. No matter how Friday happened to play out, I was sure it would be another exceptionally grueling day.

Chapter 18

I awoke a few seconds before the alarm went off. Like a frowzy gel, faint gray light seeped from the bottom edge of the window curtains. I flung off the bedclothes, catching a whiff of their stale aroma as they flapped back on the bed. When had I last changed the sheets?

Yawning, scratching at my stubble, I plodded out into the living room. In front of Anna's picture, I flung my arms wide. "Good mornin', gorgeous!" I said. Got zero response. Sometimes that girl does play hard to get. But any delay she inflicted on me made it that much better when next she appeared.

I got my blood pumping with a vigorous hike to the Seal Rock Inn at the end of Geary. I planned to breakfast on one of my tough-day staples, corned beef hash with a pair of poached eggs, washed down with half a gallon of black coffee.

I hauled a legal pad out of the back pouch of my vest, laid it to the right of my plate. As I ate, I mapped out the day's priorities. Mister Pete and Rafe Flores—together, if possible. Palmer's hospital, for an update on his condition. Cheryl Bullock, to see what muck she'd managed to rake up on Erik Eiger. Comb through Olivia's file from Desert Buttes. Talk to Cornu Cove directors and members to collect their responses to the charges I was preparing to make.

It was a safe bet the communication lines between Desert Buttes and Cornu Point offices had been burning up, last night. I chewed on my pen as I contemplated this. An interesting point. What might this make Cornu do? Would it smoke out bad guys? Would they duck for cover and hide their tracks, or try to seize the initiative, go on the offensive?

No way to know. Yet.

Final item, but so crucial I underlined it twice. I had to bring my story to the *Post-Dispatch* and make my case with Brotmann. What if he told me to just cram it where the sun don't shine? I chomped on my pen more vigorously as I pondered this all-too-real possibility. Then a solution popped into my skull: Billy Chappell, tyrant-in-residence over at the *SF Bay Sentinel!*

The *Sentinel* was a free weekly that cherished a hard-on for the *Chronicle*, the *Post-Dispatch*, and the *Mercury News*. The only thing Chappell enjoyed better than leveling criticism at the Bay's major dailies was beating them to a story. Since I could tug up the hemline of an exposé—one of seductive proportions—I felt sure Billy would allow himself to feel seriously tempted. So, should Brotmann shine me on, I'd simply offer the piece to Chappell.

Of course I'd then be summarily fired, but if Patch management didn't grab my story and run with it, my career there was obviously down the drain anyhow, no further proof required.

Frosting on this cupcake was that Chappell took pride in being an early technology adopter. Hence his weekly had a far more robust online presence than the Patch. Plenty of Bay Area youth used the *Sentinel* site as their chatroom. It could beat the Patch into the digital news stream by a day, then post up their reader feedback while the Patch was still laying out copy.

In terms of deadlines, even a third of a day is like half of infinity.

Okay, I had my plan, had a fallback position. But I didn't have any coins.

When I paid at the register, I requested five bucks in quarters. I exited through salt-misted swinging glass doors to the pay phone in the Seal Rock breezeway, a covered tunnel that led to the inn's garage. That stout old phone was flecked with rust spots from the constant swirl of sea winds, but it still worked amazingly well.

As I dialed Rafe Flores' office number, I mulled over Elle's point about me and cell phones. Probably right. But I just can't bring myself to clamp a slab of irradiating microchips up against the side of my head. My flickering brain has suffered quite enough stress, thank you very much, without adding any broiling by microwave.

I got Detective Flores' answering machine. I left him this: "Hi. It's Colm MacCay. Mister Pete, at Castello, has told you about me. If he hasn't, here's the deal. I'm a reporter for the *Post-Dispatch*. Unlike reporters you've spoken to lately, I actually deal in news. I know about Mephisto, I know about Aiano Tuato. I visited and talked with Olivia Bancroft yesterday in Vegas. I want to run my preliminary story tomorrow. Maybe we can help each other. I'll leave you my home and office numbers. If you don't get an answer, I'm out at Castello, visiting Mister Savante. Maybe you could meet me there."

Then I tried Flores' cell. Same deal, so I left the same message. Next up, Mister Pete. He answered after the first ring.

"*Buongiorno!*"

"It's MacCay."

"Yes. I was just wondering about you!"

"Wonder no more. I'm back from Sacramento and Vegas. I've got Mephisto and Olivia in the bag. Maybe more. We'll see. How you doing with Flores?"

"In tight. But he has problems of his own. He himself would benefit from a good and timely news story. Certain issues, he needs promptly addressed. Even the heat feels some heat on this one."

"Shocking. So, how timely are we talkin'? Something that runs tomorrow?"

"*Sí, eccellente.* Also, if you can help us at Castello. We need it."

"I'll show you what I've got. I left messages for Flores. I plan to come and see you. Can you round up some of your Cornu moles, but fast?"

"Yes."

I looked at my watch. "Ten o'clock this morning fast?"

"Yes."

"Can you get Flores there, too?"

"I'll try."

"*Buona fortuna.*"

"*Tu, anche.*"

Onward. Time to try Cheryl Bullock. Many rings rang before she picked up.

"Yas-ss?"

"It's MacCay. I'm back. Have you heard from Elle?"

"Yes. She's made it as far as Monterey. Should be home in a few hours."

I let out my breath in a sigh. "Good!" I said. "Well, it's happening. I'll try to get a story out tomorrow. How was your dig on Erik Eiger? Turn anything up?"

"Real good! Or bad, depending on how you see it," Cheryl said.

"Talk to me."

"Ah. Well, to start, Eiger isn't his actual name. He's Finnish, not German. His real name is Kaarlo Kriikku. He was a Finnish bodybuilder, won medals in his late teens. Whereupon he was asked to join in a film project."

"Hm. Do I hear the plop of a posing strap dropping to the floor?"

I balanced a notebook on the square top of the pay phone, readied my pen.

"That's it." Cheryl chuckled ruefully. "Ever hear of Tom of Finland?"

"Vaguely."

"An artist who painted erotic pictures of muscular, dominant, leather-clad males. After his service in World War Two."

"Okay."

"Some of those erotic images wore Nazi uniforms."

"Okay."

"Tom, whose real name was Touko Laaksonen, later repudiated those drawings. But he really hit a nerve. The whole Nazi, storm trooper, night porter stuff was an appeal to the deepest, darkest id. Even some Israelis succumbed to it. There were porn books called stalags selling well in Jerusalem in the 1960s. Block 24 at Auschwitz, where the brothels were located, was the inspiration of some pretty depraved fantasies."

"Okay," I said again.

The coffee, corned beef hash, eggs, ketchup and jelly-spread toast I'd consumed for breakfast were jostling in my stomach. It felt like they were considering a mad dash for the nearest exit.

"Are you all right, MacCay?"

"Grand and lovely," I croaked. "Continue."

"So, that's the stratum Kaarlo, or Erik, and his directors, tapped into. They produced sixteen-millimeter reels that feature Erik as the guy in an SS uniform. And all his victims, or costars if you want to call them that, were underage Finnish boys."

"Un-huh." I kept writing notes on the pad I had propped on the pay phone.

"Well, this all went down like forty years ago, MacCay. Wouldn't even be an issue today, except for one thing. Those reels were the all-time favorite movies of Jefe Hans Schaetzle. Don't know if that rings any bells. Schaetzle was a German Wehrmacht officer who fled to Peru after the war. And he started up a fundamentalist Christian compound in the mountains above Lima, called *Ciudadela de la Fe*—Citadel of the Faith.

"Anyway, it turned into quite the cult. I'll spare you an account of the abuses. But Peruvian journalists investigated Schaetzle, the authorities eventually got a clue, and he was forced to flee to Brazil. Both the news outlets and crusading officials had a heyday trying to beat each other on revelations of Schaetzle's activity at the Ciudadela. Some evidence was sealed, too inflammatory to be seen by anyone but magistrates. Are you following me here, MacCay?"

"Yes. Next, I take it, that sealed evidence was leaked?"

"Correct. It became known to connoisseurs and cognoscenti that the studly, muscle-bound SS officer in the reels was actually a young Kaarlo before he became Erik Eiger. Then the stuff went viral, became a subterranean hit in certain circles on the Internet. Have you noticed, many pedophilia busts are international in scope? Pervs have all kinds of ways of encrypting and burying material digitally. See, if you have that footage, you must keep it quiet. Not only because the images are so disturbing, but because those kids were so underage. It's a felony to even possess it."

"Wow!" I rubbed my chin. I winced at the thought that this part of the story might overshadow everything else. The last thing you want is for a reader to devour a sidebar while completely ignoring the main tale.

"After his porn phase, Kaarlo moved on to Munich, got educated in theater and acting, and reinvented himself as Erik Eiger. He won bit parts in swashbucklers and so forth, then bigger parts, and finally was discovered by a Czech director. That's the guy who did the sword-and-shield epics where Eiger built his image as the mounted knight who rides up to save the princess from a sinister threat—usually, someone in a fez or kaffiyeh. Those eventually brought Eiger to Hollywood where he had about ten good years before his career went *pffft!*"

"Whereupon he hired out as spokesman for all kinds of products and resorts and whatnot. Trading on his B-grade celebrity status. Like Reagan."

"Correct."

"I wonder if Cornu Point and 3CD Corporation just hand Eiger a check, or if they have some kind of extra hold on him because they know about the films."

Even though she was on the other end of the phone, I could almost see Cheryl's slim, shawl-clad shoulders move in a slow, graceful shrug.

"Doesn't matter. If they have that kind of grip, it won't last. This whole scandal is primed to blow. Too many know about it now. Go ahead and light the fuse. You have my blessing."

"Sure. I don't in the least mind blowing up Eiger. If that blast also inflicts powder burns on Cornu Point, I won't shed a tear. What I don't want, though, is for the mushroom cloud to overshadow everything else. But that's not your worry. It's mine. What do you have for evidence?"

"Still images pulled from those films. Actually, we've downloaded and decoded entire reels, but we don't want that known till we turn the material over to the feds. Also, we can give you translated stories from the Peruvian journalists about *Ciudadela de la Fe.* But here's the deal, MacCay. I want it made very clear in your story that what you have is the result of a C.A.P. investigation, Campaign Against Pedophilia. We get full credit, right?"

"No problemo. You can have the blame, too, if you want. That is, if any part of this winds up being wrong or if there's blow-back from his fans. Does he still have any? But yeah, what if I write: 'The Foster City-based Campaign Against Pedophilia, or C.A.P, today announced results of an investigation into child pornography films that starred a young Erik Eiger—the former Hollywood muscleman. And blah-blah-blah. You like it?"

"Sure. Except C.A.P. headquarters isn't here, it's in Oakland. How do you want the material?"

"E-mail the files to me at the *Post-Dispatch.* No, wait, send it to my personal account. Here, I'll give you that," I said. Which I did.

"Both you and Elle have been a tremendous help. I thank you from the heart. And I thank you for loaning Elle to me."

"Well, investigations are my life's work. And Elle, she wants to fight or lead a crusade of some sort. This, or some other. She enjoyed that wild-ass road trip. Elle likes you now, MacCay. Says you're all right."

"Mutual." I took a moment to bask in the convivial glow, then said, "That's it! Gotta rush to make my deadlines. I'll be in touch."

"Bye!"

I slid the receiver into the cradle. A strong gust of sea wind, bearing the low-tide reek of an Aleut picnic, swirled into the breezeway. Brr-rrr. I probably needed to go back to my apartment to grab an overcoat and a hat before heading down to Castello. And en route, stop at my bank branch to withdraw a lot of cash to pay for taxis.

Maybe it was time to buy a car.

———

Wind howled into Castello's funky parking lot. Mist from the booming surf roiled in the air like a troubled spirit, and an immense fleece of whitecaps unfurled to the horizon. But this wild weather didn't keep people away.

Two TV news trucks from channels 2 and 5 and a half-dozen shiny late-model cars looking utterly out of place were parked among the usual rusty wrecks. I figured the new ones were the cars of reps from news outlets and wire services, and as I walked up to the gate, saw that I was right.

Two beefy guys in work clothes, their arms defiantly folded, stood inside the Castello gate, and stared silently and stolidly out at a knot of people arguing with them about why they should be allowed to go out to Castello. I recognized Patch reporter Ken Stein among the supplicants. Stein was a thin, whey-faced dandy with chestnut curls, who fancied himself an expert on the seamy side of Bay Area life. Actually, he had been a decent cop shop reporter, but I couldn't stand his smug, self-important air. It reminded me too much of my own.

Outside the fence stood a pair of uniformed sheriff's deputies, also with folded arms. They observed the scene without saying much. I made my way right to the gate before Stein noticed I was there.

"MacCay! What?" Stein yelped at me. "You can't horn in on this story. It's not your assignment!"

"I'll ask when I want advice, ol' buddy," I said. "At the moment, I don't."

"So, you're MacCay?" rumbled a brute on the far side of the gate. A splendid example of Di Mastini manliness.

"The same," I told him.

We heard an automobile speed into the lot and slide to a halt in the dust. We turned to see what—or who—was being added to our mix.

The car was unmarked—except for the spotlights, radio antennas, and barely concealed emergency lights that, taken together, constitute a dead giveaway. A handsome Latino man in a rumpled suit emerged. He resembled Cesar Romero toward the end of his film career, except that his hair was salt-and-pepper instead of pure white. This guy also bore evidence of a much rougher life. His cheeks were pocked and gouged. A jagged white welt ran from his right ear to the corner of his mouth. It looked like he might've once been attacked by someone swinging a busted bottle.

"Mornin', Lieutenant," one of the deputies said, as the other nodded respectfully.

"Good morning, gentlemen," he said.

"You Rafael Flores?" I asked.

"Yes." He scrutinized me. Felt like I was being booked, and he was taking the mug shot. "MacCay?"

"Himself," I replied.

"Glad you made it. Let's go."

The Di Mastini men allowed us through the gate. One planted a broad hand square on the chest of Ken Stein who was trying to wriggle through right behind us. Stein was unceremoniously shoved back out.

"Hey! You can't touch me—that's assault!" Stein brayed. "Are you one of the guys who mugged Palmer?"

"Too bad I didn't witness that," Flores muttered. He gave me a wink.

We strolled down the path toward Castello. The first big bend afforded us a splendid overlook of Cornu Cove.

"Really kicking up out there today," I commented.

"Yeah. It can do that. But whenever it goes calm, that cove is a little slice of heaven. My pop used to drive us over from San Jose, take us surfcasting. Pisses me off now, they're trying to restrict access, make it a place for rich folks only. Native rights, that's what Pop used to say when we went down there. He thought people should try to live more like the early Californios. If we caught a big striped bass, we'd tote it back and hold a barbecue for everybody *en mi familia.*"

That's when I suspected our session at Castello might go just fine. I also wondered if I was being played. Even so, that would be all right. I was willing to try to charm Lieutenant Flores for exactly as long as he seemed willing to try to charm me.

Flores shared a bit more during our walk to the Castello square. County officials had qualms about where the Palmer assault investigation was heading. They balked at the expense of sending a detective to Samoa to collect a DNA sample from Aiano Tuato or—best possible result—persuade Tuato of the wisdom of returning stateside and turning himself in to face charges.

"Probably smart not to generalize," Flores said. "Still, I've found that when PIs—excuse me, that means Pacific Islanders—get angry, they tend to be totally furious. Next, if they feel remorse, it goes just as deep. That's what I'd try to appeal to in Tuato. Then, if it didn't work, I'd arrest him."

"So, you did find two types of blood on that pole. Some from Palmer, plus a dab from someone else."

"Yep."

"And these nameless officials who feel some reluctance. Might they have real-estate holdings rising in value because of the Cornu Point development? Or might they have good friends, supporting their careers, who possess holdings like that?"

"Yep."

"Therefore, we must have a potent story running soon, and thus convince them it's better to hop over to the red square of virtue than continue to dick around with those sordid minions of evil on the black square."

"Yep."

My turn. I told Flores we could prove Mephisto the stallion had visited California. I shared Olivia's revelations. Flores exhibited keen interest. He even tugged a little spiral-bound notebook out of his breast pocket and jotted things down. I said I wanted to call in the FBI on Olivia's probable kidnapping. Flores said he'd take care of that. Good; then I'd need a statement from the FBI announcing their investigation. Flores said I'd likely get it.

Pleased, I served dessert. I told him what Cheryl's C.A.P. group had discovered about Erik Eiger. Something that wasn't exactly a smile settled on Flores' face. His look suggested the grim satisfaction a hunter must feel, finding quarry in his crosshairs after a long and frustrating pursuit.

"You hate that you ever bought into his lie about the horse, eh?" I guessed.

"No shit!" Flores said.

On the rough cobbles of the Castello town square, we found Pete had gathered an array of folks for us to interview, some wearing the coveralls of Cornu Point ground crews. In less than an hour, both Flores and I had all the statements we needed. He also collected promises that depositions and courtroom testimony would occur on demand.

"This is an important day," Mister Pete announced to all and sundry. "It's when we find out if Castello can exist awhile longer, or whether it must soon fade away."

The Chihuahua jerked up its head and gazed at Pete with bulbous, intelligent eyes, trying to grasp the implications of his master's grave tone.

"Well, if you get booted out, you can go to a warmer place," Lieutenant Flores told Mr. Pete after the meeting. "Shorty might like it. He could take off that itchy sweater."

"No, no!" Pete protested. "He enjoys Castello, where he gets plenty of fish. Shorty loves fish. Sometimes I tell him that he must be part cat. But that sort of talk he doesn't like so much."

I told Pete I now possessed an official state summary that recapitulated the founding documents for Cornu Point and Castello in an interesting way. I'd send him a copy soon. Unless I located something better. I might be able to get my hands on an actual set of originals. If I could decipher what Olivia had said.

"Tell me."

"Uh, let me ponder it some more. If I say what I *think* I heard, you'll go buggy."

"Whatever you do, do it soon. We have a cooperating agreement with the state Chippers," Flores said. He meant California Highway Patrol troopers. "They want San Mateo County deputies to help them evict everyone from Castello. I'll need a damn good reason to say no."

"Start with tomorrow's paper."

We shook hands all around, headed back out to the gate. Guards and deputies were still present, but the crowd of disappointed newsies had evaporated. My taxi driver, bless him, remained, but Flores volunteered to drive me over to Palo Alto and the hospital so we'd have more time. I sent the cabbie off with a decent tip.

"Our statements have to come from our San Mateo County Sheriff's Department spokesman," Flores said. "I'll give you her number. Me, I can't be quoted by name in any story. Not yet."

"What if we just cite a source close to the investigation?"

"Perfect."

As he drove, I asked him if a notebook had been found with Palmer. Flores said it had, without many pages filled in. Then he mentioned that Palmer also carried a letter from Beverly Bancroft.

"The one in which Beverly talks about the founding documents?" I asked.

Flores gave me an appraising glance. "Yes. And she also provided Palmer with personal contact info for everyone on the Cornu Point board. Stuff not so easy to get nowadays."

"Can I have a copy?"

"Officially? No." Flores said firmly. "Unofficially, I'll fax you one. But stand right by the machine. Then cut my sender information off the page." A band of even, white teeth flashed in his dark face. "I must say that it gives me great pleasure to know that you're going to make those bastards squirm."

Flores dropped me off at the Palo Alto Trauma Center. I went up to Palmer's room in the neuro ICU. Asleep in a chair was a large woman whom I took to be Palmer's mom.

A tall black man in a lab coat, with combed-back silver hair and a goatee, stood right by Palmer's bedside, talking quietly to nurse

Marty, who was back on duty. Marty introduced us.

"This is Dr. Gregory David, Sebastian's neurologist. Doctor, Colm MacCay. Do I have that name right? He works with Sebastian at the paper."

"Pleasure, Doc," I said. We shook hands. "How is he?"

"He may be coming around. Not posturing anymore, which is a good sign. I just performed a level-of-consciousness test—I rubbed a knuckle over his sternum—and he reacted. Mumbled, tried to push my hand away. Doesn't mean he's conscious, but some stimulus is getting through.

"Marty here," he touched the nurse's shoulder, "told me his involuntary roving eye movements ceased early this morning. He can now track a point of light. The EEG monitoring shows a good brain-wave pattern. Later today we'll do a test called a Brain Auditory Evoked Response. That'll show us how well he's hearing sounds."

"Uh-huh." I whipped out a notebook and began scribbling. The doctor looked startled.

"You plan to put this in a story?" he asked.

"Yes. That a problem?"

"Let's talk outside." He grabbed me by the arm and guided me out the door. Once in the hall, he pushed the panels of his lab coat aside and put his hands on his hips, tucking his thumbs into a narrow lizard-skin belt.

"Sebastian was terribly beaten. It was a murderous assault, possibly gang-related. A culprit has yet to be arrested. Yes?" The doctor sounded testy. "Once healthy, Sebastian could become a witness at a criminal trial. So if you announce he's getting better, you're putting him right back at risk."

"Good point, Doc," I said. I scratched my nose with the button end of the ballpoint, thinking it over. "How about this? I know Lieutenant Flores, the lead detective on this case. I tell him your concerns, I ask him to send a deputy to stand watch. That better?"

"Yes." The doctor kept his hands on his hips. "One more thing. Any assessment of the patient's condition must come through our communications department, not me. Or, you can see if his parents want to talk to you."

I pointed my pen back at the ICU. "You're saying I should go wake up his mother?"

He grimaced. "No. She's been here since midnight. All right. Quick. What?"

"Something simple. Layman's terms."

"Sebastian Palmer is a strong young man with a healthy constitution." The doctor looked up at the ceiling. "His injuries were serious. He's not out of the woods—"

"But maybe he can glimpse the edge of the clearing?" I hazarded.

"Sure. Poetic. Use that." He glanced at his watch. "I've got to go."

"Thanks, Doc." I wrung his hand. It felt limp and reluctant. I guessed that reporters weren't among his favorite people.

I went back into Palmer's room. Nurse Marty greeted me with a smile. I stood at the bedside. I smiled too, as I thought about Palmer's improved responses to touch, light, and sound.

"Hey, pal," I said softly. "It's MacCay. Just want you to know we've got your Cornu Point story about sewn up. Should be running tomorrow. I'll come and read it to you."

I'd wager it was my imagination, but I thought I saw Palmer's lean body twitch beneath the sheets.

Chapter 19

I went back to my flat to write up the Cornu story mainbar. I'd just cleared space off my desk and opened the laptop when I suddenly saw that it made no sense at all for me to write this opus at home. Merely something I was attempting in order to put off the inevitable encounter with Brotmann. Well, screw that! Charge on in now, laddie—get hanged for a goat! I closed the laptop, stuffed it into the pouch of my vest, went for the door.

As soon I placed a hand on my doorknob, the phone rang. I walked back to answer. It was Elle.

"Colm! I was thinking."

"My heartiest congratulations."

"Knock it off! I mean, about what Olivia said."

"Go on."

"What if it wasn't separate phrases... but all part of the same sentence?"

"About underwear?"

"No, no! What if she was saying, 'under *where* Sebastian gave me Beverly's...'"

"Okay, good. But Beverly's what?"

"Exactly! Now. What're some things we know of that Sebastian gave to Beverly?"

I racked my brain. "Well, there's just one thing. Her glasses."

"Right! And where did he do it?"

"Um, probably out at the guest house on the old Bancroft estate, where the sisters lived."

"Yes!"

"Listen to me, you insolent whelp. I'm the wordsmith around here. That's the sort of work I'm supposed to do. So help me God, you keep poaching on my turf, I'll file a complaint with the union!"

Elle pursed her lips and made a prolonged farting noise into the phone. "Yeah, but I'm the cop!" she said.

I smiled. "Yes," I replied. "Yes, you are." Then a few thoughts struck me. "Hate to point out a cloud in that silver lining, kid-do, but odds are our loyal opposition has ransacked the place. They're grabbing up every hard doc they can find, which is why they needed to move Olivia. She lost access to what was in the house. They gained it."

"But we have a key!"

"Key to what? An old filing cabinet, by now busted open and jouncing about in the back of a dump truck on its way up to Ox Mountain landfill?"

She was silent. I felt sorry for dousing her enthusiasm.

"Anyway. How could we know where, exactly, in the house, Sebastian—"

"She said 'under.' Not just 'where'!"

I thought that over. "All right, granted. But should we really quibble about what a demented old woman mumbled?"

"What else do we have?"

"Plenty. And don't get me wrong, I'd like to have this, too! But know what? The only person who can say where they stood at the exact moment when he handed her those glasses is Sebastian. And he can't talk so good right now."

Elle made an inarticulate, infuriated sound.

"Don't get me wrong on that, either," I said in a gentler tone. "I just came from visiting Sebastian in the ICU. Actually, I can report to you that he's begun to show many positive signs."

I listened to her breathe. I knew she fought to regain control of her feelings. In that battle, I knew which side to be on.

"You did great," I said. "And I do think we need to check on it, what you just figured out. That's not next, however. Next is I write my piece. Get it on the street."

"All right," she said, eventually.

"Good. Okay. I'll call. Soon as I know. Anything."

"All right."

"So you're home?"

"Yeah."

"Good. I'm glad you made it. Give my best to Cheryl."

"I will."

—

My new space in the *Post-Dispatch* building was indeed like a broom closet compared to that lordly corner suite I had formerly occupied. Still, I retained access to phones, faxes, e-mail accounts, Internet lines—even library researchers should I need help grouting holes in my narrative.

A taxi dropped me at a bare spot on the curb of Mission. I walked toward the big stone pile of the Patch. Then a nagging thought hit: Last time I'd been in this building, I'd slugged Artie Davis, the Travel editor. Might our building security have been advised to employ special measures if Colm MacCay happened to darken their doorstep?

Instead of using the main entrance, perhaps I should seek another way inside. Luck was with me: I spotted John, who runs the Patch's downstairs snack bar. His pickup stood parked at the loading dock while he pulled crates of supplies out of the bed. A back door was propped open by his steel handcart.

"Top o' the mornin' to you, John!"

He swung around. "Mr. MacCay! Good morning. Haven't seen you in a while."

"Oh, I've been away. Working on a story. Got busted back down to reporter, you know. Can I give you a hand?"

I helped him wrestle crates of sodas, sandwiches, coffee grounds, fruit, and pastry onto the handcart. We went inside together.

As he pushed the loaded truck down the hall, John said, "Heard you had a disagreement with Mr. Davis."

"I forcefully indicated that I thought him an ass. Didn't hear his response."

"I see." John stopped. "Well, Mr. Davis has been one of our best customers. But, truthfully? I never liked him."

I winked, shook John's hand. Then went up the back stairs, entered my minuscule workspace, shut the door. I opened my laptop on the desk, plugged in auxiliary power, cracked my knuckles over the keyboard, and began to type.

By 1:00 p.m. my mainbar was in fair shape. Time for official Cornu Point reaction. I rang up Flores, reached him, got updates on key issues. He agreed to send a deputy to watch over Palmer. And to send Beverly's letter. I toddled over to the nearest fax machine. It obligingly spewed out Beverly's list of directors. Per Flores' request, I snipped off his sender info with scissors, returned to my desk, and began to make calls.

Most of the directors were unreachable for one reason or another, though I did speak to a few highly suspicious secretaries and wives—at least, I think they were wives. Then I hit a jackpot. J. Rupert Hadley ranted to me on his cell phone as he sat in the lounge at the Cornu Point Inn, waiting for a teenage daughter to complete her dressage lesson. Good old "Jay"—for some reason, he disliked people calling him Jasper—had enjoyed a few cocktails as he waited, didn't care who knew. He also had opinions on Cornu Point and its plans for the coast. Wanted everyone to know about those.

"Listen, MacCay," he said. "Cornu Point Association has a fabulous history of managing its land. No one does it better! Our board is local folks with a huge interest in preserving natural beauty. Our plans are tasteful, environmentally appropriate. That's what your paper should report on. Not the richly deserved fate of those lazy squatters at Castello."

"What about Wheeler and Bates, the managers? Didn't they come from Las Vegas to run your place? Didn't 3CD buy into Cornu Point after you changed your charter from nonprofit? I mean, how is Cornu Point local?"

"Look, MacCay. For a major project, you attract investment capital. It's the American way! Yes, 3CD had interest—and they had cash. Naturally, they want onsite personnel to oversee things. But we're the board. They do as we say!

"Some may whine about Cornu Point going exclusive. Well, look at the big picture. That revenue keeps our state parks system from going under. Public access can be improved elsewhere. Cornu's best for horses and horse people. Letting members of the general public wander around, well, that only makes for a bad mix."

"As shown by what happened to Beverly Bancroft?"

"Exactly. We tried to accommodate hikers, walkers, and bird watchers. Clearly, it didn't work. Of course, Bancroft was a special case. An agitator! Her death was sad, even regrettable. But Beverly walked on a horses-only trail. For whatever reason, she yelled, waved her arms, tried to scare Eiger's horse. But that horse was a stallion. Didn't frighten so easily, eh?"

"Are you saying she had it coming?"

"No! Stop putting words in my mouth. You hacks are all alike. Sure, her death was tragic, but she brought it on herself."

"And Sebastian Palmer, our reporter, beaten up near Cornu Cove?"

"Come on. That happened at Castello, not at the cove per se. Those illegal squatters clearly are the culprits. They robbed him, didn't they? Well, there you go. No one from here would bother to do that."

"I have to tell you something not yet widely known, Mr. Hadley. Palmer was pursuing a lead into the death of Beverly Bancroft. He had evidence to suggest that she was killed on a pedestrian trail. The animal involved was a show-horse named Mephisto, trained to kick on command. Mephisto works at a casino in Las Vegas—a casino also owned by 3CD Corporation. Would you care to comment on that?"

I heard air whoosh out of him. Then he grated, "That is a total media fabrication… ." He paused. I didn't hear a switch click in his head, but when he spoke again, his voice had dropped forty degrees in warmth. I was surprised his tongue didn't freeze to the roof of his mouth.

"I was wrong to speak with you, MacCay. You're not like the rest. You're worse. If you dare put anything in print that embarrasses me or my family or Cornu Point, I will be very upset. Understand?"

The line went dead.

So next it was time to ring up the Cornu Point front desk.

"Hi!" I said to the receptionist. "I'm Colm MacCay, from the *San Francisco Post-Dispatch*. Any way I can speak to Erik Eiger? No? I need to talk to his publicist first? Well, can you give me that number? Thanks. And now, how about your managers, Mr. Bates or Mr. Wheeler? Either one will do. They're not available? No, I don't want to leave a message. But you should let them know I'm just off the phone with one of your Cornu Point directors, Mr. J. Richard Hadley. And I have some fresh information that I want to double-check with them, about the *murder* of Miss Beverly Bancroft and the *kidnapping* of her sister Olivia. Yes, certainly I'll hold. Thank you."

A man's voice came on the phone, deep and raspy, like a smoker's.

"Hello? To whom am I speaking?"

"This is Colm MacCay, a reporter for the *Post-Dispatch*. I'm working on a story on Cornu Point and your situation out there at the coast. Who are you?"

"Larry Wheeler. I'm CEO here at Cornu. I believe I've already talked with Tod Ericson and Ken Stein from your paper. Have you and I spoken before? What sort of story are you working on?"

"One matter I'd like to clear up is the alleged kidnapping of Olivia Bancroft."

Wheeler chuckled dryly. "Preposterous. Olivia was never under any compulsion. She is our guest. We are paying for her care at a top-quality rest home in Nevada. Out of gratitude for all the Bancroft family has done for Cornu Point over the years. That was all announced in the media. You see, after Beverly's tragic death, her sister—"

"So, you're saying Olivia isn't being held by you against her will at Desert Buttes in Las Vegas? She's not being drugged into submission?"

He didn't chuckle this time. "Olivia is receiving the best of care," he stated. "Obviously, it's difficult to treat someone with age-related dementia—"

I interrupted him again. "Yesterday, Olivia told me that she'd been taken there and was being held against her will. That's kidnapping. Have you taken any questions from the FBI about this yet?"

There was a long silence. Then Wheeler said, "Yesterday we had a serious intrusion and disruption at our Las Vegas facility. In Olivia's ward. Her file was stolen. The Las Vegas police are investigating. Are you saying they should talk to you?"

"Olivia's file is evidence now, Larry. But that binder isn't what you want most, is it? Wouldn't you prefer to get your mitts on the Bancroft sisters' copies of the Cornu founding documents? Those just keep slipping from your grasp, right?"

Wheeler didn't answer. He was being smart. He wanted me to keep talking. He hoped to find out how much more I knew. Well, we saw eye to eye on that. I thought it might be fun to tell him. And I was fishing for what he knew, too. Such as whether or not they'd found those papers yet.

"And 3CD owns another property in Vegas, doesn't it? Big Top Casino, where Mephisto the wonder horse performs his dance. Just like he did the day Erik Eiger rode down Beverly Bancroft. So, in light of this information, do you think Bancroft's cause of death could be changed, from tragic accident to first-degree murder?"

Wheeler was a cool customer, I'll grant him that. "Please hold for just one second," he said. Then he came back on the line. He read me a name and a phone number and said, "That's our lawyer. Why don't you put your questions to him?"

"Sure thing," I replied. "Simon Winger? Used to work for Beverly, didn't he?"

A long pause.

"MacCay? One more thing. You might consider getting a lawyer of your own. I've a feeling you're about to need one."

"Oh?"

Then came the moment when Larry Wheeler lost it. He probably enjoyed making people quake in their boots back in Vegas. Couldn't let me go without trying that at least once.

"A bodyguard might not be a bad idea either," he said.

"You mean like Sebastian Palmer should've had? Larry, can you confirm that a Samoan man, Aiano Tuato, was in fact a security guard working for Cornu Point on the evening that Palmer was assaulted?"

Click.

I felt myself smiling, wondered what my face looked like. Glee ran entirely against my emotional grain. It felt utterly odd. Yet, I was starting to enjoy myself. I was doing my job, asking questions. I could not run a piece without collecting their reaction. But after long tilling of the field, getting to the harvest phase was bliss.

Onward. I dialed up Erik Eiger's publicist. She answered on the sixth ring, just as I felt sure I was going to get her machine.

"Melanie Dawkins," she drawled. In her background, I could pick up faint music, the gush and tinkle of a fountain, the distant honk of a car horn. An image of her lounging near a sparkling L.A. pool swam before my eyes. "How can I help you?" she said.

I skirted the first question that sprang to my mind, which was to inquire whether she happened to be wearing a cute little swimsuit.

"Miss Dawkins, I'm Colm MacCay from the *Post-Dispatch*, a newspaper up in the San Francisco area."

"Yes. I'm familiar with it," she snapped. Composure vanished from her tone. "We've answered all the questions we're prepared to take on the horse incident and on Mr. Eiger's work at Cornu Point. Our answers are posted online, under press information, at Mr. Eiger's official website."

I sought to imitate Larry Wheeler's, dry, humorless chuckle, and did a passable job. "Oh, I'm not trying to dig up any of that stuff," I said. "Water under the bridge! What I want to talk about is Erik's film career."

"Oh?" She was suspicious.

"Everyone knows about Erik in Hollywood," I said. "I'd like to hear about his time in Europe, when he got launched. The background you'd need for a complete profile."

"A profile? That's what you're doing?"

"I'm thinking of it. So, how many movies did he make with that Czech guy, what's-his-name?"

"Petr Zajic," she volunteered. "Close to a dozen."

"And he was a knight, or a cavalier, or a dragoon, something like that, in all of them, correct?"

"Yes. That was his image, the mighty warrior who charges into the fray and wins the day, that sort of thing. He brought that brand to Hollywood, where our producers helped him perfect it. Well, once in a while he was a highwayman or pirate or bandit, but not often. The public pretty much liked to see him just one way, sort of a John Wayne in shining armor. If you will."

"So, Erik must be, how shall I put it, quite the equestrian?"

"Mr. Eiger is an excellent horseman! It was another interest, besides bodybuilding, when he was in his teens. In his twenties, he became a competitive rider—jumping, steeplechase, and so on. Could have won international competitions, but didn't have the time. Everything had to go into his film career. But you should see him on a horse. Amazing what he can get an animal to do. There was a project green-lighted for Erik, *The Centaur,* about a Greek god, half horse and—

"Oh, I know from centaurs! Had an education in the classics. Were there any films before the Czech stuff?"

"Not much. Art projects. Maybe something at film school."

"What about short subjects, shot in his native Finland?"

"How on earth did you find out he was Finnish?" she sounded genuinely curious.

"A little bird told me. Well, let's face it, a sparrow hawk, actually, with a keen eye for certain prey. So, Melanie, do you know about the sixteen-millimeter reels Erik performed in? The Nazi-themed porn that was found at a cult compound in Peru? The stuff now circulating through pedophile rings on the Internet?"

Melanie Dawkins gasped, then went silent. For a few seconds I thought the line was dead. Then I realized I could still hear music and cars in the background.

Finally, she broke loose with, "That's the worst case of character assassination I've heard! If those accusations show up in print, I guarantee you'll mud-wrestle lawyers the rest of your life! You won't end up with a goddam dime, you fucking creep!"

"Actually, it's only defamation or slander if there's no proof," I told her. "So, anyway. Right now, I'm kinda confused. Are you saying that it's all true, or that just some of it may be possibly true, or absolutely none of it is true? Which?"

Click.

Well! These people certainly saved me time by ringing off as soon as my essential tasks were accomplished.

After I had their quotes, denials, or refusals to answer entered in the story, I checked my home e-mail account and found the photos and materials Cheryl had sent. I lingered over them long enough to verify their contents, then sent them on to the Patch's art department. Next, I rang up Hilda, the art manager, told her I might have an A-1 story running tomorrow. Could she please assign someone to format some images and enter them into the system? My thought was to get the Cornu piece in proper shape to run, then spring it on Brotmann.

Hilda said her department was overworked, and no one had told her about this project, which was par for the course, but she'd see what she could do.

Suddenly the door to my broom closet crashed open. Mr. Tom Brotmann stood there, thin-necked, crimson-faced, and bug-eyed. That is an image I shall bear joyously to my grave. He was dressed impeccably, as ever, yet he bore a remarkable resemblance to a fully enraged bronze turkey.

"MacCay! What are you doing here? You said you'd be out sick!"

"Well, I said I might. But after I stepped outside the building, I discovered that I felt much better. So I went back to work."

"Back to making trouble, you mean. Half the law firms in northern California are ringing my office! Even the Las Vegas police. You've fouled up our Cornu Point coverage!"

"Actually, I'm fixing it. Come on, Brotmann. What you ran was pretty thin soup. You carried water for the Cornu Point Association, and for 3CD.

"Here're some missing facts. The Castello men were framed for the assault on Sebastian Palmer. I can prove it. Olivia Bancroft wasn't moved to the rest home by a benign Cornu Point Association. She was kidnapped so they could grab her important papers. I can prove that, too. And, nasty of nasties, Beverly Bancroft's death was no accident. It was a murder. And the killer was that muscle-boy for hire, Erik Eiger, who also happens to be a former porn star. In Nazi-themed gay porn, at that!"

Brotmann's eyebrows worked their way up his high forehead during this *CliffsNotes* rendition of the Cornu Point epic.

"Ericson and Stein have tracked some of those wild rumors," Brotmann said stiffly. "I won't dignify them by calling them possibilities."

"Bet they've made fabulous progress," I interjected.

"We plan a comprehensive story for Sunday. Turn your notes over to the team. Bob Porteous is steering the project. We'll pick out any bits that prove out or seem useful. That's how you can help, MacCay. Not by clubbing the hornet's nest, as you have been!"

I shook my head. "No dice. Stein and Ericson aren't lead on this. I am. Let them offer me their notes, I'll see if there's anything I want. But thanks to the boost I got from Palmer's work, some serious pavement pounding, and a few lucky breaks, I'm out in front of everybody. Sunday's too long to wait. We need to lob a front-page bomb tomorrow!"

"MacCay! You are one stupendously arrogant sonofabitch! Now, I'm not suggesting you turn your notes over and stop meddling. I'm ordering you. Refuse, consider yourself fired. You'll be escorted out of here in a New York minute."

I stood, turned off my laptop. Tugged open the pouch of my vest. "Now calm down," I said. "Let's mull this over, eh?"" I glanced at my watch. "It's only 2:30 p.m.. We've still got time to figure out how to run a big exposé tomorrow."

Brotmann folded his arms into a knot, glared, and shook his head. "The only question is, will you comply with a management directive."

"Hm," I said. "No, the question is will the Patch break the story of the year? By the way, know what other reporters in the City say the motto of our paper should be? 'If it's news, it's news to us!'"

"Which is it, MacCay? Tell me now. Where are you going?"

"Bathroom. Got a nervous bladder," I told him. "You've just made it worse! I need to think. Let you know about my decision in a moment, okay?"

I went to the door, paused, and said. "While I'm gone, here's a question for *you* to ponder: Are you a real newsman, or just some money-grubbing corporate carpetbagger from out of state?"

A wonderful feature of our men's restroom on the third floor is its two entrances, opening upon different halls. I went in one door, out the other. I took the stairs down, left the building via the loading dock. Outside, scouting for a cab, I had to dally on the sidewalk longer than I wanted, but I flagged down a ride. Then I was off to the offices of the *SF Bay Sentinel*.

———

The *Sentinel* is published from a former brewery in Noe Valley. It was the inspiration of publisher Billy Chappell to leave the old beer factory's sign on the exterior of his building: a giant mug of golden brew with a head of white foam dripping down the sides — the sort of old-fashioned icon that makes you thirsty just to look at it.

Fortunately, Billy also keeps a full cooler and a full humidor in his office. He habitually offers visitors a brew and a cigar. In that way, his place suggests what entire newsrooms used to be — back when a fifth of bourbon was stashed in the bottom drawer of every other desk, and smoke spiraled up from metal ashtrays (the old caps from wire service paper rolls) to form a miasma against the ceiling while sounds of clattering typewriters, ringing phones, and shouts of "Copy!" sliced through the haze.

Billy had once worked shifts as a copy boy at the three major Bay Area dailies. He was subsequently rejected for reporting jobs at all of them. He founded the *Sentinel* on a shoestring, to exact revenge. His weekly rag prospered by running ads for massage parlors, sex clubs, porn films, and escort services, and kinky Bay Area personals at which the dailies turned up their patrician noses. He prided himself on running sex advice from the most frank, even outrageous, columnists in the erotic plenum.

Billy functioned best in the twilit realm between hard news and tabloid pandering. Though he got big stories wrong as often as he got them right, he still landed many blows over the years, and won awards for periodicals in his category. The plaques were proudly displayed on his office wall. He commonly paid only a pittance, but his paper and his website were venues for new and struggling writers across the region.

Billy resembled a larger, fleshier version of me. His distinguishing feature was a thatch of wild gray hair that decades of dedicated combat with brushes, shears, and various gels had failed to subdue. He burnished his reputation by dressing up in an elaborate highwayman outfit every Halloween, then pranced around the Noe and Castro valleys until the wee hours, painting the neighborhoods red—by plastering crimson stickers promoting his publication on plenty of things that moved, like cop cars, and nearly everything that didn't.

I sat in Billy's office, nabbing sips off an ice-cold Anchor Steam Liberty Ale as we discussed my Cornu Point copy. I'd hooked my laptop to a printer in his office, made copies of my mainbar and sidebars. Printouts were scattered on his desk. The top pages bore a wet, uneven set of Olympic rings from the bottle of Old Rasputin Imperial Stout ("Never say die") that Billy had sipped from, then set down repeatedly, after clinking bottle necks with me.

"These stories are a hundred percent legit," I told him. "I've got notes and sources to back it all up. I'll give you the contacts.

Double-check all you wish. Your sole worry is how much the Patch sees this stuff as their property, intellectual or otherwise. But we can make a case that I produced it on my own time."

"Aw, I ain't scared of their shysters!" He brandished his cigar, which traced a glyph of blue smoke as he waved it. "Got my own bad boys with briefcases. They like nothing better than a good scrap with the frickin' dailies. Bearding those twits is the name of my game, as you know, so this is a godsend, brother!"

"My sole worry is that you'll lead with that Eiger porn sidebar, play it to the max. Relegate the rest of my tale to secondary status," I told him.

His cigar froze in midair. "Why the hell not?" he boomed. "Eyeballs — it's all about luring the eyeballs! Have you seen any signs on Broadway puffing, 'Half-Dead! Fully Clothed! Old Ladies!'? You do, it'll be on the nightclub with boards nailed over the door.

"Tell you what." He jammed his cigar into an ashtray, and leaned forward, his voice dropping conspiratorially. "Let's run with it. We'll post three stories on the site tonight. The Eiger stuff, the first half of your mainbar, and one other item you can probably crank out easy."

"What might that be?"

"Your first-person account of the way the *Post-Dispatch* failed so miserably to dig up the truth about an assault on its own reporter!" As I thought this over, he continued. "I'll pay a thousand bucks up-front, another thousand for the continuation of the series tomorrow, and another for decent follows. How's that? I'm cutting open my frickin' mattress for you here, MacCay, pissing away my own retirement. Ripping out the long green with both hands! Nobody gets that kind of payout from me. If you say I did it, I swear to God I'll slit your throat!"

"Unfortunately, I must refuse all payment," I said. "If I take anything, it only worsens my position. Should I wind up in the docket, I must seem a plaster saint. Instead, can you put it toward paying Palmer's medical bills? Send it to his family. They're blue-collar stiffs. Even copays might crush them."

Billy snatched up his cigar with his left hand to flourish it, while extending his right to me for a handshake. "Done!" he proclaimed.

I leaned forward, reaching for his paw, when a latch rattled.

The door to Billy's office swung open, and a small crowd pushed their way in. Scampering around to the front was the *Sentinel's* harried receptionist, battling vainly to keep everyone out. "Billy's in a meeting! He can't be disturbed!" she cried. Paying no attention, rudely shouldering her aside, Pat Maquire, San Francisco's deputy chief-of-police strode in. Next came a tall chap who put a pricey haircut, natty suit, and shimmering wingtips on impressive display. Then Brotmann, looking grim as death.

Billy reacted with utter aplomb. "Ah! Gentlemen! To what do I owe the pleasure?" He beamed. "What brings downtown movers and shakers like you to the outlands? How about beers all around? Takers?"

The receptionist, dropping her lost cause, stuck up a weary hand. Billy plucked a frosty bottle of Red Hook ESB out of his fridge and gave it to her. He patted her fondly on the back as he sent her away.

"You are in illegal possession of intellectual and real property of the *San Francisco Post-Dispatch*," Tom Brotmann grated. He glanced over at the suit, who gave a slight nod of approval. Brotmann continued. "Your only way to avoid charges is to hand every bit of the material over to me. Immediately."

Billy nodded. "Hmm," he said. "Sounds serious. Mind if I make a quick phone call first?"

He grabbed his cell phone, flipped it open. Instead of dialing, he snapped a photograph of Brotmann and associates as they glared at him.

"Very nice," he said. "Not a whole lot of pixels, but sufficient."

Brotmann looked at me. "I'm surprised at you, MacCay," he said. "And very disappointed."

"No, you're not," I said.

Billy enthusiastically agreed. "That's right! You see, MacCay freely admits it. He's always been a shit. No one should ever trust the man! Just look at this horrible position he's put me in."

I scowled at him. He offered me a broad, unapologetic grin. My mind raced. Then I suddenly realized, now was my time to make a dramatic gesture. Silly me, I had nearly let the moment drift by. I snatched my laptop off of Billy's desk, strode to the window, then held that little black slab, crammed full of notes and stories, out over the sidewalk. We were two floors above concrete—a distance sufficient to fuel my threat.

"All I have to do is open my hand," I said. "Then this stuff ceases to be anyone's property. So let's negotiate seriously."

"Aw, he's bluffing," Maquire said. But he took only a single step forward.

"No, I'm not!" I yelped. I eyed the Patch's simmering top exec. "Mister Bossman Brotmann over there can tell you, not a scrap of this is to be found on any Patch desktop or server. Everything's in here. Now, I've leaked enough hints for Ericson and Stein to concoct a similar story in a few days, but by then, the *Chronicle,* the *Mercury News,* and hell, I don't know, the *Sacramento Bee,* will all have scooped you. Because I'll call them and spill my guts. Why should I care? I've already been fired."

Brotmann never hated me more than he did at that exact moment. An urge to curdle my cerebrospinal fluid like month-old milk was implicit in his unwavering stare.

Out of the corner of my eye, I saw Billy Chappell deftly harvest my printouts from his desk like a blackjack dealer sweeping up a deck of cards. He jammed the sheaf of paper into a top desk drawer, then slapped it shut.

"What if we run your story?" Brotmann ground that sentence out. Each syllable sounded as if it were being pried from his mouth with a crowbar.

"So am I fired, or what?"

"Not if we run it."

"Tomorrow?"

"Yes!"

"Well." I pulled my arm and the laptop back in through the window. Then I looked at Chappell. "Sorry, Billy," I said.

"No worries, mate." He grinned. "I've got mine."

"Yes," I agreed. "But not nearly so much as you might've thought." As I passed Maquire, I swatted my laptop into his protuberant belly. Maquire obliged me by instinctively grabbing on and not dropping it. I went for Billy's desk, hauled open the drawer, yanked out my wad of printouts.

"These aren't yours, they're mine!" I said, waving them. Then I glanced over at Brotmann. "I meant ours, Mr. Brotmann."

Brotmann bestowed a hairy eyeball upon Billy Chappell. "You understand, don't you Mr. Chappell, that if you do try to do anything with material you obtained illegally, you will be subject to the full penalties of the law."

"Oooh," Billy said.

"You'll have to deal with the legal might of WestWorld Media," Brotmann said. "If you happen to have an attorney on speed-dial, give him a heads-up. He's about to get very busy."

Billy just smiled.

Brotmann looked at me. "Shall we go?"

"Certainly, sir. Age before beauty." I gestured toward the door.

I was the last to exit, and as I did, I spun around to take one last look—and saw Billy Chappell pluck a digital voice recorder from his breast pocket. He switched it off, an expression of triumph on his face. I smiled, and gently shut the door. I knew Billy would now spend a lovely hour writing up all that had transpired. Let the scalawag relish his coup, I thought. Putting it up on his site would just draw more attention to the Patch, and turn his readers' vaunted eyeballs to my breaking story tomorrow morning.

Chapter 20

As we exited the *Sentinel,* I figured it was time for me to start making nice with Brotmann.

"Great Caesar's ghost, Chief! Can't believe it. How did you guys find me so fast?" I asked.

"Security cameras," Brotmann growled. "They picked you up going out the loading dock. I sent Dewayne down to follow you. He caught the cab right after yours."

"Oh. Well, just so you know, I think this is about to work out in the best possible way."

"Mmph!" Brotmann said.

He had a big, black stretch Cadillac waiting for us at the curb. I hadn't known that he or the Patch owned so fancy a rig, and I wondered if it might be another rental. I entered the car after the driver swung open the door. Within, I noted the presence of Mike Komori, one of the *Post's* top editors. I said hello, then settled down onto the plush upholstery. The attorney entered next, sat with his briefcase balanced primly on his knees. Brotmann took his spot, and the door whispered shut upon us.

"Get back to the Patch," he told the driver. Then he looked at Mike. "Almost 4 p.m.," he said curtly. "Let's go to work."

I handed the printouts to Mikey. He lowered drugstore reading glasses onto the bridge of his nose, plucked a pink highlighter and a red felt-tip from his shirt pocket. Wielding them like scalpels, he began to saw into my copy.

No one actually shouted, "Stop the presses!" But I assure you, someone did communicate the gist of that moldy newsroom cliché to the *Post-Dispatch* printing plant—which had been taken out of the main building's basement and now resided across the bay in Fremont.

Brotmann eventually revealed he had used the hour before he burst into the *Sentinel* to check into my assertions about the Cornu Point saga. He couldn't afford *not* to check them out. With mounting chagrin, he found they held water. So he had an underling phone the print shop to slam the brakes on the *Post-Dispatch*'s next edition as it hurtled toward deadline, sending figurative showers of sparks from the shrieking wheels and the rails. Then Brotmann had mounted up his posse and ridden to Chappell's spread to corral me and my errant copy.

Now, back at the *Post,* we stood clustered around a knot of desks at the center of the newsroom. Mike and I squabbled over adjectives. The company lawyers and I wrestled over my proofs. Bob Porteous, the managing editor, sought to referee amongst us—a task at which he excelled.

A squad of newsroom G.A. (general assignment) reporters were given contact numbers for everyone from Amy Blithesdale, the Vegas stable hand, to the Castello moles working at Cornu Point, and went to work conducting backup interviews on key points. Generally, the two-source rule applied, but given the gravity of this piece, Porteous preferred three.

Business reporters whom Porteous had already assigned to a backgrounder had turned up the intriguing info that 3CD Corporation was actually a multinational chartered in the Cayman Islands; there it served as a front company for a Sovereign Wealth Fund that had recently stopped buying American debt and started scooping up American property. Whether it was a SWF from China, Russia, or Dubai was at present unclear. It could even have been crime-cartel money disguised as a fund.

An FBI spokesman phoned us with the useful announcement that they had launched an investigation into the alleged kidnapping of Olivia Bancroft.

Ericson and Stein flitted in and out of this chaos like buzzing and whining horseflies. Well, I mean Ken Stein, primarily. He plunged into the role of a betrayed diva. Ericson was more professional. He'd been stiffed and outmaneuvered on stories before, and had successfully stiffed competitors and colleagues himself, so he was comparatively wry and philosophical. But Stein hyperventilated. He would dart up to complain bitterly, then vanish—presumably to go pant into a paper bag.

Meanwhile, Hilda from the art department made periodic forays with layout ideas, research librarians were dropping by with little nuggets they'd mined from the world's databases, and Gary from photo was showing us the best images he'd pulled from Internet sources and the paper's morgue. He'd found an old pic of J. Richard Hadley posed in full preppy regalia on a polo horse. He also had a publicity photo of Erik Eiger in battle armor, smiting heathen with a mace.

Downstairs, our own security guards held back a slavering pack of lawyers hired by various threatened entities, all claiming to possess injunctions and threatening apocalyptic destruction if the *Post-Dispatch* dared publish its slanders. Brotmann took it upon himself to periodically descend to the front lobby, listen to their howls, then return to our desks and relate the nub of their objections. We used this material to test the strength of our hypotheses and proofs.

That which does not kill your story makes it stronger.

We closed in upon the witching hour of 10 p.m., which Brotmann had proclaimed as the absolute, final, no if-ands-or-buts deadline. After I had wearily rewritten my lead for the umpteenth time and achieved general approval, I looked around at the grand, dysfunctional, internally feuding family that is journalism, and breathed a sigh of delight. Journalism may be a cranky, wheezing, fractious, unwieldy amalgam of the most obstreperous, independent, and feisty souls on the planet, but when the enterprise gathers itself to deliver a bolt of hot, fresh, major news to the republic, there's nothing more thrilling than being a part of it. I felt like I had come home to the trade, and—to a degree—had come home to myself.

Naturally, something had to occur to spoil the moment, which logically had to be another onslaught from Ken Stein. He trotted up to vehemently insist his name absolutely must appear first in our joint byline. He claimed he was now the assigned lead reporter on the story, and that status had been unfairly snatched away. In retrospect, I'd call it generous of Ken to make such an obvious target. I'd undergone abundant stress and needed to burn off tension—in roughly the same way that a producing oil well must flare high-pressure gas. I leapt to my feet, sending the swivel chair I'd sat upon careening across the aisle like a missile. I hammered both fists down on top of the partition, and erupted with a blast of invective guaranteed to peel paint. I had interned with the top blasphemers on the planet, U.S. Navy chiefs, and I used everything they had ever taught me. Poor Stein looked as though he'd been caught in a wind tunnel with his feet nailed to the floor.

I finished up: "The first name in our joint byline won't be yours or mine, you insufferable, namby-pamby, limp-dick, shit-for-brains, twisted little self-promoting jack-off! It's going to be Sebastian Palmer!"

The entire newsroom caught its collective breath, then erupted in a cheer. Ken froze, jerked his head in a reflexive nod of submission, then slunk off.

Brotmann drew himself up. "MacCay? Come to my office. Now."

"Sure."

He strode before me down the hall.

Brotmann sat on his side of the desk, and I on mine. We were configured just as we had been barely two weeks ago. But that earlier bout now felt a century old. I thought Brotmann would take me to task for flaying Stein so vividly. But after staring at me, he said, "We've cut you a tremendous amount of slack here, MacCay. Please don't make me regret it."

"Fair enough."

"You've astonished us all by bringing in one hell of a story. But we'll be dealing with aftershocks for months."

"I vow to do my very best to assist."

Brotmann adjusted himself in his chair, folded his hands in his lap. "You know, you ought to acknowledge some help you received from unexpected quarters."

I cocked my head. "Such as?"

"Four days ago, Artie Davis sat where you're sitting. He claimed you physically assaulted him. His appearance indicated someone had belted him pretty hard—though we had no other witnesses. Davis wants you fired. He also seeks help from WestWorld attorneys in suing you for damages."

"Ah."

"Davis made another request: He wanted to direct our Cornu Point stories, or at least, to provide guidance in shaping coverage. His rationale was that Cornu was first and foremost a resort, and he had experience in evaluating such operations. I thought that odd, so I delayed my response until I ran a few checks. I probed rumors among our staff, asked Ericson to make some calls. Turns out Davis and his wife have taken free holiday packages at the Cornu Point Inn year after year. Why are you laughing?"

"Just trying to imagine Davis sitting on a horse. Any horse. That would be a terrible way to put down an animal."

"Well, they do have a four-star restaurant at Cornu. Anyway, soon as I found that out—as you might put it—I fired his sorry butt."

"Sweet."

"So, if he's going to come after you, he'll have to do it on his own."

"Thanks."

Brotmann's chin lifted, and a measure of ferocity returned to his gaze.

"There's another matter. Before you left our building this afternoon, you raised a question as to whether or not I was a real newsman. Here's my response: Screw you, MacCay!"

"And screw you too, sir. Very much."

He smiled thinly. "Glad we understand one another. Just to finish, there's no chance in hell of you getting your column back. You stay on reporting."

I shrugged, holding both my hands out, palms up. "You're the boss," I said.

"Now go home and get some rest, MacCay. We've still got the Caddy waiting down at the curb. Why not use it?"

We both stood, then formally shook hands. He was stronger than he looked. His grip crushed down on my right hand, where the knuckles still bore wounds from my shattered mirror and shaving mug. Brotmann's lips twitched in amusement as he saw me wince.

—

The chauffeur was not amused when I plopped my tail on the limo seat and said, "Home, James."

The big black rig rolled down my street in the foggy Avenues of the outer Richmond. I saw the tattered heap of a tramp slumped on the bench in a Muni bus shelter near my flat. Unusual. Homeless men often camp under bushes in Golden Gate Park, just a few blocks south. But they rarely expose themselves to the bone-chilling mists that can blow straight down the streets here at night.

The Caddy slid up to my curb, and I asked the driver to wait while I went inside. I returned bearing two shopping bags holding every liquor bottle I had in my place, save one. Since that clinking collection of hooch amounted to roughly a $300 tip, the driver rolled off in a fabulous mood.

The last of my soldiers left was a bottle of Caol Ila single-malt whisky, distilled on the shore of the isle of Islay in Scotland's fabled Hebrides. I'd placed that one reverently on the walnut table. It was a third full, about the right dose. I planned to down it as a celebratory nightcap, while inviting Anna to appear and share the libation. Were she willing.

But I never got there.

The homeless man slouched up to me on the sidewalk, cloaked in the thick, stained felt of a moving van's old furniture blanket. I felt sorry for this guy, forced to wander so ill-clad on such a damp, cold night. I reached in my pocket and fished out a pair of fives so he could buy some hot food somewhere. If not tonight, at least sometime tomorrow. I extended the bills. He took them, mumbling words I couldn't make out. I do remember one incongruity. His face, half-hidden by the brim of a shabby baseball cap, looked cleaner and healthier than I commonly saw on people in his circumstance.

I wished him a good night, turned to enter my place. And he struck a savage blow right in the middle of my back. I was driven to my knees. I had barely registered what had happened when he whacked me again, this time a bit higher and to the left. Under the force of it, I pitched forward onto the walkway, my upper body sprawled across a low planter box where the Changs had once made a futile attempt to grow roses. The soil was still lined with a border of loose bricks, embedded in a diagonal pattern. I snatched at those bricks. As I rolled over onto my back, I held one in each hand. I saw my assailant kick his blanket away from his feet where it had fallen to the walkway. Then he came at me with a knife. I rolled again and got to my feet. The instant I was upright, he lunged. I was just able to parry his slashing blade with a brick, but I felt the sting of its keen edge on my fingers. Suddenly he spun. When he faced me again, the knife had moved to his other hand.

He lunged once more. I whacked his knife hand with my right. This time, I also managed a counterattack, slamming the brick in my left hand into the right side of his head. He went down, rolled with the agility of someone perhaps trained in aikido, then jumped up. But his hands were empty, the knife gone. He turned and sprinted away. Must not have liked the odds anymore. The sound of his footfalls rapidly faded down the foggy street. He turned a corner and disappeared, his surprise attack a failure.

Blood flowed from my left hand, streamed in sticky ribbons from my fingers. I thrust that hand into my right armpit, applied pressure by squeezing with my upper arm. I panted, shocked by the suddenness of the assault and my own adrenaline surge.

I stood frozen for a moment, then kicked at the foul old blanket, and searched around the tiny front yard till I spotted the knife. With my right hand I picked it up. It was a slim, evil-looking thing with a ribbed handle and a double-edged, matte-finish blade. Something in my brain said SAS—a vintage British commando tool.

I trotted inside, bandaged my hand tightly. Then I shrugged off the ranger vest. As I expected, I found two deep slashes in the fabric of the back panel. I opened the pouch, tugged out my mortally wounded laptop. The attacker's dagger blows had penetrated entirely through the titanium case of my IBM Thinkpad. The point had ultimately jammed into the legal pads nestled below. If not for lugging that worn vest around and toting my gear in the back, I would've been done for.

I headed for the phone, began to dial 911, then thought *no, wait, don't complete the call.* Cops would insist I stay at the scene.

There'd be lots of time to talk with the S.F. police down the line. But I knew this night might not be only about me. The opposition's nasty plans could unfold elsewhere as well. I rang up the Palo Alto Trauma Center instead, and told them to put the deputy guarding Sebastian on high alert. Then I called in the cavalry.

"Um. Hi? Hello?" Elle's voice sounded fuzzy with sleep after Cheryl woke her and handed her the receiver. That residual drowsiness whisked off like a cobweb in a gale when I told her what had happened.

"It can't be about trying to stifle the story!" I said. "Way too late. They must know that, unless they're complete idiots, which I would not rule out. But I think somebody here is in pursuit of vengeance. He's royally cranked about his shattered plans. Either that or his team is looking way ahead to court cases, and wants to start eliminating witnesses right now. But no matter what, we ought to get down to the hospital, keep an eye on things."

"I'm going! But what about Cheryl? Is she in any danger?"

"Bring her. Or, if you can, have her stay with friends, neighbors. All right?"

"I'm on it."

"Good. You'll get there first. But I'll be right along."

Chapter 21

The nurse who wasn't Marty leaned out the door of Palmer's ICU room. "All done with his sponge bath!" she said. "You can come in and see him. And he might even be able to see you!"

"See? What do you mean?" Elle and I blurted variations on this question simultaneously.

"Sebastian's eyes are starting to stay open. He can track things better," the nurse said. "Dr. David said he's coming down to examine him."

Elle and I exchanged wide-eyed glances.

In the wee hours of the morning, we had arrived at the center and had a quick chat with the young deputy assigned to stand guard. He told us the only person he'd seen, other than the night nurse, was Palmer's dad, who had come at midnight to spell the mom, and now slept on a chair in the room. We had peeked inside, noted all was calm, and proceeded to establish our own hangout by the receptionist's desk. Elle and I alternately talked and dozed. I borrowed her cell phone to call Flores. Didn't reach him, but left a long message about the attack at my place. Around sunrise, I roused myself, ventured out to a coin box on the street, and proudly returned with four copies of the *Post-Dispatch* front page. Our team owned all the real estate on A-1 above the fold. But I couldn't bring the sections in to Palmer right then, because the nurse had suddenly chosen that time for his bath.

Now she was giving us even better news than what was on the Patch front page. We hurried straight in.

Palmer's dad, a tall, raw-boned man dressed in clean work khakis with the shirtsleeves rolled up, stood at the bedside. He was saying something to Sebastian in a low voice. He turned as we entered. "You're Sebastian's dad," I said.

"Right," he said. "Sean Palmer."

"Colm MacCay. I worked with Sebastian on the story. This one!" I held up the papers. "And here's Elle Jatobá, a friend of Sebastian's. She helped. Considerably."

"How do you do?" he said politely. We all shook hands. I was impressed with his firm grip, the sheer roughness of his hide. Felt like he could sand a board just by rubbing his hands on it. Sean Palmer had a thin patch of red-brown hair shellacked to his scalp, the rusty eye-whites of someone who had spent too many hours squinting into bright sun. Tattoos were starting to shrivel on his tanned forearms. On the left was a USMC globe with anchor and eagle. On his right, a snarling bulldog wore a sailor hat at a jaunty tilt.

"Might you be in the building trades?" I inquired.

"Yes," he said. "I own a small construction firm in Two Egg, Florida, just a little ways west of Tallahassee. Sebastian used to help out as a carpenter during the summers. This was the first summer he didn't stay home."

I sensed a bit of blame in that remark, decided to leave it alone. "So, how is our young man?" I said. "Improving?"

Sebastian's IV lines had been removed, but wires still ran from sensors on his skull and chest over to monitors that displayed vital signs in glowing wave forms. His head was still heavily bandaged. A blood-pressure cuff wrapped around his left arm. On his right, a fiberglass cast reached from his fingers to several inches above the elbow. His pallor was lit from beneath by a rosier hue. His face remained slack, but his hazel eyes would wander toward us, focus for a second, then wander off.

"Yes. Much better, praise the Lord," Mr. Palmer said. "He gazes at me a bit longer when I talk."

"Great!" I said. "Mind if I speak to him, then? Read something?" I held up the newspaper.

"Go ahead," he said. His chest heaved as he took a deep breath. "But first, I need to say something."

I braced myself for an indictment, an angry screed about the way I had abandoned his boy in an hour of need, leaving him open to assault. I could see muscles work in Sean Palmer's bony face as he got ready to speak his mind.

"Just have to tell you both," he said, "how pleased I am that you took on my son's fight. I truly appreciate that. Proud to know you." Elle and I exchanged startled looks. I felt a curious lightness. Behind my eyes, something was changing, but I could not have said what.

"It was my honor," I said.

"Me, too!" Elle said.

"Awright," he said, and grinned. He slapped me on the shoulder, gave a respectful nod of his head to Elle. "So let's hear what you got!"

I cleared my throat, stepped to one side of the bed.

"Sebastian, I hope you can get all this! Your first front-page story for the *Post-Dispatch* is right here in my hand. I'm going to read it."

" 'Murder and Mayhem Called Part of Resort Development Scheme—Authorities probe deeper into Cornu Point scandals.' Okay, that's the head and deck. Now, here we go.

> *Cornu Point, a ritzy horsemen's enclave near Half Moon Bay, was the scene of the violent death of an elderly activist two weeks ago. The vicious assault of a young reporter from this paper took place nearby on Monday. Now investigators with the San Mateo County Sheriff's Department are calling the death of Beverly Bancroft a possible murder, and indicating that a new suspect may soon face charges in the attack on Sebastian Palmer.*
>
> *They say both episodes are linked to a campaign by 3CD Corporation from Las Vegas, The Cornu Point Association, and other entities, to create and profit from a recreation empire being developed on a long stretch of the California Coast.*

I glanced down from the paper. Sebastian's hazel eyes were fastened on me. Looked like someone might be home, way down in there. Then his lips moved.

"All this great music," Sebastian mumbled. "Do you hear it?"

His eyelids fluttered down like curtains. A shudder rippled through his body from head to toe. He lay utterly still once again.

"Holy shit! He talked!" I said.

"Praise God!" Sean Palmer cried.

"Sebastian!" Elle yelped.

"Wonderful," a deep voice came from behind us. It was Dr. David, the neurologist.

"What's that mean?" I asked.

Dr. David smiled. "Sebastian's getting much closer to rejoining us," he said.

"What did he say about music?" Elle wondered.

"Ah. That rod. Fractured his skull behind the right ear, and damaged Herschel's Gyrus, the part of the brain that processes hearing," Dr. David said. "If it gets hurt, a patient can experience auditory hallucination. How long it might last we don't know, but Sebastian may hear music when he hears words. He might even hear your words as music! Hard to know. Bottom line, it should clear up. He'll be all right."

"Good," Sebastian murmured in a low voice. His eyes stayed closed.

Elle looked startled, then leaned forward to take Sebastian by the hand. The nurse moved swiftly to stop Elle. The doctor changed the nurse's mind by raising an admonitory finger and giving a slight shake of his head. Then he smiled at them both, as if to say, it's all right.

"Sebastian!" Elle said.

"Hi." Sebastian opened his eyes.

Elle looked at the doctor. "Can I ask him a question?"

The doctor hesitated. Then nodded and leaned forward. I knew he truly cared about Sebastian. Yet at that moment, I could see pure forensic curiosity was uppermost in his mind.

"Sebastian. Look at me. This is important," Elle said. "When you gave Beverly's green plastic glasses to Olivia, where were you standing?"

"Wow," Sebastian said. "Beethoven."

"Oh, Sebastian." Elle looked at him, pity in her eyes. Glint of tears, too.

"On the porch," Sebastian said.

"What? Of the house?" She grew excited.

"Mm-hm." He closed his eyes. "Right at the door."

He gave another of those strange full-body shudders, then lay still. Dr. David put his hand on Elle's shoulder. She looked up, and he gestured with his eyes: time to move away.

"We'll be back. Real soon, Sebastian. I promise."

When she looked at me, her eyes smoldered. I smiled.

"Don't mind going out there at all," I said. "If we find something cool at Olivia's house? That'll give me tomorrow's lead."

—

The Crossfire's wheels squeaked around curves of the Coast Highway as we rose out of Pacifica, swirled past Devil's Slide, then roared on south through Montara. Elle had both windows rolled down, flaming beats on the stereo. Her unbound hair whipped in the wind.

"You've got the key, right?" She looked at me.

"Oh, sure. Yeah." I pointed down. "In my sock!"

We came up the rise to Cornu Point. Elle threw the car into a left. We slipped on gravel and pine needles a tad, then the tires grabbed, and we zoomed up a narrow drive of lumped and twisting asphalt. After a score or so of dizzying turns, we glided into a triangular clearing under tall, swaying redwoods. We stopped, and Elle switched off the engine. She pointed through the windshield at a jumble of rubble. A set of brick stairs led up to the ragged mound. "I think that's where the house was," she said. "They must've knocked it down."

"What about over there?" I pointed at a midden of rocks scraped together under an old, dense, more shadowy grove of redwoods.

"Nope. Here. Definitely."

We got out.

"All right." I led the way up the steps. "This is what's left."

A heap of bulldozed house, a haphazard windfall of shattered sticks and shingles, spread away from our toes.

"The door would be right here."

"Fine."

"She said, 'under.'"

"What?"

"Under where Sebastian gave her Beverly's glasses."

"You mean somewhere down below this giant heap of crap?"

"No. Just right here."

I looked past our feet at the random I Ching cast of debris that washed up against the steps, grabbed a few pieces, tugged. Elle did, too. We worked our way down the high side of the steps, the part nearest the fallen house. Suddenly I saw the seam of a hatch, a metal door, set into the back of those steps.

"Here, here!"

Elle dug with me.

"Look!"

A two-foot-square slab of painted metal had been set on a hinge in the back of the stairs. There must've been a trapdoor in the living room floor that led straight down to this place. The lock on the right side of the hatch looked like the kind that might require a short brass key.

"In your sock?"

"Kidding."

I reached in my pocket, pulled out Olivia's key. It worked. The metal door creaked open to reveal two shelves. Each bore a pair of oblong boxes wrapped in loose black plastic.

"Garbage bags," Elle said. "They look new. Bet you Beverly changed them every so often."

She reached in, pulled one out, set it atop the steps. Then I heard a damp whack, like someone hitting a melon with a bat, followed by a cough, a short pneumatic concussion. Elle flopped over on top of the sheathed box. I saw, with horror, a red hibiscus of blood spread on her back. Her body slipped limply off the steps, collapsed down into the hole we had made in the rubble.

Reflexively, I turned to face the direction the sound had come from, heard another sharp percussive puff. A sudden pain seared the side of my head. It became hard to concentrate. I fell on top of Elle. I knew I could not, should not, let myself fall into unconsciousness. Elle was thrashing under me, making angry sounds, trying to get up.

"No, no, no, no! Man with a gun! Don't move!" She heard me, stopped. I cautiously raised my head till I could peer out between shards of debris. Coming out from the edge of the woods, a bald man walked toward us. A long-barreled pistol dangled from his right hand, with the bulge of a silencer on it. He was in no hurry. He saw me look at him, but did not hasten his gait or raise the pistol. He knew he had us.

I searched for something, anything, a pipe, a free piece of wood, to use for a weapon, a shield. I desperately imagined wrenching that small steel door off its hinges. I curled my fingers around it and heaved. It creaked, but did not loosen. I saw Elle's eyes, wide and wild, stare up at me.

The man had drawn closer. I now saw a familiar face, one wearing a smile, tight and triumphant. It was the same guy who had attacked me outside my apartment. Something else ripped through the air, a sharp, high-velocity crack, like a bullwhip. The bald man immediately staggered. He dropped the gun, clutched both hands to his abdomen. Ruddy fluids suddenly gushed out between his fingers, running in streams down his legs. He turned back toward the forest. That whip-crack sounded once more, and the back of his head burst, a crimson geyser sprayed out a halo, and he slumped to the ground in a heap.

"It's okay! We're safe!" I announced to Elle. "I think. Somebody dropped him."

She was pale. Shock was setting in. The back of her shirt was blood-soaked.

"Where's your bandanna?"

"In my pocket. Right hip."

I pulled it out, wadded it up. Looked like the entry wound was on her left shoulder blade. No exit, so her muscle and bone must've stopped the round. I pressed the yellow cloth against the hole in her back and leaned on it.

"Your face..." she said.

I raised my free hand to my head and it came away sticky. Scalp wounds always bleed like a sonofabitch.

"Looks like hell, I know. But if it wasn't a graze, I'd be dead. I'm probably all right. You are, too. Hang in there. Don't let yourself fade. Stay with us."

Lieutenant Flores came jogging out of the woods, holding a Colt AR-15 rifle, its slim, black barrel pointed at the sky. He stopped at the body of the man on the ground, poked it with the end of the muzzle, then, carrying the rifle by its pistol grip, walked the rest of the way over to us.

"Jesus," he said. He carefully laid his weapon on the lowest step, then pulled a tiny, hand-held radio from his jacket and ordered us an ambulance. Other sirens were already wailing out on the Coast Highway.

Flores looked at me. "What do you need?" he asked quietly.

"I think we're good till the medics get here," I told him.

"I have an emergency kit in the car. I'll go get it." He picked up the rifle.

"Wait," I said. I pointed. "Who was he?"

"Dick Prichard," Flores said. "The Cornu security chief. He used many versions of that name. Phil Richards was the one that went furthest back, far as I could trace."

"How did you know we were here?"

"Saw you leave the hospital! So did he. He was waiting. You both set a hell of a pace! All I could do to keep up." He smiled, his teeth a white stripe in his dark face. "Now relax, stay quiet. Don't move much. I'm going for that kit."

"Rafe. Thanks."

"Of course!"

Carrying his weapon once again at port arms, Flores loped back the way he had come. The approaching sirens that had been growing louder had now fallen silent. I assumed a posse of cop cars were now parked back where Flores had left his.

Elle groaned and shifted under my hand.

"Shit, Colm! Stop pushing down so hard! That hurts!"

"Sorry, kid! Need to do it until you stop leaking. Got to keep your insides where they belong. You may be expendable to Lieutenant Flores, but you aren't to me."

She was silent for a long moment. When she spoke, her tone was soft and amazed.

"What's that supposed to mean?"

"It means Flores could've ordered a felony stop on Prichard at some point on any road between the hospital and here. But he didn't. So what happened is likely what he wanted to happen."

"He wanted us to get *shot*?"

"Not exactly. He wanted a reason and a chance to shoot Prichard. That's what we gave him."

"But why?"

I sighed. "Lieutenant Flores has a huge pile of obligations. Some overlap, some may conflict. He's hunting for the best outcome for the greatest number of people. Especially all coastal locals. Prichard was way overdue to exit the scene. Should've tried to liquidate his assets instead of us. Then he should have fled. Alive and staying around this neighborhood, Prichard would only make a bigger mess. Especially if he got arrested, then was forced to testify."

"If that's how you think, why did you thank Flores just now?"

"Oh. He could've let Prichard finish us off. Instead, Flores took him out midway. For that, I'd say he deserves a measure of gratitude. Since us being dead wouldn't have hurt the overall outcome he wants."

"My God! Colm, you are completely batso. You must be the most cynical man I ever met. Or the most paranoid. Or both!"

"Really? I don't feel that way. Want to know how I feel, right now? Lucky."

I looked around the forest clearing. Cool air was wafting up from the ocean, making the redwoods sway and carrying their spicy, tannic scent to my nostrils. There was a sough of that sea breeze in the high branches, and the echo of distant bird calls. Beams of tawny sunlight fanned down between the shaggy russet tree trunks.

"Lucky, and glad to be alive," I said.

I looked down at Elle. She had an odd expression on her face, something that was half grimace and half grin.

"You are truly a piece of work, Colm MacCay," she said.

Postlude

C heryl Bullock had been right on the money when she said breaking a story about Erik Eiger's long-ago fling in Nazi porn would be like lighting a fuse. That most salacious segment of the Cornu saga did indeed fly around our scandal-hungry globe with a rocket in its ass.

The rest of our A-section suite of stories mainly set off a shit-storm right here in California. They prompted a media feeding frenzy of epic proportions. All the various Bay Area media out-lets competed to see which of them could delve down first to the next revelation.

Boxes from the tiny vault below the steps of the Bancroft sis-ters' cottage were my ace in the hole. Since we had found them, the sheriff graciously let me announce the contents. Naturally, I doled them out one by one. The first held a lifetime of correspon-dence between Max Bancroft and Rudy Wyatt. A book contract was soon let for someone to write an account of one of the great friendships (nowadays I guess they'd call it a real-life "bromance") from Hollywood's golden era. Not me. (The fortune-favored writ-er would be *Post-Dispatch* movie critic Leiff Jensen.)

The second box was chockfull of Morgan silver dollars, high-purity coins struck from Comstock Lode ore by the U.S. Mint in the period 1878–1921. I don't know whose mad money it was, but that pristine collection made modern-day coin buffs fairly hot under the collar. As well as hot in every other place where their clothing was tight.

The third box held bundles of love letters tied with ribbon, one set written from various beaus to Olivia, the other written by a single besotted college lad to Beverly.

And yes, the fourth and final box did contain notarized copies of the original Cornu Point founding documents. They said everything Beverly had told Sebastian they did. The day we ran that piece, the California State Resources Agency chose to announce that it had finally located its own Cornu Point originals, and they would soon be returned to the archives. In an unrelated story, a deputy secretary of resources announced his resignation, so he could take a newly created job as environmental ambassador-at-large for the U.S. State Department.

The Assembly Water, Parks & Wildlife Committee promptly launched a series of investigative hearings. Bay Area politicians took turns banging upon desks to condemn wrongdoing, while vigorously demanding justice. Upshot was a new bill revoking the state's contract with the Cornu Point Association, for cause. It would restore all the Cornu land to state park oversight, restrict the equestrian op to the existing footprint, and launch competitive bids for a new concessionaire to run the joint. It squirted through the entire state Legislature like grass through a goose. And yes, it established the village of Castello as a special use district, a living history center. Citizens there could collectively lease the land in perpetuity—at 1933 prices.

If you'd like to know what happened to the bad guys, Dick Prichard, AKA "Whoever," proved nearly as hard to nail down after death as he'd been in life. He had employed a trick of slightly altering his name and Social Security number one letter or digit at a time, which allowed him to either call the result a mistake, and turn back, or proceed with the new identity, depending on need. The documented part of his trail included service in the Texas Air National Guard, a stint with the DEA, participation in Plan Colombia, then a job with Durst-Attels, a military contractor in Iraq. His final role had been as partner in Huffenhutt Security, in which capacity 3CD and the association hired him to protect their show at Cornu Point.

Prichard's investment firm, Velocity Trader, did hold options for sale of the farms around Castello. These proved of marginal worth after it grew certain that Castello and its citizens would stay put. Those options had close expiration dates anyhow, which then duly expired. And the FBI struggles on to learn the names of Prichard's co-investors.

No friends or relations ever claimed Prichard's body. He was buried in pauper's row at a cemetery in Colma. I'd hoped to see him cremated, then his ashes molded into a missile, which I intended to call Dick's Brick. I planned to hurl it through windows of the 3CD corporate offices in Las Vegas. No one listened to me on this.

Erik Eiger's dimmed star-power did flare into nova one last time—the night he was slapped in steel bracelets and guided through a perp walk to San Mateo County Courthouse, to be booked for murder and conspiracy. Camera flashes and TV floodlights made it look like Oscar night. But the glow faded after Eiger slipped out on a massive bail, to retreat under terms of house arrest and await trial behind the walls of his Beverly Hills estate.

What finished him were those Nazi-themed porn shorts from his debut in the performing arts. Eiger swiftly became the butt of the blogosphere, a piñata for radio's barking heads, a running gag in late-night talk shows. Shreds of his macho image turned into a pile of maggot-riddled scat. When he glanced under that noisome heap, he couldn't even locate dust. Not much liking the exit scene handed to him, Eiger proceeded to script his own. He gobbled a fistful of barbiturates, washed them down with an icy bottle of 1996 Moët et Chandon. And that was a wrap. Cut. Lose the lights. Lose the set.

Larry Wheeler was indicted for conspiracy, kidnapping, false imprisonment, and accessory to murder. 3CD corporate lawyers maneuvered to get him out on an insanely high bail, paid by 3CD, whereupon he promptly vanished, despite a tracking ankle bracelet. Some say he escaped to a *finca* in Latin America. I prefer to think of him as supplying fertilizer to cactus roots in some patch of Nevada desert—this retirement plan courtesy of his former employers.

That left Tom Bates and Simon Winger to face bars of the same music. Since all Bates knew about was promotion, sales, and development, his floundering and thrashing on the witness stand tended to exonerate him while not harming anyone else. But Winger was forced to cut a deal. On one hand, he was promptly disbarred. On the other hand, he became fully barred—in the federal prison at Lompoc.

Aiano Tuato returned to the States on his own. His aunt was an avatar of South Seas culture who lived in Fremont—where she directed a West Coast association of outrigger canoe clubs. She reached him through family contacts in Samoa. She told him about the Cornu Point news stories and where they were going, and persuaded Tuato to turn himself in.

Finally grasping that Prichard had duped him into attacking Palmer, Tuato expressed profound remorse. He copped a plea for assault with intent to inflict grievous bodily harm, and was given the minimum sentence. As soon as he had the chance, he made a heartfelt personal apology to Palmer. The big lug even had tears running down his cheeks.

On to the good guys. I mean, the other good guys. All things considered, I thought Aiano managed to redeem himself.

Elle needed reconstructive surgery on her left scapula. They extracted a .25 caliber bullet, stapled the bone, sewed up the tissue, and sent her off to physical therapy. Cheryl, since she'd had practice with medical adventures, proved a stellar caregiver. She excelled at reminding Elle to keep up with her boring exercises. She also persuaded Elle that it was high time she applied to enter the POST (Police Officer Standards and Training) curriculum at a local community college.

Sebastian, like Lazarus, rose from his litter after a month to resume a semblance of normal life. Brotmann had granted him medical leave until Christmas. Sebastian insisted on returning to the Patch much sooner, to launch into what he saw as light duty—helping our rag boost its online self an iota further out of the digital Dark Ages.

Olivia earned her own provision in the Cornu Point Restoration Act, affirming her right to live out her days at site of the old estate. A Bay Area law firm, founded by a friend of her father's, won a substantial settlement from 3CD. A trust fund was established, and Olivia was moved back into the rebuilt Bancroft guest cottage, with round-the-clock nursing care. A similar care deal was made for Jessup, Beverly's cocker spaniel. Olivia wanted him to come back home too.

Then, there's me. Number me with the good guys or not, as you please. I don't care either way. I felt exhausted. Sure, I put on a reasonably good show for weeks as I helped the Patch churn out many needed follow-ups to the Cornu Point saga. I worried that I might've vaulted up from my bleak limbo, only to lapse back into it as the challenge wound down. Under duress, I had reinflated my ability. Now I wondered if that buoying blast of hot air would squeak out of my survival raft.

The most odd and curious development was that I failed to resume serious drinking. Not for lack of an attempt. After Elle and I shared our ambulance ride, after I'd gotten my scalp shaved and stitched back up from the bullet crease at my medical home away from home, the Palo Alto Trauma Center, I returned late to my flat.

I lit a few candles in front of the framed portrait of Anna, plinked down two crystal shot glasses. I loosened my belt, untucked my shirt, pulled off my shoes, and sat. I poured golden fluid into the glasses, enjoying the subtle music of a *glick-glick-glick* as Caol Ila slowly chuckled from my bottle of artisanal single-malt.

I savored an eentsy sip from my shot, then splashed the rest off my tonsils in one gulp. A delicious, familiar warmth slowly spread through my body, while peaty, peppery aromas drifted upward to tease my palate.

I raised Anna's glass to her photograph, "Here's to you, kid!" I said, and took a sip of hers.

But she remained within her picture, laughing, vibrant, and utterly frozen, locked away within that bygone moment, a damselfly in amber.

"You've certainly been quite the tease of late," I told her. "Can't be because I've disappointed you! Or can it?"

Anna made no reply. I felt irritated.

"Come on. It's hardly fair! Of all you've asked of me, what have I left undone?"

Nothing came back. Then a thought raised hair all over my scalp and neck.

"You haven't left me, have you?" I demanded. "With not so much as a word of farewell? Anna, that's cruel!"

No matter what I tried, no matter what I said, I could not dislodge her from that carved wood frame and pane of glass. That put me in a desolate mood, but strangely, I did not guzzle all the rest of the whisky.

Instead, I cast my mind back to the moment I had first laid eyes on the ravishing Anna Gardiner, raven tresses gleaming against her alabaster skin, at that table in the Fairmont. I thought of all the hours and days we had spent in this very apartment, entangling then disentangling ourselves from the twisted-up bedclothes. Dinners at romantic little Bay Area *boites* where we felt we could dine and dance unobserved—or at least unrecognized. Those fascinating, endless conversations, where we could complete each other's thoughts, sometimes with little more than a quirk of the lips, a wink, or lift of an eyebrow.

"Is this what it will be like from now on?" I demanded of her picture. "Must I do it all myself?"

No answer. Tears moistening my eyes, I stood up, gently blew out her candles. Drained her shot. Stuffed the cork back into the neck of the Caol Ila. It was now down to a quarter full, nowhere near enough to mount a proper rampage. I toyed with a temptation to run out to a little all-night market six blocks away, for a fresh fifth of something cheap. Instead, I decided to toddle to bed. If I got snockered, it would likely only drive her further off, whereas if I played it smart and sober, there might be a chance she'd return.

Well, neither happened on any subsequent night. I did not proceed to get soused, and I did not visit with Anna. And steadily, I withdrew from the alcoholic compulsion. By day, hard work provided a badly needed distraction. During commutes to and from, I would meditate upon the things that were changing. My recent adventures had reset some internal mechanism, demons had been sated or exorcised.

I had always known visits with Anna were not true séances, but visions, waking dreams, wherein I heard messages that resonated with my memories of her, extrapolations of those memories, perhaps. They could easily have been truths I needed to hear from a deeper self. A voice of health, or soul, or a form of psychic homeostasis if you will. It's just that these visions were far more cathartic and pleasurable when I let myself drift toward imagining that she was actually present.

Such shifts in perception may sound sane, even enjoyable, but I assure you I did not get off that easily. My first few nights of full withdrawal were especially horrendous. Sleep, if it came, was fitful, and riddled with bizarre fantasy. Hieronymus Bosch would have paid cash money for a balcony seat in my cranium. I could usually only manage an hour or two of uneasy slumber before jolting awake, sheathed in a sweat, the sheets knotted, pillows flung across the room. Next came an interminable wait for dawn, the numbing passage of time marked by the periodic wheeze of air brakes and diesel rumble of infrequent Muni buses lurching past the nearby stop on the street.

But here was the interesting thing, the phenomenon that made it all seem worthwhile, that encouraged me with a sense that I was on the right track. There was now a solid floor beneath my feet. It was not that my dark, beckoning abyss had closed or vanished, but that I no longer floated dangerously above it, or saw myself plunging down into it. The black option was there, but now it seemed more like a vertical doorway, positioned off to one side. Now I would have to choose to walk into it rather than simply let myself drop. It was a difference that reassured.

Meantime, inside the sandstone hulk of the *San Francisco Post-Dispatch,* the work of journalism staggered on. While WestWorld Media continued to whack budgets and trim staff, the need to craft stories and meet deadlines didn't drop in the slightest. Instead, it ratcheted upward.

A job in media is like being married to a nymphomaniac—the instant you think you ought to be done, you're forced to start all over again.

Mr. Tom Brotmann challenged us all to "work smarter," accomplish more with less. During Cornu Point, he and I had reached a rapprochement. But we still had the occasional set-to. I said he should stand up to the execs back in Denver, and invest in the paper's future, not just try to cut his way to solvency—a loser's game, in my view.

"Can't accomplish anything if you don't stay in business," Brotmann harrumphed.

I retorted, "Of all the ways to go out of business, the surest must be not having a product!"

And I wondered about that night when our whole newsroom had rallied to launch our A-1, Cornu Point blockbuster. Was it the last time I'd witness that sort of thing? All pistons furiously pounding on a giant media locomotive while it charges a grade? The rousing climax of a sprawling investigative report as it neared deadline? The thought that I might have seen the finale of that sort of triumph tired me. And after that last month, I was running on fumes anyhow, so I startled Brotmann by asking to take a six month's leave without pay. During this time, I intended to figure out what I'd do with the rest of my life. Of course, I didn't mention that part to Brotmann. I wanted a position kept ready and waiting for me at the Patch, something to glom onto should my inclination turn that way once more.

All of which made the celebration held one week later among the pastel houses of Castello a pivotal event. Felt like the end of an era.

It felt luminous as well. The air was hushed, the ocean flat and still. The entire cove had that held-breath feeling of North Coast evenings in late September and early October, when the world considers diving into winter but isn't quite ready to leap.

The sun swayed down to fatten and glow on the horizon, then slipped into darkness with a final bright wink. Lighting duties at Castello were taken up by paper lanterns strung across the plaza and pathways. Santa Fe-style luminaria plopped outside the doors of homes, and kerosene lanterns hung in windows. Castello received power from its solar panels and wind turbines, but didn't waste much of it on exterior lighting. The old way of illuminating did fine, and generated a warm rose-and-gold hue.

As I approached I heard strains of music wafting from the village. Sounded vaguely gypsy-like, with plenty of furious fiddling. Over the course of this evening, many different genres figured in the soundtrack. There were folksongs in Italian, a few well-delivered arias, a sea chanty or two that I guessed had to be legacies from the fo'c's'le of the schooner *Cornu Arietis*. Even some big-band torch songs, and Perry Como, Dean Martin, and Tony Bennett tunes.

Once down in the plaza, my other senses absorbed other atmosphere. There was a spicy aroma of calamari being flash-fried with olive oil, black pepper and garlic in huge woks perched atop propane burners. Pungent tomato sauce. Chopped fresh basil flung over hot pasta. I even fancied I smelled the musk of hearty red wine, spiraling out of the glasses, mugs, and cups that everyone seemed to hold.

The first two people I recognized in that half-lit crowd were Cheryl and Elle, gripping hands as they sat on a bench at the edge of the plaza. I went over to chat with them. Sebastian Palmer then strolled up with a dark-haired lass on his arm. She looked like either a denizen of Castello or a descendant of one.

"So, how do you feel now, Colm?" Cheryl asked me.

"Oh, we all should be pleased as punch. I'm proud of everyone," I said.

"No, I mean you. How do you feel? Look what you pulled off!"

"Ah, our enterprise was collective." I felt my eyes narrow involuntarily as I looked down at her, sought to guess what she might be driving at. "Besides, as the archdruid David Brower said of our environment: All victories are temporary."

"Every party has a pooper," Elle sang. "That's why we invited you, party pooper!" Then she laughed.

"Hey! I believe in the noble chore of us ink-stained wretches. But strong investigative pieces are becoming rare! Do you realize how close our story came to never seeing light of day? Can you see the consequences had our story not run?"

Cheryl and Elle exchanged puzzled looks.

"Colm," Elle said. "It *did* run."

"Sure, right. But did it go deep enough? Far enough? A painting is never finished, artists say, only stopped. Well, stories, especially investigative stories, are just like that. It's not a matter of fingering a few obvious miscreants. Who are the real bad guys? Where are they? How many?

"These horse people, all they ever wanted was a place of their own where they could admire each other and be admired without any interference. There's the locals, made irrationally exuberant by a chance to cash in. Then 3CD Corporation, looking for a secure and fertile spot to plant a wad of money and watch it grow. They hired tough guys like Wheeler and Prichard to keep eyes on the prize. They needed a pitchman like Erik Eiger to stick on a happy face and sell, sell, sell. Sure, Wheeler and Prichard were amoral and evil, but they were only mid-level operatives. Eiger didn't even get that far. He was just an empty vessel, happy to carry whatever purpose anyone wanted to pour in. An idiot sociopath. When he lost the image that won him fame and approval, he lost everything. Like Gertrude Stein said of Oakland, there was not even a there *there*.

"Did we catch every culprit? Did we even get the main ones? Thrilling as it would be to find and nail a top puppet-master, there may not be one. No Goldfinger, no Dr. Evil, no Ernst Stavro Blofeld. Just the relentless viral urge of a heap of money to double itself. Plus all the human ushers that money drew to its side to ease its path. Were people directing the process, or simply getting heaved along in the torrent? Did Wheeler and Prichard get detailed orders, or were they just fulfilling wishes, using any means they thought necessary? Perhaps one day we'll know for certain. I doubt it.

"Evil's most enduring victories occur when all the conniving small operators can remain concealed behind the curtain, ready and willing to join in the next project. And exactly who are they? How did that Sovereign Wealth Fund acquire power? Well, if it's from an oil-producing state, it got dough from people irresponsibly burning up petrol decade after decade. If it came from Asia, it got dough from the export of our industrial base to their shores, and our endless lust to import cheap goods. Damn the balance of trade, full speed ahead! Did we think ill effects could never proceed from dumb collective decisions? Why should it come as a shock if our very own Boobsy Twins, Cupidity and Stupidity, thrown out into the world, circle around to bite us on the ass?"

At that point, I had to push PAUSE on my rant. For three reasons: I realized that I *was* ranting; I had pretty much run out of breath; and all my listeners were laughing at me. Elle, in fact, had a finger to her lips and was saying, "Shhh!" in the same manner one might use to try to silence a wailing babe.

"No, wait," Sebastian said to Elle. "Cut him some slack, Elle. Mac's right. Journalism must be a process, not an event. Its whole function is ongoing feedback. Social, political, and economic feedback. That's what gives people a chance to correct course. That's what keeps us sane. So the feedback should never end. The challenge of producing it stays constant."

I thanked him with a look. Then I took a deep breath in order to resume.

"But the sad fact is, it could end. The clean, clear-eyed, hard sort, at any rate. More and more, we get blind-sided by disaster because our faltering press, the whole dysfunctional media apparatus, plus our government, can barely keep the people informed of all the galloping symptoms, let alone the root causes of our disease.

"And the scant ability we had a decade ago has steadily diminished. Mere opinion is replacing it. Who wants to read bad news? And especially, who wants to pay to read it? Journalists may soldier on with particular stories, but it's like trying to fight a monsoon flood by bailing with thimbles. It's... mmphh!"

At that point, I could say no more. This was because Elle had jumped to her feet to confront me. She slapped one hand on the back of my neck and clamped her other over my mouth, her thumb hooked below my chin. Everyone laughed some more.

"Mmph!"

"Hush!" Elle gently shook my head. Her gray eyes regarded me with astonishing tenderness. "Colm. Listen to me. Maybe journalism isn't dying. Could be it's only going through a bottleneck. But tonight, let's not care! Why not just enjoy the heck out of this moment, when it all worked?

"Here. Look," she said. "Get yourself a plate of this absolutely amazing seafood. Glass of wine. Sit. Relax. Enjoy the party, huh?"

She released me. I smiled, bowed, and complied. Mostly.

I did walk to the serving tables, equipped myself with dinner and beverage, then munched and quaffed. But I did so standing, with my plate on the cover of a rain barrel, while I watched the dancers twirl all around on the flattest part of the plaza. There went Mister Pete, cutting quite a caper with two ladies at once. Shorty was hard-pressed to keep out from underfoot. There went Sebastian and his date. I saw him spin her rather adeptly through swing moves. He looked healed, except for the bandage on the side of his head and a short cast on his right forearm. Elle and Cheryl stood close, gently swaying together in time to the music.

I felt separate from the scene, however, as though I were in an orchestra pit, watching this party occur onstage. It wasn't that I felt alienated from the festivities, but simply that I was not yet ready to participate with a full heart. This was my sense of how I would proceed through this large change: two steps forward, one back.

Besides, I'd already concocted a different plan. I was aimed at a trip down the coast for one of my biannual visits with Brother Brother at his monastery in Big Sur. This time I would not need to beg a ride or take a bus. Out in the Castello parking lot sat my new car. Or rather, my newly bought, very used pickup, a Ford Ranger with fading blue paint and a camper shell on the back.

I finished my food, dumped the paper plate, and quietly made my way through the whirling throng and out under the strings of colored lanterns. As I departed the plaza, I noticed Lieutenant Flores sitting on a bench in the shadows with a few of the younger Castello guys. I'd seen him at many of the formal proceedings, but at all of them we were unable to engage in any informal chats. The stakes were too high. Flores saw me pass, hoisted a wineglass in salute with one hand, and flashed me something that was either a peace sign or a "V" for victory with the other. I responded with a wave, but pondered his gesture as I walked away.

At the final bend in the trail to the dusty parking lot, I stopped to gaze back at Castello. Its blaze of light, music, and chatter was reduced to a tiny spark, a dot of crackling campfire, bravely holding forth against black night's boundless dome.

One Di Mastini man was posted at the gate. I nodded at him in friendly fashion, then cranked up my truck. Leaving Cornu Cove, I drove south along the darkened coast. I breakfasted in Monterey at dawn, then lurched onward, as I re-familiarized myself with the operation of a standard transmission, moving past Carmel and on to Big Sur.

Play of rising light and brightening clouds above the sprawling sea brought balm to my disordered soul, and, dare I say it, a touch of humility. Before such oceanic vastness, I was a bug. How important could one human insect's troubles truly be? That feeling was heightened as I passed the naval station and light at Point Sur, a cluster of spindly human structures perched on a grand roil of rock rearing high above the measureless Pacific.

Steering through all those Big Sur highway bends provided a smooth and soothing rhythm. Just past the Lucia Inn, I found the monastery driveway heading inland, where a weathered wooden cross poked up from the coastal scrub.

I worked my way two miles upward on a narrow, winding ribbon of pavement. Abruptly, New Camaldoli Hermitage appeared as a collection of low buildings and one lofty chapel, before which a dozen or more transplanted Mediterranean cypresses towered. Van Gogh's vision made such cypresses writhe like demonic flames. These stood as still and calm as sentinel angels.

Fine place for contemplatives. These monks are generally enjoined to silence. Prevailing sounds consist of bird calls and an infrequent ringing of bells. Devout visitors are welcome to some ceremonies and rituals, and a small number can stay here on retreat.

I checked in at the monastery's modest bookstore, a cubicle that shelves classics by Thomas Merton and Bede Griffiths, and newer commentaries on spirituality and Catholicism as well. I wandered the aisles and poked at books I seemed to recall. Connor walked up to me.

"Colm! Bless your heart. Grand to see you. You look well."

"Connor, come on. Shouldn't you be a truth-teller in this joint?"

I could never make myself call him Brother Romauld, the name he took upon entering the OSB religious order. Which is why I call him Brother Brother, or just Connor. I thrust out my hands, gripped him by his knobby, fleshless shoulders, gazed at his thin face with its wisp of white beard. Into those familiar eyes, with irises formed from a higher grade of lapis lazuli chips than my own.

"But you, you look all right, for such a crusty old anchorite. If a bit emaciated. Been fasting for peace in the Holy Land? Thankless job. Or endless, anyhow. Come, jump in my truck. I'll run you to Cambria. Fill you up with ribs and beer and ice cream."

"Ah, the same old Colm!" he reproved. "Voice of temptation."

"In his infinite wisdom, God himself offered me that role. Holiness should always be tested. What would Anthony have achieved without his imps? Or Augustine, without his pimps? Or Job, without all those nattering village busybodies?"

Connor shook his head and chuckled—somewhat ruefully. He never liked it when I mentioned his illustrious forebears with anything less than utter reverence.

"So," he said, changing the subject. "That invitation must mean that you're finally driving again?"

"Yep! Your little brother's big adventure produced a car key as one of its outputs. I'm a reporter again, too. Pretty rusty at both. Afraid I savaged the clutch, driving down. But I made it! We'll see how I get back. The other big change? Seems like I'm finally off the sauce. Either that, or taking an amazingly lengthy break from it."

"That's grand, Colm."

Then good Brother Brother and I went on a walk around the monastery grounds. As we ambled, he told me about the imminent publication of his new book of Gospel-based meditations. Other than that, he had no news. Things didn't change much up there. I replied with book and verse on the Cornu saga. He shook his head over the ways of the world. I fingered the round ritual object I carried in my trouser pocket, and pressed its small sharp knob hard into a fingertip.

"I've lost her, Connor," I suddenly blurted out. "I've lost Anna."

His head jerked up, and his blue eyes scrutinized me.

"Anna died, what, thirty years ago?" he said.

I felt surprised to find that my own vision was beginning to blur. I was tearing up.

"Yes. Even so, it felt like she would still come by for a visit occasionally. Now she's stopped. Haven't seen her in weeks."

He didn't have a response for that, not at first. Then he asked gently, "What does that mean?"

"I guess it means that now I'm forced to finally let her go. All the way." I didn't much enjoy the quaver I heard in my voice. Sounded a bit too much like a weepy child.

Connor raised his thin hand, squeezed my upper arm.

"Why don't you rest up from your trip?" he said.

He led me to the cloister behind the chapel, to a row of plain concrete-block cubicles that formed the monks' individual cells. Connor put me up in an empty. I lay down upon the cot—just a thin mattress unrolled on a board shelf—to relax for a bit. But I fell into a heavy, dreamless sleep.

I awoke refreshed, yet also somewhat disoriented. Took a minute or so to remember where I was. I left the chamber to wander the walkways, till a monk took me in hand and brought me to Connor.

"Rest well?" he inquired.

"Amazingly," I said.

"Camaldoli tends to do well at slowing folks down. Want to take the next step? Come join us at Vespers, Colm. We're about to start."

The monastery chapel was as I remembered. An entry led into a small hall lined with yellow leaded-glass windows, where straight-backed chairs stood in rows for use by the faithful. Air in the chapel held notes of perfume from beeswax candles and stale incense vapors.

Purely from reflex, I dipped a finger into the cool puddle of holy water offered to visitors at the entry, then made the sign of the cross. To my surprise, a small shiver ran through me. I suppose, once you've been sealed into the Faith, you never get yourself quite unstuck.

That first hall of the chapel led to an inner sanctum, an austere octagonal chamber with a skylight that showered sunbeams down around a suspended crucifix. Here, polished red-granite tiles flanked a nine-sided floor of rough gray granite. A stone altar stood directly below the cross. The only other furnishings were two wooden benches, beneath which were stuffed a dozen zafus—Buddhist meditation cushions. That seemed new. Maybe some spiritual cross-pollination was underway.

I went back out to the hall. About twenty monks had gathered. A handful of the laity modestly occupied the rear seats. I installed myself right near the door, just in case I felt seized by an impulse to bolt. There was a moment of stillness. Then, "O God, come to my assistance," a cantor monk chanted.

"O Lord, make haste to help me," the chorus of monks sang in response. They were using tones and cadences similar to Gregorian chant. I missed the actual Latin of my youth.

But generally, formulaic prayer makes me feel impatient. The mere introduction to this service felt like a more than sufficient dose. I edged out the door. As I departed the chapel, I went past a large, six-sided window that opened up onto a view of a steep brushy slope and the sea far below. A breeze blew in that aperture, carrying herbal scents from hillside vegetation and the sporadic twilight twitter of birds.

Fingering the diamond ring in my trouser pocket, I walked back down the monastery drive. I saw a bench perched by the road. It was too close to the chapel; I could still hear the monks. Went on to the next bench. It tilted uncomfortably to the left.

I found further progress barred by a large, soot-hued lizard lounging on a patch of warm asphalt. The reptile calmly tilted its beady eye up at me. Normally such things frantically skitter away. Not this one. He waited until I had almost stepped on him before sauntering off.

I passed up three more benches, till I found a sturdy, level number facing south, placed at the high point of a bluff, near a sharp bend in the road.

I crunched up to it through dirt and gravel, then plopped my posterior down. The sunset tonight was nowhere near as dramatic as the previous one. The high western sky was a gauze of clouds, and daylight simply faded to a darker gray.

Directly above, however, a glitter of stars began to switch on. I fished the engagement ring I had bought for Anna out of my pocket. Held it at arm's length. The gem also sparkled in the faint light. I'd walked out here with a notion of pitching the thing into the sea, but now it seemed obvious that, no matter how hard I flung it, it would never reach the water. It would merely bounce into the brush. Instead, I pulled the ring over the tip of the little finger on my left hand. The finger I had used to measure the diameter of Anna's ring finger, hoping to get the fit right, so I might surprise her later.

I cupped my right hand tightly over the ring, felt the metal band and its jutting stone bite into my palm.

I still sat there when Brother Brother found me, an hour later. He sank down onto the bench at my side, asked how I was. I told him: calm, sad, and empty. I held up the ring.

"I've carried this for a long while," I said. "I bought it for Anna. Guess it's time to get rid of it."

Connor regarded me soberly. "It may be that you're right about that," he said. "You know, Colm, I've been carrying something for a long time, too. And the only way I can be rid of it is to tell you. I think you may finally be ready. Anyway. It's now or never."

"What?"

That simple inquiry unlocked a dark vault of family history.

Connor began by telling me that our father had not turned gay in San Francisco. That transition had begun back in Ireland, long, long before, when Brian was an altar boy and had been seduced by our parish priest. Their clandestine relationship lasted for years. Only as a young man had our father finally struggled to break free. He did it by courting and marrying the lovely Lily, and starting a family.

But even that did not free him. The rectory housekeeper caught the priest and Da in a compromising position one day. The debacle of this discovery scandalized all of Lahinch.

"So, you remember none of this?" Connor probed.

"No! I was so young. And I was young when we left. Why have you kept this from me all these years?"

"We ... thought it was for the best."

"We?"

"Da and I. Because—"

"Why?"

"Colm, you remember how Mum died?"

"I was always told she had a heart problem!"

"That she did. A broken heart. And ... she hanged herself. With an electrical cord. In a closet of our house."

Connor's face, pale and gaunt, stared at me out of the deepening gloom, and the moving air off the ocean made wisps of his white hair and beard flounce around the stillness of his gaze.

"Who found her?" The voice I heard say that did not sound like it came from me.

Connor reached out his skinny arms and held me by both shoulders.

"You did, Colm."

—

Mysteries reside in the formation of each of us, I suppose. I cannot say who is more fortunate, the one who careens through life without knowing or acknowledging the roots of his mystery, or the one able to make the discovery that shocks, that astounds.

I now saw the true nature of the abyss that had haunted me over the run of all my days. It was nothing more or less than a black slot formed by a gaping closet door. I would like to say that this discovery solved everything. It didn't, of course. Though through it ran all my lines to the dead.

There came no rush of repressed memory or emotional trauma, no titanic and cathartic release of feeling upon Connor's act of revelation. That, I supposed, would occur later, would descend upon me at its own glacial speed, yet also march with the inevitability of sunrise—a prospect that terrified me. But on this night, I felt only the soft *snick* of a piece of understanding falling into place. And a general grief for the woeful world. For an Irish country girl who had loved and married with a whole, pure, and innocent heart, only to find herself confronted by the utter demolition of all she felt, knew, and believed. For a husband torn between two lives, who saw his own confusion lead to tragedy, who sought salvation by trying to raise a pair of sons as best he knew how—but ultimately was fated to complete the act of orphaning them.

Connor and I sat, talked, clung to each other, wiped away tears, then talked some more. I got him to wait right there on the bench while I walked to my truck and returned with the final quarter-bottle of the Caol Ila. Following my first sips, I prepared to hurl the diamond engagement ring out into the night. But Connor halted me, persuading me that it made much more sense to accomplish some good with the ring by giving it away, to drop it into the monastery poor box at the chapel doorway.

I agreed. Then I smiled, wondering what the monk who happened to find it might think.

"I must do something else, then." I blurted it out suddenly, a surprise to myself as well. "How about this? I want you to hear my confession."

Connor fixed me with a gimlet eye. "That would hardly be appropriate," he said.

"Why?"

He pointed at the bottle of scotch.

"Now, you true believers often sip wine at communion, do you not?" I challenged him.

He would not concede my point. "We call confession the Sacrament of Reconciliation now," he said. "You should approach it reverently. If you still feel this way tomorrow, we can discuss it.

How long has it been since your last good confession?"

I rummaged through memory. "About forty years," I said. "Give or take a few. Well, all right. Something else, then."

I abruptly stood, and raised the bottle. "To my true lost loves!" I declaimed. "To you, Lily, to you, Da, and to Anna. Farewell, my darlings. May flights of angels sing you to your rest." And then I poured the rest of the scotch out onto the earth, making a dark and fragrant mark.

"May all souls rest in the great peace, in the bosom of Christ," Connor said.

He raised his bony hand to make a sign of the cross, and sent a blessing out into the boundless night.

About the Author

PAUL McHUGH reported news for The *San Francisco Chronicle* and other journals for more than 20 years. His main beats were outdoor sport, resource use, and environmental issues. He launched several investigative series during his time at the paper. He continues to string for the *New York Times, Washington Post, Bay Nature* magazine, and other publications. McHugh is an award-winning writer, an avid adventurer and outdoor sportsman. He currently lives near Stanford, California, with his wife, Dawn Garcia. *Deadlines* is McHugh's third book and his second novel. Discover more about his life and works at **www.paulmchugh.net.**

FSC

Mixed Sources

Product group from well-managed
forests and other controlled sources

Cert no. SW-COC-002283
www.fsc.org
© 1996 Forest Stewardship Council